Magic's Source

The Essence of Magic

By

Michelle Ermens

Dedication

To Arthur and Julia,
My Fionn and Mori.

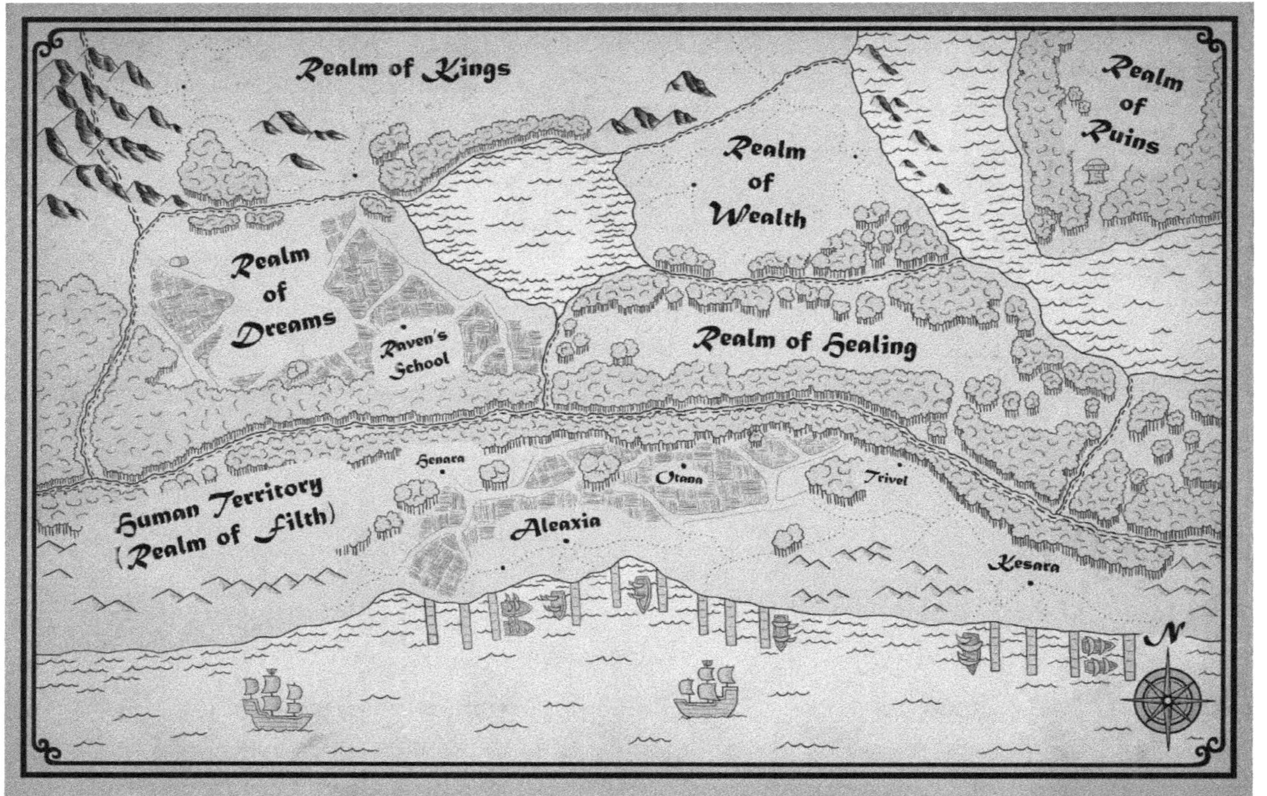

Realm of Kings
Realm of Ruins
Realm of Wealth
Realm of Dreams
Raven's School
Realm of Healing
Henara
Otana
Trivel
Aleaxia
Kesara
Human Territory (Realm of Filth)
N

1

"Fionn! Mori! Dinner is ready! Where's Thera? I already called her fifteen minutes ago!" Dad walked back inside and slammed the door behind him, while my younger brother, Fionn, who was hiding behind a small stack of big rocks, put his hand against his mouth to stop his laughter from escaping. I sat on one of the bigger rocks beside him and couldn't hide a small, somewhat surprised chuckle myself.

"Why are you hiding from Dad? You've been running around all day, aren't you hungry?" I asked.

Fionn's joy disappeared, and he folded his arms with a grumpy look on his face, which ironically made him look exactly like our father.

"It's the third time this week we're eating mashed potatoes, and I hate it."

I lifted an eyebrow. "What are you talking about? You love potatoes."

"Yeah, if they're baked, but they get all soft and slimy when they're mashed, it's gross."

I suppressed another laugh.

"Whatever, can we go? I'm bored, and I don't want to wait here until it gets dark and cold like last time," Mori sighed.

I looked at her over my shoulder. She was sitting on a flat spot on the rock above Fionn and me and pretended to look at her nails as if they were more interesting than us. Pretty much the definition of puberty. Although her tone annoyed me, I did agree with her. The year was coming to an end, the sun went down earlier every day, and with the night came the first signs of winter. If we'd go along with Fionn's tomfoolery for too long, all three of us would pay for it with a cold.

I got up, slapped the dirt off my pants, and pulled Fionn up by his hand, cleaning the dirt off him as well. I held out my hand to Mori, offering to clean her up a bit too, but she ignored it and walked right past Fionn and me towards our home.

"Mori has been mean lately." Fionn inadvertently spoke my mind, and I shrugged.

"That's just what happens when you start growing up." I put my hand on his wild head of dark hair. "Don't worry, in a few years, she'll be too grown up to be embarrassed about literally everything, and she'll be our usual, sweet sister again."

He shook his head in disbelief. "Sounds like a lot of trouble, if that's how you become a grown-up, then I'd rather stay like this."

I grinned. "If only."

He suddenly looked up at me. "Does that mean that you were mean too when you were growing up?"

I stopped laughing. "You know, I'm not so old that I've stopped growing up completely."

He gave me a teasing, crooked smile. "You look old enough to me."

He avoided my fist that softly swung towards his arm and ran away laughing until he disappeared into the house before me.

"No hitting the little ones Thera." Mom appeared from the shadow on the left side of the house, a basket of eggs under one arm.

"Somebody should. You and Dad can't because that would be child abuse, but it's okay if I do it. It's just brothers and sisters messing with each other." Perfectly sound logic.

Mom seemed to disagree, though, and pinched my arm.

"Hey!" I rubbed it. "That really hurt."

She gave me her sweetest smile. "It's not child abuse because you're already over eighteen, so it's okay if I do it."

I sighed, using perfect logic to even out my perfect logic; Mom always knew what she was doing. I rolled my eyes to admit defeat and followed her into the house.

The scent of potatoes and meat floated my way, and I breathed it in deeply. Unlike Fionn, who could be a rather picky eater, I loved food.

I gave Dad an apologetic nod as I sat down next to him at the dark, wooden table. He tapped his finger on that table with an annoyed expression but managed to keep himself from saying something. My dad was funny and silently kind, but he had the devil's patience.

"Urgh, it's all cold." Fionn, who hadn't been able to wait for us anymore, had put a big scoop of mashed potatoes in his mouth and screwed his face up in disgust. I saw Dad's frown deepen as he bit his tongue not to yell at his shameless son, and I had to try really hard not to show my amusement.

"Just eat it Fionn, it's your own fault for hiding for so long." Mom used a stern tone, but I could see that she was having trouble not laughing.

"But mooom…" Fionn wined the way only kids could and rebelliously stirred his mashed potatoes in a wild motion.

"Finish every last bit of it, Fionn." This time Mom was less amused.

"Yeah, you don't want the specials to come find you and take your soul while you're sleeping." Mori grinned as she mocked her little brother, but everybody else at the table fell completely silent.

"Where did you hear that, Mori?" Mom's voice was soft as if she were too afraid of both the question itself and the answer she might have received.

Mori shuffled in her chair as she looked from our mom to our dad and back.

"I…" she hesitated for a second, "from the other kids at school." She looked at our dad again, hoping for backup.

"Yeah," Fionn put his spoon back in the mashed potatoes again, "my friends say it too. Their parents always say it when they don't want to eat their vegetables or go to bed." He started to scoop his mashed potatoes to the middle of his plate. "They say that the specials especially love the souls of disobedient children."

He shook his head and shrugged while lifting his hands in disbelieve. "It's all stupid though because if that was true, they would've taken Jackos' soul a long time ago. He's the worst kid ever."

He waited for the laugh that he normally would've gotten, but my parents looked at each other worriedly. Not being able to take the silence anymore, I decided to give Fionn what he was waiting for and forced myself to laugh, although it came out more like a screech.

"You're right," I kept my eyes lowered while scooping up some cold mashed potatoes, "Jackos is the worst, and if he still has his soul, then there's no way it's true. Right?"

I looked at Mom, trying to calm her down with my eyes. "Remember when Jackos came to Fionn's birthday party and stole all the eggs from under the chickens and started what he called an 'eggfight' with the rest of those kids he hangs around with?"

Mom's eyes immediately spit fire. The anger she still felt over that incident was enough to distract her. "That little jerk," she mumbled while she stuffed far too big a scoop of mashed potatoes in her mouth.

The rest of the dinner was eaten mostly in silence, only Fionn didn't seem to have realized our parents' strange reaction to Mori's words and talked as much as always, mostly about all the pranks Jackos pulled at school and how funny it was when they backfired on him.

I listened to him with half an ear and nodded every now and then while keeping an eye on my parents, who mostly kept their eyes on their plates and ate a lot faster than they usually did.

Specials hadn't been seen here for hundreds of years. For most humans, just like Fionn and Mori and their friends, they'd become nothing but legends. But it was different for Mom and Dad and me. Specials didn't come here, and humans never set foot in their territory, but the subject still made us nervous.

I joined Mom in doing the dishes when dinner was finally over, and to my surprise, Dad did as well. He hated doing the dishes. He claimed the slimy feel on his hands made him gag, but he wasn't a half-bad cook, so their deal for as long as I could remember was that he would prepare dinner, and Mom would do the dishes. Mori and I would usually take turns helping them. Fionn didn't do much as he would get too distracted and only end up dropping either plates or cups or our entire dinner.

"Thera," Dad started, his arms folded in front of his chest, his eyes uncomfortably aimed at the other side of the room. "I just wanted to say," he glanced at Mom, "we just wanted to say…" He stopped again.

Mom saved him by putting a wet arm around my shoulder and leaning against me, forcing me to partly support her to keep her from falling.

"You know how much we love you, right, Ther?" She put the side of her head against mine. "All three of you kids," she added with confident warmth.

I chuckled. "Of course I know that, now can you stand up straight again? You're going to make us both fall."

She grinned and complied. I let out an extra loud sigh of relief and looked down at my clothes. "Ah gross, there's dirty dishwater all over my sweater now."

Mom laughed again. "Perfect, then you can go wash that and the rest of the dirty laundry after we're done with the dishes."

I sighed again; I'd walked right into that one.

Dad heartedly slapped me on my shoulder. "Come on, I'll help."

I followed him outside, where we kept the tile in which we did our laundry. Dad wasn't the type to easily say things like 'I love you' the way Mom did, but he always managed to show it somehow. He sat across from me at the other side of the tile and hummed to himself while he rubbed our clothes on the wash rack.

"Oh," he suddenly looked up, "my ax broke this morning," he leaned closer to me so I could hear him whisper, "could you finish cutting the wood for me tonight?"

I hesitated for a moment. "I-I'm not sure I should, Dad… what if Fionn or Mori saw me?"

I lowered my voice. "What if someone from the village saw me?"

He looked disappointed at my hesitance but forced himself to nod, nonetheless. "You're right. I'm sorry. I shouldn't have asked." He pulled another piece of wet clothing out of the tile and started rubbing it against the wash rack, faster than he'd done before. "I'll go into town tomorrow to get the ax fixed. We've got enough firewood to keep us warm tonight anyway."

I smiled gratefully. "I'll help you cut and put it away to dry when the ax is fixed, Dad. It's not that I don't want to help; I just think it's better that way."

He put his hand, covered in bubbles, over mine. "I know."

I got ready for bed with a feeling of disappointment gnawing at my stomach. I got so lost in thought that I brushed my teeth for about ten minutes until Mom eventually poked her finger in my cheek and told me I wouldn't have any teeth left if I kept going.

After I rinsed, she followed me into my room and held up my blankets for me with a warm smile.

I rolled my eyes. "Mom, you don't have to tuck me in. How old do you think I am?"

She pulled up an eyebrow and tilted her head without giving me an answer, and I laughed as I crawled into bed and rolled myself into a tiny ball. That's how I fell asleep almost every night, but somehow, I always woke up with my arms and legs spread in every direction, in the least feminine way imaginable. Fionn often woke me up by making fun of the position he'd find me in the following morning.

Mom tucked in my blankets to the point that I could barely move anymore and sat down on the bed next to me, stroking my hair.

"You want me to sing you a lullaby?" She asked me, half teasing, half serious.

"Come on, Mom…" If I'd been able to, I would've turned around so she wouldn't have been able to see my face.

She chuckled and poked my cheek again. "Sleep tight, sweetie." She stroked my hair and then got up and quietly left the room.

I woke up from a light pressure pushing down on my stomach. I opened my eyes and blinked a few times to clear my blurry vision. It was still the middle of the night. Only a few rays of moonlight shone through my window, enabling me to see a tall, thin, extremely light-skinned man sitting on my stomach.

"Your younger sister is very cute." His voice was light and melodious. It would've been pleasant if he hadn't snuck into my room in the middle of the night and sat on top of me.

In a panic, I tried lifting my hands to push him off me, but he'd placed his knees on my forearms, making it impossible for me to move.

"Do you love them, your family?" He asked me in a monotonous voice.

"Who are you? Get off me before I kill you!" I snarled but tried to keep my voice down; Dad would've had a heart attack if he walked into my room and saw some stranger sitting on top of me.

"Do you love them or not?"

I was still moving around, struggling to find an opening in his airtight hold on me.

"Of course I love them!" I started to get out of breath.

"Even though you're not related to them by blood?"

I stopped moving and looked up at him. It was the first time I'd actually looked at his face, the part that I could see, that is. The lower half was small and V-shaped; I could barely see stubble or any sign of facial hair at all. His skin was light, lighter than anything I'd ever seen; the color was closer to that of milk than to that of my own skin. His lips were also a noticeably light, almost pink color. His nose was small and straight. If I could've seen his entire face, I would've thought he was dainty but beautiful. Not handsome, beautiful. But the top part of his face, including his eyes, was covered by a small, colorful mask, set in with gemstones and topped with three feathers that flowed off to the side. It reminded me of the villagers' masks for carnival, but of better quality and probably much more expensive.

The mask had holes for his eyes, but they were covered with a thin gauze-like fabric. It probably enabled him to see through it but made it unable for me to see his eyes, of which I had a creeping suspicion they were beautiful as well.

All this time that I was staring at him, he'd stayed perfectly still, waiting for my answer.

"How do you know that?" I asked him quietly.

It had been very clear to me from a young age that I was adopted, and when I finally dared to confront my parents about it, they'd simply admitted it and asked me to keep quiet about it to others. So, all my life, it had been a secret that only me and my parents knew.

"Answer the question. Do you love them, even if they're not blood relatives?"

I narrowed my eyes, about to snap. "Of course I do. They're my family, no matter what."

The left corner of his mouth lifted a little, almost as if he were smiling, although I couldn't help but feel like he was mocking me.

"Then you should get them to safety before it's too late."

My eyes widened. "What? What does that mean? What are you going to do to them?"

With a single, gracious move, he jumped off me and landed next to the open window behind my bed.

I looked at his feet. They were clad in soft leather that I didn't recognize, but that wasn't enough to explain the complete silence in his movements.

He quietly placed a foot on the windowsill and looked at me over his shoulder.

"Do it tonight. If they don't leave, they won't survive." With those words, he jumped out of the window, although it almost seemed like he floated out and disappeared into the night.

2

I fought myself out of my blankets, jumped out of bed and started walking from one end of my room to the other. Who had that guy been? Where had he come from? How had he known the truth? What was it that he warned me for? And most important of all, should I believe him?

I stopped in the middle of the room. There was a very, very big chance that he was some sad, deranged guy who had some sort of episode right when he passed by our house and saw my window was open. And honestly, I would be deranged as well if I listened to him and ran my family out of the house in the middle of the night.

I turned towards the door and opened it. Yet somehow, there had been something about him that made me feel like it would be a mistake to ignore his warning. What I'd risk by ignoring him was too much, too precious. There was no way I could take that chance.

I ran to my parents' room and knocked on their door.

"Mom! Dad! Wake up! We have to leave!" I pulled on the doorknob and slammed the door open to see Mom sitting up in her bed, a sleepy expression on her face. She shook Dad, who was still sound asleep, by his shoulder.

"Thera?" She gave up on waking up Dad and rubbed one eye while looking at me half asleep. "Waz wrong?"

I ran into the room and grabbed her arm, pulling it towards me, forcing her to turn around and look me straight in the eye. The sudden and somewhat aggressive action seemed to wake her up instantly.

"I have no time to explain, but you have to trust me." I let go of her arm. "Wake up Dad, I'll go grab Fionn and Mori. We have to get out of here right now and head for the forest." I didn't stay to wait for her answer, I knew my mom, and she knew me; she would believe me.

I ran towards the room that Fionn and Mori shared and slammed open the door the same way I'd done in my parents' room. Fionn sat up straight in his bed with a sleepy face, the same way Mom had done, but Mori had already gotten out of bed and put on a sweater over her nightgown. Had she been awake even before I started screaming through the house, or had she just instantly listened to me? I followed her example and grabbed a warm sweater out of Fionn's closet and pulled it over his head while he was still sitting up in his bed, his eyes only half-open.

I pulled his feet out from under the blankets and put his shoes on, after which I mercilessly lifted him out of his comfortable bed and put him to his feet. I took his hand and held my other hand out to Mori. She accepted it to my surprise, and I ran towards the back door, dragging both of them behind me. Our parents were already waiting for us there. Mom held all three of our winter coats in her arms, and we quickly put them on.

The first death scream of many we would hear that night tore through the air at the very moment Dad opened the door. All of us froze and turned our heads towards the village, which was only a few hundred yards away from our home.

I turned back and pushed Fionn and Mori against their backs, towards the door.

"Don't listen to it, just run. Run and don't look back." I looked at Mom, who gave me a short nod and put her hand on Fionn's shoulder as she led the two of them out of the house. I followed in their footsteps, and Dad closed our little formation.

"What is happening?" Mori ran in front of all of us, although she already sounded out of breath, which worried me more than the second death scream of that night.

"Keep running, Mori!" Dad yelled.

"Thera," he lowered his voice, so only I could hear him, "what on earth is happening?"

I shook my head. "I don't know, Dad. All I know is that we have to get out of here as fast as we can."

"And then what?"

I just shook my head a second time and kept running, until after a third and fourth and tenth scream from far away in the village, the edge of the forest finally came in sight.

I sighed with relief, and I think the rest picked up on that, as Mori immediately slowed down. The moment we reached the forest and the big deciduous trees blocked the moonlight above us, she stopped and leaned against one of those trees, desperately trying to catch her breath. I stopped as well and anxiously watched her. How could such a young, healthy girl have so little stamina?

I looked at the rest. Fionn seemed fine, but he was used to running around all day. Mom was breathing heavier than normal, but she wasn't in as bad a shape as Mori. And Dad wasn't as unaffected as I was, but he didn't seem tired by far yet.

Good, if it was only Mori, carrying her the rest of the way shouldn't be a problem. I started walking towards her, but Dad grabbed me by my arm to stop me.

"Thera." He stared at the village over his shoulder. We could hear an almost non-stop string of horrifying screams. He turned back to me, a desperate look in his eyes. "I don't understand what happened or what is going on, but those people are dying."

I tensed up as I looked at him.

Mori started crying behind us. "Sara, Jena…" She put her hands against her face and sobbed silently.

Dad had been worried that I didn't know what was going on in the village, but all his words had done was make Mori realize that her friends were among those people, that one of those screams we'd heard probably belonged to one of them.

Mom put her arms around my little sister and hugged her tightly. I turned to Dad, ready to get mad at him, but instead of seeing the look of guilt on his face I expected, he was the one who stared at me in anger.

"You have to go back." His voice wasn't soft anymore. "You have to go back and help them."

I stared at him in disbelief. "Dad… I-"

"You have to, Thera!" He interrupted me, his voice far too high pitched. "They are our friends, the people we grew up with, the people *you* grew up with! You have the power to save them. How can you turn your back on them and just run away?" He grabbed my arm tightly, and I felt waves of guilt crushing down on me.

"I'm not just running away, Dad," I heard the trembling of my own voice. I could barely get the words out, "I'm trying to get you all to safety. Do you think I want to let them get hurt or die? But I don't know what's happening, I don't know if I'm even able to do anything! Except get you guys as far away from any danger as I can! Shouldn't that be the most important thing?"

Dad opened his mouth, but Mom put her hand over the one he was still holding me with.

"She's right, Creig," she glanced towards the village, so quick that I'm pretty sure I was the only one who saw it, "no matter what happens, our family is most important. Our first priority is to protect each other."

She looked over her shoulder to Fionn and Mori and gave them a small, comforting smile before turning back to Dad. "So, let's go, okay?"

"I can't." Dad straightened his back. He wasn't used to going against Mom, but when he did, he knew he'd have to give it everything he had. But instead of talking to her, he turned to me.

"I'm sorry, honey, you're right. Protecting our family is what's most important," he took a step closer to me and put his hand on my shoulder, giving it a gentle squeeze, "so, please protect them for me from here on out, no matter what."

He looked at Mom, unable to let go of my shoulder. "I'm so sorry, darling. I have to go back and help them."

She burst out in tears. "You'll die! Can't you hear them? Whatever is attacking them is clearly too strong to fight."

Dad was now clenching my shoulder so hard that my arm turned numb. "I'm so sorry," he repeated, "I love you."

He let go of me, walked over to Fionn and Mori, and put his arms around both of them. "I love all of you."

He held them like that for a moment, both of them frozen in place, then he turned and started running.

"Creig!" Mom yelled his name through the night, and I unwittingly flinched. Would the attackers hear her scream from so far away?

I stared at Dad's back, which slowly faded into the dark night, and then looked past that to the dancing orange light that came from the village. Had it been set on fire?

I turned back to Mom and saw the question in her eyes that I knew she would never ask me out loud. I swallowed and then nodded hesitantly as I took a step back from the three of them. Fionn noticed and tried to reach out to me with his little hand, but Mom stopped him and pulled him close to her.

I somehow managed to plaster a confident expression on my face. "Don't worry, Fionn, I'm only going to make sure Dad doesn't get hurt. You guys stay hidden under the trees and keep going straight. We'll catch up to you in no time."

I honestly wasn't sure if I was a great liar or believed my own words, but somehow, they came out convincing enough to make Fionn believe me.

I turned to Mori, who was still hiding her face in Mom's coat and then to Mom herself, who simply stared back at me with a resolute face.

I looked her straight in the eye, trying not to show my fear. "Take care of them. Don't stop until we find you again."

She nodded once, and with that, I turned away from them and ran off in the same direction Dad had gone.

The closer I got to the village, the louder the screams and cries became and the more poignant the scent of ash and burning straw and flesh.

The first movement I saw as I reached the village came from a creature right out of a nightmare. They were like misshapen humans with extremely long arms and legs, but short, almost round torsos and small horns sticking out of their shoulders and head, but none of them at the same place. Some of them had hair on their heads like us, but most were bald. Their skin was a blueish kind of beige but became much darker around their horns and back. Their coloration reminded me of lizards, but their skin seemed similar to ours, maybe a little leatherier.

I felt my fear growing, and my stomach turned as I watched them rip doors and pieces of roof off houses and set fire to the straw and wood while they killed everyone inside with their bare hands.

None of them were wearing weapons; they clearly didn't need them. They didn't have claws or huge fangs or anything either, but the unlikely strength they seemed to possess made them more than deadly enough. A strength that I recognized, and had there only been one of them, I wouldn't have been scared to face them head-on at all, but there were at least ten in my vision alone. Who knew how many more were all over the village? How on earth would we ever be able to take them out?

"Thera! Behind you!" A somewhat familiar voice called out to me, but I didn't have time to think about who it was. All I could do was turn around, just fast enough to avoid a long, beige-blue arm that came swinging my way. A swing most normal humans wouldn't have been fast enough to evade, and the creature standing in front of me seemed to realize that as well. He tilted his head, and a big smile appeared on his face as he took a step forward, closer to me. I instinctively took a step back.

He didn't have a row of sharp, glittering teeth. If anything, they seemed rounder and blunter than mine. They reminded me of sheep's teeth. Could these things be vegetarians?

His surprisingly bright blue eyes, which were already too big compared to his face, became even bigger for a split second, and I knew he was coming for me, no holds barred.

I leaned back and waited as if to pull him in and at the moment he jumped forward and lashed out at me, I stepped aside and hit him with my elbow, pushing him off balance and to the ground.

Instead of hitting the ground as hard and painful as I hoped he would, he simply rolled over and jumped up, releasing a low hissing sound from his mouth, jumping at me again before I had any time to react.

He hit me in the stomach. His fist was as hard and heavy as a block of concrete. I fell to my knees, grasping my stomach, desperately trying to catch my breath. He slammed his knee into my face. A terrifying, disgusting, cracking sound filled my ears as I flew backward and landed on my back in the sickeningly warm, bloodied mud.

The creature stepped over me, one leg on each side of my body and like the masked stranger had done earlier, he sat down on my stomach. This being had much more weight and much less delicacy to him than that stranger, so for the second time, I found myself desperately gasping for air.

A light, high cackling escaped the creature's mouth as he looked down on me and leaned over to bring his face closer to mine. So close that I could feel the warmth of his breath on my face. I could smell the iron scent it had, a scent I knew very well.

"I got you." Three small words, in a soft but light voice. Only three words, but it set my brain afire. This creature could speak. And if it could speak, if it could form words and sentences, if it could speak our language, that meant it was intelligent. It could think like us.

I looked up at the dark splashes of red on his body that contrasted his skin's light, blueish color. If it could think like us, then how could it do this?

I'd been raised relatively peacefully. I'd never known real sadness or real anger or any specifically deep emotions that you could only feel in these kinds of situations, but I felt them at that moment, all of them. They gathered inside me, whirled around like a storm that I was unable to control and in what must've been less than a second, they came bursting out in a feat of strength that I never even knew I had. I lifted my hands, placed them on both sides of the creature's head and simply pulled.

A loud cracking accompanied by a disgusting sucking and spattering sound filled my ears as his head came off his body with ease. A yellowish-green liquid squirted out of his neck from both his body and his head and rained down on me as I pulled the head past my own, watching the look of horror and surprise in the creature's blue eyes, and threw it as far behind me as possible.

The head landed in the mud with a watery splash, and the body, which was still sitting on top of me, slowly started to fall to the side. I quickly got up. Adrenaline was pumping through my veins, and I dreaded the moment it would stop, and I would start thinking like a normal human being again.

But until that moment came, all I could do was take down as many of these monsters as I could until I'd find my dad.

"Thera!" The same voice that had warned me before called out to me again, and this time I was able to find the person it belonged to.

Because I was so different from the rest of the villagers, my parents had raised me as far away from them as possible, but I recognized the boy who had called out to me. Steav. He had graduated a few years ago from the same school that I'd been to.

I'd never particularly liked or disliked him. Still, on the rare occasions I'd spoken to him, he'd always managed to make me laugh, so it shocked and angered me to see him down on the ground, covered in blood and mud, using the last of his strength to fight off the monster that was hanging over him excitedly.

I was next to them in three big steps. I pulled my arm all the way back behind my head and swung my fist against the side of the creature's face. The hit hurt my hand more than I could've imagined, like hitting a brick wall as hard as you can, but much to my surprise, the creature flew off Steav and slammed against the nearly burnt down wooden wall of one of the nearby houses. The wall gave in, and the creature fell through it, inside the burning house, which couldn't seem to take any more than that and collapsed on top of it.

Part of me wasn't sure if that would be enough to kill it, but rather than going over there and checking if he was really dead, it seemed more important to get Steav to safety.

After over twenty years of hiding my abilities from everybody, I simply picked him off the ground, threw him over my shoulder and ran away. He was bleeding but didn't have any excessively big cuts. He was probably more in shock than anything else. I lay him down in the grass far enough outside of the village for him to probably be safe.

"Steav, have you seen my Dad?" I leaned over him to make sure he heard my question, and I saw him cringe. The memory of the previous person who had leaned over him like this was probably still very fresh in his memory. I immediately leaned back, so the only thing he saw while looking up was the night sky. But I couldn't cut him some slack yet.

"Steav, please, have you seen my Dad?" I heard the impatient tone of my voice, and I tried to control myself.

He shook his head quickly at first, but then slower, and eventually, he stopped and nodded instead.

My eyes widened. "You did? Where?"

"Barn…" It was the first word he had said after screaming my name earlier, but it would have to do; I didn't have time to wait for more.

"Thank you, Steav. Stay here, don't make a sound, wait for someone to come get you. You'll be okay."

I got up and started running towards the village again. There were two big barns close to each other in the vicinity of where I found Steav. Dad had to be near one of those two.

I ran over to the first one as fast as I could. The smoke coming from the fires all over the village had become so thick that I could barely breathe anymore, but at least it kept me hidden as I reached the first barn.

My heart sank as I stopped and looked up at the towering flames that devoured the barn at an alarming rate.

"Dad!" I yelled at the top of my lungs, but my voice was barely discernible amongst the deafening roar of the fire.

"The…ra…"

My heart jumped, and I ran towards the direction of his voice. I pulled aside several pieces of burning wood and stone, causing my hands to painfully blister in the process.

"Dad! Please answer me, Dad! Dad!" I yelled until I couldn't use my voice anymore. I was sure my lungs had completely filled with black smoke, so much so that I barely heard him call out to me over the sound of my coughing.

I pulled the last pieces of smoldering wood off him and kneeled next to him, trying not to look at the horrible burn marks all over his body. I'd never seen something so bad before, was that something a human being could survive?

"Dad…" I tried holding back my tears as I slid my left hand under his neck, trying to lift him up a little. He moaned in intense pain and shook his head.

I bit my lip, trying not to show how bad it was on my face, as I carefully lowered him to the ground again. This time, I forced myself to carefully inspect his body.

His right hand covered a wound on his stomach that I hadn't even noticed before. Blood dripped through his fingers, down his body and onto the ground. I shook my head again, fighting back the tears.

"I'm… sorry…" He looked up to me, his eyes were watery, his voice barely more than a whisper. "I knew it was… useless… but I couldn't… abandon… them."

He lifted his hand, and I clasped it with both of mine. His hand was warm and sticky from the blood that he had been trying to stop from spilling out. I pressed it against me, close to my face, holding onto it for dear life.

"No, I'm sorry," I cried, "I'm the one who's sorry Dad if I'd just come with you right away… if I'd protected you…"

He used what could only be the last of his strength to softly squeeze my hand.

"It's okay… honey… you were right… the ones you should protect…" he started coughing, and splatters of blood hit my arms. He lifted his free, shaking hand and wiped the blood off his face while he used his other hand to pull me closer.

"Protect them, Thera… stay together… no matter what…" He closed his eyes. "I… love… y…" His breath left his body before he could finish his sentence, and I leaned over him, pressing my forehead against the burnt skin of his chest, unable to let go of his hand. Unable to even cry anymore.

"Did you check all the houses?" The same kind of light voice I heard from the first creature I killed reached me through the thick smoke.

"Of course we did! Let's get out of here already!"

I looked up. Had they surrounded the barn? Were they going to come in here? I had been able to kill two of them when I fought them one on one, but I wasn't certain I would survive facing two or more at the same time.

I looked down at Dad's lifeless body. I couldn't leave him.

I slowly, carefully let go of his hand, placing it on his stomach, and slid my left hand under his shoulders while placing my right hand underneath his knees. Without any effort, I got on one knee and lifted him up.

I strained my ears, but apart from the two I'd heard talking earlier, it didn't seem as though there were any of them in the direction of the forest. Steadily, I started walking backward. One step at a time, tightly pressing Dad against my chest, scared we would be found out, scared they would take him from me with every step I took.

I'm not sure how long I spent slowly walking backward through the dark, suffocating smoke until eventually the air cleared up and I saw the flames in the village starting to shrink down. In an instant I turned around and started running, as fast as my legs could carry me. The view was clear from here. If they saw me now, it would be over the second they caught up to me.

I headed towards the edge of the forest but stopped the moment I passed our home. It wasn't a problem for me to carry a grown man, even if I had to run for miles with him in my arms, but then what? Should I take him to Mom like this? To Fionn and Mori? Seeing Dad burned and cut open was the most horrible thing I'd ever seen in my entire life. How could I possibly put those three through that as well?

I looked over my shoulder; it seemed like the other monsters had listened to the one who had suggested that they'd leave because none of them had followed me, and I couldn't discern much movement in the still quietly burning village.

I passed through the low, wooden front gate and kneeled in the middle of our big garden, completely covered in wildflowers. Mom had always disliked them and teased Dad by saying they looked more like weeds, but he'd always loved them and adoringly taken care of them.

I ignored the tears that started streaming down my face again as I begrudgingly placed him on the cold earth, between those wildflowers. The hard ground would be difficult to dig in, but at least it might give him some relief for his burnt skin. I got up and looked towards the shed behind the house. There were shovels in there, but to get them, I'd have to leave Dad here, all alone.

I hesitated for a moment but then kneeled next to him again and started digging in the ground beside him with my bare hands.

I dug the hole faster than any human could have and carefully placed Dad in it. He fit too perfectly. Looking at him like that made it impossible for me to keep moving.

I looked at the scoop of dirt in my own blistered hands. I'd been able to dig the hole, I'd even been able to put him in it, but to cover him up was just too… How did other people do this? How could they bear to bury their loved one's underneath layers of cold, dark dirt?

I let the sand fall through my fingers, back on the earth, and looked at him. His body was maimed, covered in boils and blood, but his face had remained strangely untouched. I leaned over him and softly stroked the side of his chin. He hadn't shaved today; I could feel the stubble beneath my hands. I closed his blue eyes that were staring up at the night sky. The same blue eyes both Fionn and Mori had.

Mom had always bragged about how handsome Dad had been when he was younger. 'A little rough around the edges, but such a handsome face', was what she always said.

I picked one of the wildflowers surrounding us and then another one. I'm not sure how long it took me to pick enough to completely cover him, or if he would've agreed with what I was doing to his garden, but if it were in the flowers he loved so much, I could at least stand to bury him.

3

I found Mom and Fionn and Mori not long after tearing myself away from Dad's grave. They had obediently listened to my words and kept running as much and as far as they could. One look at their faces told me that they were exhausted, and they wouldn't be able to go on much longer.

All I could do was thank the gods that those monsters had left the village in the opposite direction. If they hadn't, they probably would've caught up with Mom and the kids even at a walking pace.

The second Mom saw me, she put Fionn, whom she'd been carrying, down and ran towards me, putting her arms around me.

"Oh, Thera!"

I never liked to be hugged all that much, but at that moment, I found myself hoping she would never let go. Partly because I'd never felt so relieved to see her alive and well, but mostly because I was too scared of the moment she'd stop. Because that's when I had to tell them.

"Where's Dad?" Mori stood next to us, looking behind me.

Mom froze, instantly understanding the situation, and slowly let go of me. For a second, I considered letting her tell Fionn and Mori, but I couldn't let her take on that burden.

"Mori," I looked at my little sister while simultaneously gathering the courage to look at Fionn, "Dad is… he's not coming back."

Fionn stepped forward and grabbed my sleeve with a confused look on his face. "Why? What's happening in the village? Why is he staying behind?"

I swallowed the pain in my throat, wishing I had the strength to at least softly put my hand on his head to comfort him. "No. I'm so sorry, Fionn, but he didn't make it. The creatures that attacked the village… they killed him."

Every word I said was like a knife I was stabbing him with. He started shaking as he looked up at me.

"But you promised." His grip on my sleeve became tighter as his voice became louder but more broken. "You said you'd make sure he wouldn't get hurt!"

I didn't respond; I couldn't have even if I'd wanted to. His words cut deep into my soul and painfully resonated with my own crushing feelings of guilt and sorrow.

"Fionn…" Mom stepped forward and put her arms around Fionn, pulling him close the same way she'd done with me only moments before. He started crying loudly and uncontrollably while leaning against Mom with his whole weight.

"It's not her fault, Fionn. Thera did everything she could. Please don't blame her; she lost her father too tonight." Her words were soft and warm and kind, but somehow, they hurt even more than Fionn's words had done.

"Did she?"

Mom and I both turned towards Mori, who stood in front of us, her shoulders pulled up high, her entire body trembling. She was clearly fighting back her tears with all her might and had instead decided to turn those feelings of pain into anger. Anger that was aimed at me.

I silently stared at her. Mori acted like a spoiled teenager most of the time, but this wasn't the first time I noticed she was much more perceptive than she liked to let on.

Her anger hurt as much as Fionn's accusation had, but I also felt grateful for some reason. I knew Fionn had just yelled the first thing that came to mind without thinking about it, and even if Mom agreed with him, she would never let me notice, but Mori's anger was a conscious decision, something she'd given thought to.

I waited, a hundred possibilities of what she could say to me next crossed my mind, each of them more hurtful than the other, but nothing came. It seemed that asking us that one question, giving us that one little clue that she knew the truth, was all she could push herself to do.

I took a step closer to her, worried she'd move away from me, but she stayed still, waiting for me.

"Mori…" I reached out my hands to her and carefully put my arms around her, giving her a chance to push me away until the very last moment. And when she didn't, I pulled her close the same way Mom was holding Fionn.

"Mori, Dad was as much my father as you are my sister, as Fionn is my brother, and Mom is my mother, no matter what." I put my head against her soft, dark hair as I felt my shoulder get wet from her silent tears.

"I'm so sorry." I quietly whispered it in her hair, and her silent sobbing changed into loud, soul-crushing crying.

"What now?" Mom had lifted up Fionn and walked closer towards Mori and me. Her face wasn't wet like theirs, but her eyes were red. "Can we go back home?"

I looked up from Mori's head to the village. "...I don't think that's a good idea."

She nodded, her question had been hopeful, but she'd probably already known the answer.

I looked past her to the darkness between the trees, leading deeper into the forest. What now was a good question. There were several choices. Normally the safest direction would be east, past our village, deeper into human territory. But it was only human territory on contested ground. It might've been mostly inhabited by humans, but technically nobody owned it. And the fact that those monsters had shown up here scared me.

Specials were creatures of legends and bedtime stories; they weren't supposed to be real. Humans knew not to go beyond the border, and I'd never known a human that had.

But those blue monsters had changed that. Were more coming? Had they decided to take this land from us, even though they hadn't set foot on it for hundreds of years? Then why now? Had they already conquered the land behind our village without us knowing? For now, we couldn't risk going in the same direction as those monsters.

The second and worst possible option would be to keep going straight to where we were heading, north, special territory. Even though no human had seen one for decades, those tall tales about specials couldn't all be made up. At the very least, they had to have some truth to them at their core. Besides, if those monsters that had destroyed our village were, in fact, a kind of special, then what other kind of horrors would be waiting for us in their own land?

The only two options that seemed somewhat possible at this point were going west or south. Out of those two, South was probably safest. West would eventually just lead into special territory.

So, we pretty much didn't have any other choice than to go south. The problem with that was that in the south, there was only ocean. We'd have to cross that ocean to reach the human continent, but not only was that more expensive than we could ever afford, the people offering those trips had also conceived ways to detect specials, making sure none would ever pass the ocean to poison humanity with their presence, or even worse, their genes. And the truth was that not even I knew exactly what I was. All I knew was that they would never let me on a ship.

I looked at my mother again and saw her staring south with a desperate look on her face. I guess she'd reached the same conclusion.

I looked at the kids, Fionn had fallen asleep a while ago, and even Mori had become like dead weight in my arms. I loosened my embrace, so she could nestle herself against my shoulder.

"The three of you should go south." I could barely get the words out. The thought of letting them cross the ocean without me, the thought of letting them face whatever was waiting on the other side alone, nauseated me.

Mom glared at me; I could only imagine what she wanted to say.

"It's no use, Mom." I forced myself to reassuringly smile at her. "I'll offer to work for them to pay for your passage. They might not let me on their ships, but they definitely won't pass on having a worker like me on the docks." I looked down and patted Mori's dark hair. "I just need you three to be safe." My voice broke. "I promised him."

I looked up at her. She hesitated, but she wasn't saying no, and I hated myself for it, but it hurt.

I wanted her to tell me she wouldn't leave without me, no matter what, even if it meant facing whatever dangers awaited us in the west. I wanted her to tell me to swim to the other side of the world if that was what it would take for the four of us to be together.

She suddenly sighed and shook her head. She moved Fionn a little to the right to free up her left arm and put her hand on my head, stroking my hair, the same way I was still unconsciously stroking Mori's hair. "The best way to keep us safe is to keep us together."

A compassionate look gleamed in her eyes as she stared at me. "Oh, my baby," her voice was soft, "we'll figure out a way for all four of us to go there, so please forget I ever made you look at me like that, even for a second."

She pressed her hand against my cheek, and I gratefully, greedily pressed my own hand against it.

We stayed like that for a moment before she let go and sat down on the ground while carefully placing Fionn on her lap. Only now that she'd sat down did my eye catch something she'd been blocking from my view up until that moment. It was too dark in the forest to distinguish anything clearly, but there was something over there, hanging from a tree. Small but big enough to catch and reflect some of the moonlight that shone through the canopy.

I tilted my head and squinted my eyes but couldn't discern more than a shimmer. A shimmer that had somehow captured all of my attention, that was inexplicably trying to pull me in. I carefully lifted Mori and sat her down next to Mom, who gave me a questioning look.

I got up and started walking towards the shimmer that seemed to be calling out to me. I stopped less than a yard before it. It was his mask. The mask that had covered the top half of his face and his eyes as he'd warned me about what was about to come.

I took it off the small branch he'd hung it on, and the scent of oranges floated towards me as I brought it closer to me. I'd completely forgotten about him with everything that had happened, but the truth was that we owed our lives to him. So, where was he now? Why had he left this here? Had something happened to him because he'd come to warn me? And why warn only me?

"It's hanging to the north."

I turned around, shocked as if I were awoken from a deep sleep. I blinked my eyes a few times and turned to Mom. She'd leaned both Fionn and Mori to a tree close to us and had walked up behind me, her eyes fixated on the mask in my hands.

"Thera, that mask looks like magic." She noticeably pulled up her nose as if she were talking about something disgusting.

I looked at the colorful mask in my hands. She was right. It had definitely been spelled or charmed. It would explain the intensity to which I'd been attracted to it and the haze it had put me in. I hadn't exactly planned on telling Mom about what had happened until I understood it a little better myself, but there was no point in hiding it now.

"There was a man in my room earlier tonight; he warned me about what was about to happen," I reluctantly handed her the mask, "this belongs to him."

She took it and stared at it with a puzzled expression.

"He told you what was going to happen?"

I shook my head. "He told me to grab you guys and run away. He said you wouldn't survive if you stayed." I sighed. "I didn't really believe him, but a part of me just…" I shrugged. "I just listened."

She nodded slowly. "I don't think this is someone we can trust…" she looked up at me, "but if he saved our lives…" She turned her head to the left, staring into the darkness that led to the north, to special territory. "Maybe we should follow his directions, Ther. He might be able to help us. He might have some answers."

I stared at her with wide eyes, not sure if she was serious or not. "What answers? Who cares about any of that? All we have to do is get to safety."

She turned back to me with a look of disbelief, as if I'd said something incredibly stupid. "This man knew you, Thera. He sought *you* out, only you. Don't you want to know why, how?" She took my hand and pinched it. "I love you more than anything, and you've been my daughter, *mine*, since the day we found you, but… what if this man has answers about you, about where you came from?" She looked me straight in the eye with an almost painfully understanding look. "Isn't there at least a part of you that wants to know? That wants to finally understand?"

Of course there was. Of course there was a part of me that wanted to know. How could there not be? But… "Not as big as the part of me that wants to get us to safety, far away from here." This time it was my turn to pinch her. I wasn't going to discuss this; my mind had been made up.

"We're letting them sleep for a few more hours, and then we'll head towards the docks at sunrise. If we're lucky, we can get you guys a passage on a ship before the next nightfall." My voice's tone was stern, no room for doubt or discussion, even though I was talking to my mom.

She looked at me in silence for a moment but then handed me the mask back.

"Okay, we'll head south right before dawn."

4

Aleaxia, the port city, was bustling. It had always been a busy city, full of life. People from all over either arrived to find a home here, leaving their home and departing for a new life, or merchants stopping here on their way to somewhere else, trying to trade or sell whatever wares they had in the cargo hold of their ship.

The city was about half a day's walk from our own village, and either me and Mom or me and Dad had made the trip many times ever since I was a kid. For me, this place had always had something magical to it. There were so many things I'd never seen before. Colorful spices, strange animals, more scents than I had words to describe, each one as exotic and enticing as the next.

That day though, I felt like an outsider coming to this vivacious place. It somehow made everything that had happened last night seem far away, as nothing more than a dream. All these people around me were strolling along, talking, and laughing as if a village only half a day away from them hadn't just been destroyed by monsters.

I looked around. There was no way that they hadn't gotten word of it already, so why was nobody panicking? Why weren't they taking extra security measures?

I kept walking down the side of the road to avoid the crowds, closely followed by Mori and Fionn, with Mom at the back. Should I go warn someone? But those monsters had left in the opposite direction of Aleaxia. Maybe everyone here really was safe. Maybe they had already sent a battalion of soldiers after them.

I looked to my left, where tons of ships were floating in the harbor. The most important thing, for now, was to get these three on a ship to somewhere far away from here. After that, I'd figure out how to best warn the rest of this city.

"Hey!"

I jumped and pulled Mori and Fionn behind me while I turned around. A tanned woman in a loose white shirt and tight-fitting leather pants stood on the edge of the harbor, clearly staring at me with bright, brown eyes. Her long black hair blew in the wind, and I could smell the pungent scent of wood wax and sweet lemonade for some strange reason. It was a revolting and, at the same time, enticing smell that pulled me in.

She moved her head back, motioning for me to come over. I looked at Mom, who nodded slightly and walked over to the woman, holding my hand up behind me to gesture the rest to wait. I stopped at a reasonable distance from her. Close enough to have a conversation, but enough space between us for me to either flee or strike when necessary.

"You looking for passage?" Her voice had a rich, commanding timbre, despite the rude tone she spoke in.

I raised an eyebrow. "How did you know?"

She shrugged uninterestedly. "You got a scared look in your eyes like you need to get outta here."

I narrowed my eyes. I wasn't quite sure what to make of this person.

"Yesterday our vi-" I started, but she lifted her hand in the air to stop me with a slight grin.

"I ain't really interested. If you're in a hurry, there's some room left on my ship." She gestured her head to the right, and I looked past her at a relatively big ship contently floating on the calm sea. I didn't know much about ships, but one look was enough to tell me that this definitely wasn't the best ship around. However, it seemed to be well maintained and clean, and we didn't have the time to be picky.

I looked back at the woman in front of me and then opened my mouth to ask for her price, but she lifted her hand to stop me from talking again. It irritated me, but I swallowed every reaction that came to mind.

"Before you ask me anything, contracts and payments are handled by the guild," she gave me an icy stare, "and so is the permission you need to get aboard any ship in this harbor."

She pointed behind me. I turned around and followed her finger with my eyes. A small, short building, almost hidden between the many big warehouses all over the place. It was built from dark red stone, square and sturdy. The only thing that gave away that this was the guild building was an oblong piece of light wood hanging next to the door with the words 'Aleaxia Seafaring Guild' painted on it in dark red letters.

I turned back to the rundown ship captain, but she'd already walked away from me and was now talking to a man wearing only loose red pants, no shirt; probably one of the sailors on her ship.

I guess that meant our conversation was over. Either the guild would allow us to board her ship, or they wouldn't.

I turned around and walked back, sticking my hand out to Fionn, who immediately took it. I prayed that I looked as untroubled as I tried to act, but I knew very well what would happen inside that small guild building. All I could hope for was that they would grant at least Mom, Fionn, and Mori permission to board that ship.

I lifted my hand to knock on the door but stopped halfway. There was too much noise coming from within the building for anyone to hear my knocking. Clearly, this wasn't only a place of business. I grabbed the door handle and pushed the door open slightly, so I was the only one who was able to glance inside at first.

A room that seemed to cover almost the entire first floor spread out in front of me. Round wooden tables were scattered across it. A tall, flamboyantly dressed lady stood on a wooden podium on the back, singing a song accompanied by a rough-looking man on an instrument I didn't recognize. The scent of beer, tobacco smoke and sweat made its way to me, especially from the long bar covering almost the entire right side of the room.

The place was gross and filled with loud drunks that completely drowned out the singer's voice.

I reluctantly pushed the door open a little more. A big, intimidating-looking man sitting in the right corner had caught my attention. He leaned back on a chair next to a stairway leading to the second floor.

I sighed. Clearly, we had to make our way through this rancid place to get to the people we needed.

I opened the door completely and stepped into the room, followed by Mom and the kids. A few people turned their heads towards us, and I felt disgusted as their eyes moved all over me and, to my dismay, all over Mori as well. I quickly took a step to the left, hiding her from their sight, and stayed close to her as we made our way through the room. I stopped in front of the guy who was guarding the entrance to the stairway.

He looked up at me without changing his expression, not saying anything.

It wasn't easy to give him my most disarming smile. "Hello. We're looking for passage on a ship. One of the captains we spoke to told us to come here."

The man didn't move, he didn't say anything, he just stared me up and down for a second, then looked at Mom, Fionn, and Mori, and then back to me again. I stared him straight in the eyes for what felt like an eternity until he eventually nodded his head to the left, a short, but clear sign that we could pass him. I didn't wait for any more than that but quickly pushed everyone onto the stairs.

We nervously walked up and stopped in front of a wooden door that was painted the same dark red as the letters on the plank in front of the building. I could hear some noises coming from the other side as well, but not nearly as much or as loud as in the room below us, which made me feel more hopeful as I knocked.

A light voice yelled from the other side of the door that "it was open" and "you can come on in", so we did.

This room was a lot smaller than the one on the first floor and a lot cleaner. Two people sat on one side of a small desk under the window on the right side of the room. Two empty chairs waited for visitors opposite of them. A warm, crackling fire in the big hearth on the left side of the room invited us in much friendlier than the people in the room had done. A young man was warming himself in a rocking chair in front of the fire, leaving temporary tracks in the thick rug beneath him. He didn't even look up from the paper he was reading as we entered. Very much unlike the three people in the middle of the room, who were standing behind a big, dark wooden table, staring at us intently.

"Come in, take a seat, please." The same light voice that had told us to come in. It belonged to one of those three people, a young man on the right. He sat down and leaned back in his seat, gesturing us to sit down on the opposite side of the table.

Relieved to meet what seemed to be a kind person, we followed his request and sat down on the wooden chairs placed on all four sides of the table.

"Four people for passage to Herodia?" He opened a big, black, leather-bound book and flipped through it until he reached a page that had only been filled halfway.

I nodded, and he moved his finger over the first half of the page, which seemed to be a time schedule.

"There's some room left on the *Winged Survivor* if you want to leave today. It's not a very big ship, but it's sturdy, and the captain is a decent person." He showed me a compassionate expression. "She's willing to accept labor as way of payment."

I felt the blood rushing to my face. Was that how terrible we looked?

I swallowed. I knew there was enough Mom could and would do on a ship, and the same went for me, but…

"If you could place your hand on the crystal one by one and hold it there for at least twenty seconds." The man in the middle, a much older, more grumpy looking man, lifted a piece of dark red fabric that I'd clearly mistaken for a tablecloth to uncover a small, light red, almost orange crystal that had been mounted in the table, so you only saw the top half of it. It had been polished smooth and was semi see-through, but there was a vast swirl of color inside it.

The young man on the right had taken a pen out of the inner pocket of his jacket and looked up at us.

"Please state your first and last name and place your hand on the crystal until I ask you to take it off again."

I stared at the crystal. I had no idea how it worked or how it could be so beautiful, but I knew exactly what it was for and what it would reveal about me. What should I do? Could I make up an excuse, tell them there was no need for me to touch it because I wasn't going to cross the sea anyway? Was there a way for me to secure passage without having to do this? I felt my hand twitch slightly. Should I touch that crystal and find out the truth once and for all?

Mom had been right. There had always been a small part of me that wanted to know, that wanted certainty. This was a way for me to get it.

I lifted my hand and slowly moved it towards the crystal.

"Thera Moralis." I softly stated my name, took a deep breath, and nearly slammed my hand on the crystal. From the corner of my eye, I saw Mom's shocked expression, but I ignored it and focused all my attention on the crystal instead. It felt cold underneath my hand, much colder than I expected, closer to ice. I expected it to feel smooth with how clear it looked, but it was somehow soft to the touch. I wasn't exactly sure how to explain it. It was like I was touching a pillow that wouldn't budge. Even with everything I had riding on this, I couldn't stop thinking how amazing it would feel to have a bed made from this crystal in hot summers. I wondered where they got it from and if they could get more of it.

I was the first one who noticed a slight change in the coloring of the crystal. My hand started tingling, but it was a pleasant feeling, almost like a friendly exchange. I don't know what it was or how it happened, but something flowed from me into the crystal and back into me. I couldn't hide a smile. Was this something everybody who placed their hands on the crystal felt? Or was this just me? It felt natural, nostalgic almost, like something I recognized.

"Very good, thank you, you can take your hand… off… the…" The man on the right stopped talking, staring at the crystal with wide eyes.

Almost. I'd almost made it through twenty seconds, but right before I was allowed to take my hand off, the swirling color inside of it had started to move very, very slowly. And not just that, a small line of light red, orange light started to appear on the outline of my hand, as if the crystal were marking the exact place where I was touching it.

"You!" The old man in the middle jumped up. The grumpy look on his face had made a place for one of shock and fear. The two people on both his sides and the two people behind the small desk next to the window and the man reading the paper by the fire followed his example.

I felt myself shrink. This had been a mistake, this had been one big, stupid mistake. There had been so many other choices I could have made, so many things I could have done to avoid this, to find a better way to handle this and now my selfishness, my one moment of weakness, had ruined it all.

I got up too, slowly, not to scare anyone.

"Please, at least listen to-" A high, deafening scream reached us through the window on the right side of the room and cut me off.

I turned my head to the window as the world seemed to slow down. I recognized that scream. I had heard it more times than I could bear as I'd watched our village burn to the ground. Someone was dying.

I ran to the window and looked outside. Flames crawled up the warehouse next to us, and people were running over the street in a panic, trying to find cover from what seemed to be small, floating sparks that were scattered all throughout the air.

"Thera!" Mom had gotten up and grabbed both Mori and Fionn's hands. "What's happening?"

I shook my head. "The warehouse next to us is on fire, and more things seem to be catching fire all over town. Take Mori and Fionn and run towards the water. Jump into it if you have to." I put a foot on the window pain. "I'm going to see what's happening and if there's something I can do."

"So, this wasn't you?"

I stopped, already halfway out of the window, and turned around. The young man who had been talking to us so casually before stood behind the table, clutching it in fear, staring at me with big eyes.

I hesitated for a second, this was exactly why my parents had made me keep quiet about this all my life, and I regretted that the truth had come out this way, but I had no time to deal with it now. And neither did they. So instead of trying to talk to him, I turned around and jumped out of the window, first against the wall of the burning building and then against the wall of the guild, after which I landed on the ground.

"Run! Take cover near the water!" The captain that had shown us to the guild was standing on the street, gesturing people in the direction of the water. Some people listened, one person whose clothes were on fire even jumped in, but most people kept running in every direction in a blind panic.

The captain cursed and yelled some orders to her sailors in a language I didn't recognize. I ran towards her as the sailors she'd been screaming at moments earlier started hoisting buckets of water out of the sea and simply throwing it wildly around them.

More people around me started to catch on fire. I instinctively grabbed two of them that were screaming and crying in pain and threw them on the ground, hitting out the flames that were eating at them until one of the sparks hit me. I swiftly reached out my hands and caught it.

Even though it seemed like a small flame, it wasn't too hot or painful. Quite the opposite, it felt warm and pleasant. It moved in the palm of my hand, and I opened it slightly.

My eyes widened as I stared at it. It wasn't a spark or even a real flame I was holding; it was a small person-like creature.

"Don' hurt me! I don' wanna die!" It looked like a little girl that was somehow dressed in fire. A raging fire was swirling around her, from the top of her head, down her back and chest, and part of her legs, leaving her face, arms, and the bottom part of her legs open, which had a light red color. I stared at her in disbelief. She was hitting her tiny fists against my palm in an attempt to free herself. She was pretty in an adorable way, and even though she was the cause of the horror that was unfolding around us, she didn't seem to be doing it on purpose or to have much control over it.

I lifted an eyebrow, everything but my hand.

50

"What are you doing? If you catch one, put it in the water!" The captain had run over to me with a bucket of water. She grabbed my hand that held the small fire creature and stuck it into the cold seawater before I could stop her.

"No!" I pulled out my hand as fast as possible and opened it to see if the tiny creature was okay, but it was too late. Its fire had gone out, and its skin had turned to a dark kind of grey. I just stared at it, too shocked to say anything.

"What do you mean no? These things are destroying everything. We have to kill them before there's nothing left!" She pushed the bucket against my chest, forcing me to take it from her, and then got up and left.

I got up as well, the bucket of water in one hand, the dead fire creature in the other. The captain was right. Even if they didn't mean to, these little creatures were causing horrible destruction. But was there really no other way to stop them?

"Thera!" Mom came running out of the guild towards me, closely followed by Fionn and Mori and most of the people that had been on the first floor.

"Keep your heads down!" I yelled at them. I grabbed Mom by her arm and pulled her close to me and the ground at the same time.

"Douse yourself with a bucket of water and run out of the village, but don't go into the woods!" I let go of her arm and pointed to the sailors who were still lifting buckets of water out of the sea at a rapid pace. "I'm going to find a way to help them."

She looked at me with worried eyes. "Thera, you don't have to do this again. Let's go together."

I shook my head. "Please go ahead. I promise I'll follow shortly."

She hesitated, but at that same moment, someone not even a yard away from us caught fire and screamed in agony as they fell to the ground, rolling left to right in a desperate attempt to put out the fire. Mori let out a high-pitched scream and grabbed Mom's arm. That seemed enough for her to cast all her doubts aside.

She put her hand against my face. "Follow us within the hour, or I *will* come back for you, no matter what."

She took her hand off my face and pulled Mori and Fionn along as she ran towards the sailors and, after they poured a bucket of water over them, along the edge of the wharf out of the city. I didn't give myself time to watch them leave all the way. Instead, I kneeled next to the man who was still rolling around on the ground. I used my hands to help him slap out the fire. He had some pretty horrendous blisters, and I could smell the nauseating scent of burning flesh. It brought back flashes of Dad, but I pushed them away and helped the man up after the fire had gone out.

I looked up at the sky. More and more fire creatures seemed to be filling the air every second. It wasn't hard for me to jump up and grab another. The moment I closed my hand around it, I turned around and ran into a small alley between two warehouses. It wasn't a very safe place to hide, but I had to try and talk to one of them before the captain, or anyone else would extinguish it again.

I opened my hand slightly and looked at the little humanlike fire creature, a little boy this time.

"Hey." Probably best to start simple.

"Leggo of me!" Like the little girl earlier, he was hitting and kicking the palm of my hand. "I gotta go, gotta find a place ta hide!"

I lifted an eyebrow. "Hide? From what?"

"Leggo! Leggo! I need ta go!" His little fists hit less than pinpricks against my skin.

"Hey, talk to me. What are you hiding from? Why are you here?" I tried to keep my voice calm, moving my face closer to my hand to ensure it would hear me, but it kept on ignoring me and hitting and kicking.

I frowned, stopping myself from poking him. "Come on, buddy, if you tell me, maybe I can help you."

As I'd expected, it still ignored me, which made me think it really couldn't understand or hear me for some reason.

I sighed, and at that moment, an entire swarm of them came soaring down, landing on my hand. They all started pulling on my fingers, trying to save their friend.

I was sure no number of these tiny creatures would have been able to take on my strength, but I opened my hand to set my little captive free, nonetheless.

"You!"

I turned around, and even though I still believed they couldn't understand it, the swarm of fire creatures around me followed my example. The young man from the guild stood in the opening of the alley, looking at me as if he were looking at a monster.

"You did this!" His eyes were spread wide open as if he were too scared to even blink. "Why would you? What have we ever done to you?"

He bent over and picked up a rock from the street, which he bravely lifted above his head. "Stop this! Send those strange sparks away! Douse these fires!"

He lifted the rock up higher. I wasn't sure if he believed that he could actually use it as a weapon against me or if he was just plain desperate.

"Listen," I kept my voice soft and reassuring as I took a step closer to him, "this wasn't me, but I'm trying to find a way to help."

"Liar!" He spat that word at me, and I stopped moving immediately.

We stood there in silence for a second, then he lowered the rock slightly. "How are you going to help us?"

I kept myself from sighing with relief. "I don't know. They won't talk to me."

"They?" The look on his face darkened, and he lifted the rock up higher again. "I knew it; you are one of them, you monster!"

That pissed me off. "I told you I didn't do this; I didn't have anything to do with this!"

"It doesn't matter!" He pulled his arm back and threw the rock at me. "You're still one of them!"

It was purely coincidental that the sharpest part of the rock hit me right above my eye. I was stronger and tougher than humans, but even I wasn't impervious to sharp edges. The skin above my eye broke, and a small stream of blood dripped down my face. It seemed to shock that guy more than me. He stared at it with a terrified look on his face for a moment but then bent over to grab another rock.

"What're you doing, you idiot?" The female captain, the very person I'd tried to hide from by coming here, appeared behind him, and hit the new rock out of his hand.

"But she is-"

"So what?" She mercilessly cut him off, and he took a step back. "Is she the one setting our city on fire? Get outta here and go help douse the flames and kill these creatures!"

The man just stood there silently, staring at her, while keeping an uncertain eye on me at the same time.

The captain took a step closer to him. He instinctively moved back, and after one last look at me, he turned around and ran away.

The captain took three big, angry steps to get to me and grabbed me by my arm. "And you," she seemed barely able to contain her anger, "get outta this city."

I tried to shake my arm loose from her grip, but she was stronger than any human I'd ever met. "I had nothing to do with this!"

She snorted. "Well, they sure didn't show up till the second you set foot in this city!"

I folded my arms as best as I could, with her still holding my upper arm. "That's a coincidence, not evidence," I mumbled.

She reacted by squeezing my arm to the point that it hurt. I looked down and grabbed her wrist to free myself forcefully, but only at that point did I see the countless red, painful-looking blisters on her hands. I stared at them with mixed feelings. How many of these creatures must she have grabbed out of the air and dunked into the water? How many human lives did she save by killing these small specials?

She let go of me when she saw me looking at her hands. "You heard me." She hid her hands behind her back and gave me a dangerous glare. "Get out of Aleaxia."

I took a step back and nodded slowly. I didn't believe she was right, but I didn't really believe my own words either.

I took another step back as I watched the captain turn around and run away, catching more fire creatures in the process.

It pained me to run. Even if those fire creatures would leave because of that, it was probably still too late. This city was going to go up in flames, just like our home.

I started running, but not far from the city, I stopped and turned around. Every single ship in the harbor was set aflame. This wasn't an exception to the rule anymore. Something bad was happening, something unbelievably bad, and our only hope of getting out of here safely was burning down right in front of my eyes. I turned my back to the city and walked in the direction I'd told Mom and the kids to run in while I took the feathered mask out of the inner pocket of my coat.

I stroked my finger over the sparkling gems. I'd hated myself for not having been able to leave it behind in the woods, but at that moment, I was also glad that I hadn't. Mom had been right; it was time to go get some answers.

5

"Thera! Oh, thank the gods!" Mom jumped up and came running towards me as soon as she caught sight of me. She wrapped her arms around me before I had a chance to talk and pulled me close. I closed my eyes and let my head rest against her shoulder. For a second, I allowed myself to stand there and feel safe in her arms.

After that second, I put my hands on her arms to free myself from her embrace and leaned to the right, so I could look past her at Fionn and Mori, who both seemed exhausted.

I couldn't really blame them. Mom had taken my words to heart and had run a lot farther than I'd expected them to. They'd stayed close to the water line and had moved from the smoothly paved streets of Alaexia to the loose white sand of the beach next to the city. Halfway across the beach, they had taken cover in the dry, high grass between some of the bigger dunes. The woods weren't far behind, but Mom had clearly heeded my warning against entering them. I gratefully turned back to her to see her standing in front of me with her arms folded and a stern look on her face, aimed at me.

"Are you ready now to accept that we should stay together, all four of us like I said?" She used that tone of voice to put me in my place that only a mother could.

I nodded obediently. From the moment all of this started until right now, I'd been making all the decisions. I somehow thought I was the only one eligible to do so because I was different from them.

I carefully looked up at her again. I wasn't the only one who was eligible, but I wasn't blind. Mom was as hurt, shocked, confused, and terrified as I was. We were both reaching in the dark. Seeing her struggle the same way I had, I'd simply decided to do what I thought was best. She had accepted it, and it had ended in complete failure.

I scraped my throat lightly. Now that I'd decided on a new course of action that I thought was best, would she accept it again? Because I knew I didn't have the strength to go against her after all that.

"Wait. Why did you say 'all four of us' like that?" Fionn pushed himself to get up, despite his clearly tired legs. "Were you going to leave us too?"

My breath stopped in my throat. Dad wasn't here anymore, and now, not even a day later, I was trying to leave them too. The feeling of betrayal was written across his face.

"Of course not," Mom put her arm around my shoulder, "there's no way Ther would leave us, sweetie. That's not what I meant by saying it like that."

Mori scoffed, clearly not buying into Mom's lie, but she was sensible enough this time not to say anything.

"Anyway," Mom quickly spoke over Mori's mocking reaction, "I guess we're going north after all?"

She looked down at the mask I was still clutching in my hand. I hadn't even realized how tightly I had been squeezing it until I saw how my knuckles had turned almost completely white. I quickly loosened my grip and looked up at her.

"We don't have to." I kept my voice soft, although I was fairly sure that both Fionn and Mori were following every word of our conversation.

"Well," Mom forced a smile, "we can't go home, we can't cross the sea, and like I said yesterday, if that man warned you about what happened, he might have some other answers for us. I'm not very delighted by the thought of heading towards special territory, but right now, I can't think of a better option."

She looked at Fionn and Mori from the corner of her eye and lowered her voice. "But from now on, no more running off, no more sending us away and trying to do everything on your own. I don't care how much stronger or whatever you are than us. We stay together. Understood?"

I nodded obediently.

I took a deep breath to try and collect myself as best as I could and then turned to Fionn and Mori. "Let's go."

From the look on their faces, I expected a waterfall of complaints, but both of them agreed quietly and got up. They looked so worn out it made me wish they would've complained. At least it would've proven they still had some fight left in them.

I looked over my shoulder, unnoted. Even from this distance, I could still see the orange glow hanging over Alaexia. I could still smell smoke. I turned back to the kids. Were we at a safe enough distance to give them some time to rest? Maybe I could catch some fish and at least feed them something.

As if she'd read my mind, Mom put her hand against my back and pushed me towards the woods. "Let's go." She repeated my earlier words.

She clearly didn't think we were at a safe enough distance, and if she believed Fionn and Mori were able to keep going for now, then I gladly trusted her on that.

The woods gave us some more cover, but I honestly have no idea how much longer we kept walking after that. Fionn's legs gave up on him sometime before dawn, and I carried him on my back. Mori bravely kept walking, but as it started to get dark, her steps started getting smaller and slower.

I turned to Mom, and she nodded at me without a moment of doubt. We didn't even go out of our way to find a proper place to sleep. We just sat down next to the closest tree, where the kids curled up against Mom and fell asleep.

I allowed a relieved sigh to escape. It had been a long, hard day, we barely ate, and it wasn't freezing anymore, but it was still extremely cold.

I managed to start a small fire, even though I knew from the start that I wouldn't be able to stay awake long enough to keep it going, and sat down next to Mori, leaning her head against my shoulder and wrapping my arms around her. Secretly, I was relieved she was asleep since she normally wouldn't let anybody get close like this to her anymore. She always said she was too old for hugs, unlike Fionn, who was always hanging around my neck.

I looked at him. He'd curled up as close to Mom as he possibly could, and she'd wrapped her own coat around him, the same way she had done with Mori. Despite everything, I wasn't as worried about him catching a cold, or worse, as I was about Mori. Fionn spent most of his days outside in the cold for hours on end, and he was always fine. Mori, on the other hand, liked to spend her days inside the house, as close to the fireplace as possible, until our mom or dad would tell her to go outside and get some fresh air every once in a while.

I closed my eyes, trying to picture those moments. Trying to picture Dad's face as he would shake his head when Mori refused to go out, without having the heart to actually push her into listening to him.

I was pretty sure I slept at least a few hours, but it didn't feel that way when I was awakened by a sharp whistling sound. I sat up straight and rubbed my eyes, under heavy protest of my thoroughly cold and stiff arms.

The whistling sound reached me for a second time, and it gave me goosebumps, even though I'd never heard it before. I wasn't sure if I should call it instinct or rational thinking, but I was completely sure that whatever that sound was, it was bad news. I reached out to wake Mom up but stopped before I touched her. She'd pressed her left hand against her face and was quietly sobbing.

I pulled my hand back as I choked up. "Oh, Mom…"

She stopped sobbing and lifted her head to look at me with wet, bloodshot eyes. She averted her face the moment our eyes met, and she quickly wiped her tears away with her hand as she coughed softly to explain the hoarseness of her voice.

I shook my head as I took her trembling hand. "Mom, I-" I stopped as the whistling rang in my ears again.

Mom leaned closer to me, a worried expression on her face. "Thera?"

"Ssht," I pressed my finger against my lips to stop her from saying anything else, scared of how well the hearing of whatever was close by was. "Do you hear that? I think we have to leave right now."

She quickly looked around, scanning our surroundings, and let out a barely audible sigh of relief after determining that whatever I was talking about wasn't close enough to be seen yet. She then woke up Fionn and Mori.

The whistling reached me again, louder and higher-pitched this time.

I turned back to Mom. "What do you think it is?"

She slightly lifted an eyebrow. "What what is?"

I looked over my shoulder and back. "The whistling."

If her first reaction hadn't been enough to tell me already, the surprised look in her eyes certainly was. She wasn't able to hear it. I looked at Fionn and Mori, but they stared at me with the same blank expression.

She put her hand on my shoulder. "Are you sure you heard something? It's been a long day, and you haven't slept much…"

I shook my head to stop her. I knew she didn't mean it in a bad way, but the worried look in her eyes frustrated me. "I'm not making this up, Mom."

She softly pinched my shoulder to calm me down. "No, I know, I wasn't trying to say that." She took her hand off my shoulder and held it out to Fionn, who gratefully accepted it. She turned back to me. "Let's go. The sun will start rising any moment now anyway."

And with that, she started walking north. Walking, not running. Part of me wanted to push her to move faster, but I controlled myself. I knew she wasn't doing it on purpose. They hadn't nearly slept long enough, and I was forcing them to leave as soon as they'd woken up, without even giving them a chance to eat anything. Not that we had anything.

I looked over my shoulder. The whistling became louder and more frequent. I wasn't sure what was out there. I wasn't even sure if they were after us or not, but there was definitely more than one, and they were moving in the same direction as we were at a higher pace. They would catch up to us before long.

I turned back, just in time to stop myself from falling over Fionn, who had tripped on a root and fallen face first in the thawed, but no doubt ice-cold mud. Mom quickly pulled him on his feet and vigorously tried to wipe the mud off him.

"Maybe we should all do that?"

Both Mom and I turned to Mori in surprise. It was the first time she'd spoken all day. She stared back at us with an uncertain look on her face.

"You know, how the hunters cover themselves in mud, so the animals won't be able to smell them?" Her voice was small, and her cheeks turned red as if she were embarrassed about coming up with the idea.

I looked at Fionn, it was true that his scent had become distinctively weaker than that of Mori or Mom, but would that be enough to throw whoever was following us off our trails?

I rubbed my hand over my forehead, there was too much I didn't know about them, but there was no time to figure anything out.

I turned to Mori and nodded. "I think that's a good idea, Mori. Let's do it." I turned to Mom and Fionn. "I don't know if it will help, so we have to keep going as fast as we can, but if there is a possibility that it works, we should at least try."

Mori smiled proudly after hearing my praise and bowed down to pick up two handfuls of mud without waiting for Mom's reaction. Against all my expectations of my usual dirt-fearing little sister, she slapped the mud against her face and stomach without a moment's hesitation.

Mom suppressed an equally surprised look and followed her example, and so did I. The mud was as cold as I'd expected it to be, and despite it being overall liquid, I could feel little frozen clumps within, painfully scrubbing against my skin.

After covering most parts of our bodies, we started walking again. There was no need for me to push them to move faster this time, everybody instinctively walked as fast as they could to keep themselves warm, and I secretly wondered if we'd made a mistake. Even if this somehow managed to help us escape whatever was behind us, how long would it be before we could warm up? Were we all going to die from hypothermia before any creature even had the chance to kill us? Should I have taken the chance and faced whatever was behind us? I looked at Fionn and Mori's fragile bodies walking in front of me. If they got separated from me so close to the border to special territory, how were they ever going to survive?

A new whistle soared through the air, loud this time, louder than any of the other whistles before that. I turned around; I wouldn't have been surprised if whatever creature made that sound would be standing right behind us at that moment. It wasn't, but I knew that would only be a matter of time.

"Run." I whispered the words, even though I was pretty sure by now that the creatures were following us, and they were very aware of where we were.

All three of them turned around and looked at me with big eyes, simultaneously scared and hesitant.

I ignored it. "Run now, as fast as you can."

We sprinted, and I heard all three of them gasping for air next to me, but I couldn't allow myself to give them time to rest.

A new whistle started up, even closer than before, but was suddenly cut off halfway. I stopped and turned around. Mom and the kids stopped too, bending over, sucking in as much cold air as they could.

I narrowed my eyes and tried to look through the trees that were too close together to reveal anything at all. Why had it stopped right in the middle? Had it got cut off? By whom? And why?

I turned my head, trying to focus my hearing. There was another whistle in reaction to the earlier one that had gotten cut off, but it sounded a lot farther away. And very softly, from even farther away, a second reaction. I had no idea what had happened, but one thing was for sure, the creatures had changed direction and were now going in the opposite direction to us.

All of a sudden, all my tension disappeared from my body, and my legs gave in. I fell on my knees on a patch of wet moss. For the third time in a forty-eight-hour period, I'd thought we were going to die.

"Thera?" Mom softly put her hand on my hair and leaned over so she could look at my face. "Are you okay? What happened?"

I let out a little laugh. "Yeah." I got up and properly smiled at her and the kids. "It's okay now. I think we're safe." For now, I thought.

Fionn let out a big sigh of relief and flopped on the ground with a soft thud. Mori followed his example. I looked at our mom, half and half expecting her to plop down too, but she seemed to be able to keep standing somehow.

"Hey, isn't there a lot of green here?" Mori leaned forward and plucked some of the moss around her.

I looked down and then around me. She was right. It wasn't very consistent, but there were big patches of bright green moss all over the place.

Fionn lay down on his back. "And the mud is warmer here than before." He scooped up a hand full of it and rubbed it over the dried-up layer of cold mud already on his stomach.

Mori lifted an eyebrow but followed his example, immediately showing us a look of delight. "He's right!"

I hid my surprise and stared ahead of us. It wasn't just this spot. The farther I looked, the more green I saw.

"It's special territory."

I turned to Mom. She didn't look nearly as happy as Fionn and Mori. "They must've spelled it somehow to keep the winter away."

I lifted an eyebrow. "Spelled nature? There's no way they can do that."

She shook her head. "We have no idea what they're capable of."

I felt my stomach cramp up in response.

Mori got up. "We can't go back anymore now, can we?" She looked toward special territory over her shoulder. "If we can't, then maybe we should just go ahead to where it's at least warmer."

She looked at me, waiting for my approval, and I looked at Mom, who nodded slightly. Good enough. Every part of my being resisted the idea of going farther into special territory, but every part of my being also resisted the idea of going back. If every part of my being couldn't make up its mind, then Mori was right. We should at least think over our options in a warmer place.

Something strange fell over us the farther we walked. I wasn't exactly sure what it was. I couldn't touch it; it was something inside me. But it had a certain scent that I couldn't place. It was pleasant, welcoming almost.

I stopped when Fionn suddenly put his hand on my arm. I looked over my shoulder to see that Mom and Mori had turned around and started walking in the opposite direction, back to where we came from. Fionn was pulling at my arm, trying to get me to join them.

"Fionn?" I pulled him closer to me. "Mom! Mori! What are you doing?"

Neither of them reacted, and Fionn gasped softly. I looked down at him. He blinked his eyes, which had a distant look in them, a few times.

"Ther?" He lifted his head. "What…"

I held onto his hand while I dragged him with me to stop Mom and Mori. It was magic. That feeling that had rolled over us, that feeling that had smelled so welcoming to me, it was some sort of magic. Magic that only seemed to affect humans.

I grabbed Mori's arm. "Mori! Mom!"

They both stopped walking and turned around to me, tilting their heads, clearly trying to focus on me.

"Thera? Why are you stopping us?" Mom put her hand on my arm. "We should keep going until we're at least in a warmer spot to talk."

I pulled Mori a little closer to me. "That's what we were doing before the three of you turned around and started going back."

I stared her straight in the eyes. "Mom, look at me. Are you okay?"

She blinked a few times, just like Fionn had done, and then the glassy look in her eyes cleared up. "What happened?"

I exhaled and shook my head. "I don't know but stay close to me. I'll pull you through."

She nodded and tightened her grip on my arm while I held onto Fionn and Mori.

"It was so weird," Fionn spoke softly. "My head became warm all of a sudden, and I couldn't think anymore. The only thing I knew was that we had to turn back."

He looked up at me. "But you weren't coming with us."

He squeezed my hand tightly, moving closer to me.

I squeezed back. "It's okay, Fionn. I'm not leaving you. We'll all stay together no matter what."

He nodded quietly. I glanced at Mori, who walked on my other side. She'd been listening to us, but she hadn't said a word. Just like Fionn, I could see her fighting whatever it was that was trying to mess with her head. But when I squeezed her hand as well, she softly squeezed back.

We didn't even have to walk that much farther. Within a few minutes, the magic that had tried to chase Mom and Fionn and Mori away faded, and they regained full control over their thoughts again.

I had no other choice but to assume that meant we were officially in special territory. Although I felt nervous about what other kinds of magic were waiting for us. Would I be able to pull them through that easily every time?

We continued for little more than an hour until the temperature had raised several degrees and a nice, summerlike breeze started blowing against our faces. Less than a second hour later, we'd truly reached summer. The air was nice and warm, we walked on soft, green grass, and the trees all around us were covered in vibrant green leaves, letting through the occasional bright sunbeam.

No matter how aware we all were of the dangerous place we'd entered, I think that was the moment we all subconsciously started to feel safe. I shook my head. Just those few rays of sunlight had made all the difference.

Fionn suddenly stopped. He let himself fall down on a nearby rock protruding out of the ground. After he'd sat down, he looked up at Mom and me with a defiant look in his eyes, as if he dared us to tell him to get up and keep walking. Neither of us had the heart to do that, though. Even I was about to collapse. I could only imagine how they must've felt.

Mom sat Mori down next to Fionn and turned to me with an almost excusatory look. "I will make us a fire, but…"

"It's okay," I stopped her by softly putting my hand on her shoulder for a moment; I'll find us something to eat."

I turned around and started to walk away but then stopped and turned back. "Don't leave each other's side and if something happens, run away if you can. If you can't, call out for me as loud as possible. I'll make sure to stay close enough to hear you."

All three of them simultaneously nodded in response, and I walked away. I'd heard the sound of water while we'd been walking, and even though I knew both Fionn and Mori didn't like fish very much, it seemed like the safest bet.

I didn't have to walk too far to find a small, babbling brook that led to a relatively small but beautifully turquoise lake. I stopped at the water's edge and stared at it in awe. The water was so clear I could see the flowing green plants growing on the bottom, with small fish swimming between them. And with no trees to block the sky, the sun shone directly on the water, which reflected it so brightly that it nearly blinded me, but I still gratefully took it in.

I leaned over and stuck my hand in the water. It was cold compared to the summer air, but nothing compared to the icy mud in the forest, not even a day away from here.

Without a moment's hesitation, I stepped into the water and let myself fall in it. I almost felt guilty about the huge amount of dirt that came flowing off me, clouding the water, but I quickly pushed that feeling down. I scrubbed my clothes hastily. I would take some time to wash them decently after I'd gotten Mom and the kids something to eat, but for now, it felt good to see some white fabric again. I got out of the water and took my clothes off, keeping only my underwear on, squeezed the water out of them and hung them over the nearest branch.

Then I looked for the sharpest stick I could find and walked back into the lake. I walked far enough that the water reached above my belly button at first but then lowered myself into it completely. I held my breath as I wiped my hands over my face and arms, and chest, trying to wash as much dirt off as I could until I needed to come up for air.

I stood up straight again, took a deep breath and closed my eyes, leaning my head back, giving myself a few seconds to enjoy the feel of the fresh water against my legs and belly and the warmth of the sun on my face and back.

"Water seems nice."

I turned around, shocked. He was nonchalantly sitting on a branch of the tree I'd hung my clothes on, far too high above the ground to be safe, mostly covered by the shadow from the leaves around him.

I covered my breasts with my arms and turned my back to him. I felt anger rising within me. Not only had he somehow managed to sneak up on me, but how long had he been sitting there staring? The worst part though was that I was annoyed that he, despite that he was staring at me like that, didn't act the least bit affected or even interested.

"I found your mask; it's somewhere in my coat over there. I forgot about it, though, so I'm pretty sure it got wet." Part of me wanted to turn around and look him straight in the eye, especially now that he wasn't wearing his mask. Who cared if he saw me naked again if he wasn't interested anyway? *I* was interested, more than a little bit, in seeing the face of our mysterious savior.

"That's okay; I already got a new one."

In a reflex, I really did turn around that time. He wasn't lying. A new mask decorated his face, this one a lot more elegant than the previous. It had a checkered pattern of black and silver running over three-quarters of it. The last quarter, running diagonally from top to bottom, was all black, the sides laid in with small, sparkling crystals. It didn't catch your attention as much as the last one, but I liked this one better. Not that that mattered at that moment, though.

I quickly turned my back towards him again, although I made sure to keep my eye on him over my shoulder.

"Why are you wearing those? Are you hiding some hideous scar or something?" I chuckled.

"Yes."

I immediately stopped laughing and stared at him in silence.

"It runs all the way from my left temple," he moved his hand from the left side of his face to the right, "across my eyes, to my right temple." He leaned back against the tree. "Anything else about me you want to make fun of?"

I looked down, ashamed about my thoughtless comment and even more about laughing about it. I should've left it alone, instead of trying to hurt him back, just because I got offended by his disinterest in me.

A soft rustling made me turn around and stare in shock as he pushed his hands against the branch he was sitting on and jumped down with one fell swoop, landing as softly and gracefully as a trained dancer. He walked towards the edge of the water with a big grin on his face, and I slowly felt my cheeks turn red, embarrassed that I'd let myself fall for it.

"You were lying."

He snickered, and his shoulders slightly moved up and down with his melodious laugh.

"That should teach you something about making fun of people's deformities."

I felt myself get angry again, but knowing he was right, I couldn't let myself express it. Instead, I turned my back again, strengthening my grip on the stick in my hand and searching the lake for nearby fish.

"Whatever." I could barely get it out of my mouth, "Did you come to give me some answers? Because if you're not, just leave me alone. I have to concentrate."

I waited and listened. I didn't hear any footsteps leading away from me, but by now, it was clear that that didn't mean anything with this guy, as both times I'd met him, I hadn't heard or felt him coming.

Suddenly the water rippled behind me, and I looked over my shoulder to see him come closer to me. He didn't wade like I'd done; he moved with quiet ease. He hadn't even taken the time to take off his clothes or even his shoes; he'd simply stepped into the water the same way I'd done at first.

"Stop!" The memory of him sitting on my stomach, pushing me down on my bed, vividly flashed through my head, and I yelled the word before I even realized it.

He immediately obeyed and stopped behind me, close enough for me to feel his warm breath against my neck as he leaned forward, bringing his face closer to mine. Even though the mask he'd left me behind had smelled like oranges, he didn't have any scent himself.

"I'm glad you're still alive, Thera." He whispered the words in my ear, and they sent an unauthorized shiver down my spine, making my legs weak.

He grinned, clearly enjoying my reaction.

"Put on some clothes if you don't want to talk to me naked. I'm not going to wait until you're done fishing."

I pulled up my shoulders but didn't say anything. I disliked how he spoke to me and disliked how he made me tremble even more, but the last time this man came to talk to me, he literally saved my family and me. Ignoring him or sending him away could be dangerous, and the truth was that I was desperate for any kind of help or instruction. Wasn't finding this guy the entire reason we'd dared to enter special territory, to begin with?

I looked down, making sure my breasts were completely covered by my arm, and then walked out of the lake, trying very hard to keep my back turned towards him at all times while still being able to keep an eye on him.

I put down the stick, close enough that it remained within my reach, and clumsily put my heavy, wet clothes on again, trying to make sure to keep as much of my body covered in the process since he didn't once have the decency to look away.

"Why were you covered in mud anyway?" He asked.

So, he really had been sitting there from the start. I cursed at myself for not noticing.

"We were blocking our scent," I answered reluctantly, fairly sure of how he would react.

"Hah... you think those guys found you only based on your scent?"

I tensed up. "How am I supposed to know what they use, or even what they were? It's not as if this kind of thing happens every day, you know."

He walked out of the water, up to me. "Well, it's true they can use scent, and broken twigs, and body warmth, and the sensation of a special without magic you leave behind. Honestly, it's not that hard to track an untouched at all if you know what to look for."

I glared at him. "An untouched? What's that supposed to mean?"

He showed me an amused grin. "Not what you're clearly thinking, you perv."

I didn't have anything to say back to that since he was, once again, mostly right.

I folded my arms. "So, then what is it?"

He leaned against the tree next to us, covering himself in shadow, and shrugged nonchalantly. "Just someone who hasn't received their magic yet."

I gasped and unconsciously took a step closer to him. "Received? I thought you were born with magic."

He gasped as well, clearly mocking me. "Who told you that?"

I immediately took a step back again, ready to say something back in an equally mocking tone, but then I stopped myself and thought about it. No one had ever *told* me that. It was something I'd assumed, something we'd all assumed.

It seems my answer was visible on my face because he snickered again. "Well, you were wrong. You're not born with magic, you have to ask for it, and if you're lucky, you receive it. Well," he shrugged, "maybe not really lucky, since I don't know anyone but you who doesn't have it."

I didn't respond. If magic was something that was received, didn't that mean *I* could receive it as well? Automatically my eyes moved in the direction where I knew Mom and the kids were waiting for me. Imagine what I would be able to do for them if I had magic. They would never have to run or be afraid of anything again.

"You'd have to receive it first, you know?"

He interrupted my train of thought, and I suppressed a scowl. "How do I do that?"

He pressed his lips together, as though deep in thought. "You have to ask for it, but…"

He pushed himself away from the tree and moved closer to me while ensuring he stayed in the shadows. "I've never seen anyone receive it at such a late age. Even if it will be given to you, there's a chance your body will either reject it or simply won't be able to take it and break down."

I scoffed. "Neither of those things will happen."

He didn't grin or mock me as I thought he would. It was actually the first time I saw a serious look on his face. "How do you know that?"

I shrugged. "I don't know. I'll make sure of it."

He stared at me from behind that mask for a moment but then suddenly covered his mouth with his hand to hide his laughter.

Without saying anything, he turned around and walked back to the tree he'd been sitting in before and picked up a backpack he'd hidden behind it. He threw it in my arms with a small arc.

I looked down at the light brown leather bag. I didn't need to have heightened senses to know what was in it. Food. And not just any food, good food. Good smelling food. My stomach instantly started to rumble with a violence I'd never heard.

I looked up, grateful enough to let down my guard and thank him abundantly, but he was nowhere in sight. I made a full turn looking all around me for him, including up in the trees above us this time, but he'd completely disappeared.

I cursed. Where had he gone? And how? I'd been standing right in front of him. I turned around and started walking back to where mom and the kids had set up camp. There was so much more I needed to ask him, but I completely blew it. When was a chance like that going to come around again? Should I tell Mom? She was going to know something happened as soon as she would see the backpack anyway.

I sighed and put it on my back, after which I took the mask out of the inner pocket of my coat. He hadn't taken it with him. Did that mean he really didn't want it anymore? Or was he going to come back for it again?

6

"Oh, gods." Fionn closed his eyes while taking an enormous bite out of a kind of meat that I didn't recognize, but that was incredibly tender and smelled amazing.

Several pieces of this meat, wrapped in big green leaves, were spread out in front of us. I'd just finished one myself and was now biting on a big, almost yellow, smoked carrot. I had no idea if it were my hunger, the way it was prepared, or if this carrot was really that amazing, but it was honestly the best thing I'd ever had after that piece of meat.

Immediately after we were done eating every last thing that had been in that backpack, I took all three of them with me to the little lake, and they jumped in as gratefully as I'd done, washing both their clothes and themselves. After that, they stripped down to their underwear, hung their clothes to dry over the same branch I'd done and sat down on the warm grass at the edge of the lake. Fionn and Mori managed to stay seated for maybe a full second before they lay down, closed their eyes, and immediately fell asleep.

I grinned and lay down too. If I closed my eyes now, I was pretty sure I'd be able to sleep for at least two days on end.

"So, what did he tell you?"

I turned my head to see Mom staring at me, her eyebrows slightly lifted.

"What?" I sat up straight again, aiming my eyes at the grass by my feet, trying to feign ignorance.

She laughed, surprised that I even tried. "Sweetie, you not only came back from hunting washed and in a good mood but also with a bag full of prepared food." She gave me a stern look. "And I know you're more responsible than to accept something like that from a complete stranger."

I sighed. "It's not like he isn't a stranger."

She nodded, clearly agreeing with that. "But since he saved our lives before…"

I nodded too. "I'm sorry, Mom, he didn't really tell me anything. He just… came out of nowhere and talked to me about magic. Then he handed me this bag, and the second I looked up, he'd disappeared again."

I plucked at the grass around my feet. "All I know is that…" I clenched the blades of grass in my fist, "I think that our village got attacked because of me. And Alaexia as well. And even those creatures in the woods yesterday."

I carefully looked at Mom from the corner of my eye, trying to see how she'd take that revelation. She barely showed me a reaction; it didn't seem to be much of a revelation to her at all.

I lifted an eyebrow. "You knew?"

She avoided my eyes. "I wasn't sure, but…" she lowered her head, "I've known there was something about you from the moment I found you on my doorstep, Thera."

"Something like what?"

She shrugged slightly. "I honestly don't know. I mean, we obviously figured out very quickly that you weren't like us, but you weren't exactly like any specials we'd ever heard of either. I've always thought that you were different, even among specials." She gave me a sorrowful smile but then turned her head away from me, staring at the lake, as if she could see something beneath the surface that I couldn't.

"Your dad…" she swallowed, "he never wanted to talk about it. He told me that we should be happy that we had you and not question it. We should keep you close to us and far away from… this place."

I felt a pain pressing down on my chest and blinked my eyes a few times. That was so typically Dad, just trying to keep me close, to keep all of us close together, and not try to think about what I might've left behind or what might've been waiting for me far away. I wonder if he ever tried to take us over the sea to human territory. I looked at Mom from the corner of my eyes again. I bet she wouldn't have agreed with it if he tried. Did they argue about it? Had she ever tried to find out where I came from or why I was abandoned? Had Dad tried to stop her from doing so?

Question after question came flowing in my mind, but somehow, I didn't dare to ask any of them.

"He knew my name."

Mom kept silent for a bit. "He could've heard it somewhere when he first came to the village."

I shook my head. "It didn't feel like that. Besides, if that was the case, then why come and warn only me?"

She shrugged again. "I don't know. We don't know a lot of things."

I sighed, but then I suddenly remembered something. "He asked me if I loved you all, even though you weren't related to me by blood. And only after I told him I did, he warned me to get out of the village and bring you guys to safety."

She lifted her eyebrows and then put her hand against her chin to thoroughly think about that.

She frowned. "Next time, don't let him get away, no matter what."

"And until then? Apparently, it's really easy to find someone who doesn't have any magic, and you guys are human. We're sitting ducks here."

"There's a house."

Mom and I turned around to Fionn, who had woken up and sat up straight. He looked at me and blinked a few times as if he weren't quite sure if he really was awake or not.

"There's a house not far from here." He cleared up his earlier statement without truly clearing anything up at all.

I leaned closer to him. "What makes you think that?"

He tilted his head as if he had to think about it. "I was dreaming about… I don't remember, but there was this man, he walked into my dream and then suddenly he knew who I was, who we all were, and he told me to come to his home."

I stared at him in shock. Someone entered his dream? What kind of magic was that? And trying to convince someone to come to his house like that, wasn't that the worst possible way to try to earn someone's trust?

"Which way did he tell you to go?" I could barely get the words out. Who was this person? How was he able to reach Fionn? And even worse, did he know where we were? Was he close?

Fionn lifted up his hand and pointed his finger across the lake. "It's close by."

I turned to Mom. "Let's go the other way, as far as we possibly can. He might need to be close for his magic to reach us."

I had no idea what to think or expect. All this whole ordeal had taught me was that I knew pretty much nothing about magic.

She nodded, and we both got to our feet. She ran to the tree to grab our clothes, and I softly shook Mori's shoulder to wake her up. Mori groaned and tried to push away my hand. She had been sleeping deeply but clearly not for long enough. And how could she have? None of us had. I pushed her again, and after she opened her eyes, I took her arm to help her to her feet. Her eyes were still half-closed, but she obediently dressed after Mom handed her her clothes, unlike Fionn.

Mom was standing opposite of him, holding his clothes out to him, but he didn't accept them and stared at her with his shoulders pulled up high and his fists clenched.

"I think we should listen to him!" His voice was high pitched; it clearly wasn't easy for him to go against our mom like that.

I walked over to them, closely followed by Mori. "Fionn, what are you talking about?"

Fionn turned from Mom to me, straightening his back. "It's just… he was nice. He wants to help us. Why shouldn't we let him?"

I frowned. "Because we can't trust him."

He folded his arms in front of his chest, looking closer to tears than angry at that point. "Why not? You trusted that guy who gave us all that food. He was only trying to help us too."

He got me there. "I don't trust him either, Fionn."

"You trusted him enough to let us eat the food he gave you, though." Mori mixed herself into the conversation.

That shut me up. What was I supposed to say back to that? I took a breath and tried to calm myself. We didn't have time for this, but it seemed I pushed them too much the past few days. They weren't going to keep running away again and again just because I told them to.

"Think about it," I tried to put on my most reasonable voice, "how has any creature we've met up until now with magic treated us? The only reason I believed that other guy was because he warned us; he saved our lives and the only magic I could feel from him came from this thing." I pulled his mask out of my coat and held it up for them to see. "But Fionn, this man that showed up in your dream, your *dream*, uses what I can only describe as incredibly manipulative magic to lure us to his house. Do you really think we should obey him?"

I looked at Mom from the corner of my eye. She clearly agreed with me. I looked at Mori as well. She seemed unsure. Lastly, I turned back to Fionn, he still had a defiant look on his face, but I could tell from the look in his eyes that he knew I was right.

"I mean… if I think about it like that…" He admitted it begrudgingly, lowering his head.

I sighed with relief and put my hand on his shoulder. "I'm sorry, Fionn, I'm just trying to look out for us."

He nodded but refused to look at me. It didn't matter. I would talk to him again about this, more seriously, when we would've reached a hopefully safe distance from this place. I pinched his shoulder encouragingly. "Let's go."

He nodded again and got dressed, pulling himself away from my hand on his shoulder. That hit me where it hurt, but I tried not to show it on my face and quietly waited for him instead.

"Wait!" We hadn't even taken a single step when someone yelled out to us in a voice that sounded like he was gurgling water. And only a fraction of a second later, a small wave of water shot past us and spread out vertically right in front of us, blocking our way with a small, thin, flowing wall of water.

I suppressed a scream and grabbed Fionn by the collar of his shirt and pulled him safely behind me. Mom and Mori stepped behind me as well, and all three of them moved closer to look at the wall of water in front of us over my shoulder.

The water started to shrink, or rather, clump together until it was more like a moving blob. Then it stopped and stayed there like that, a flowing orb of water.

I carefully took a step closer to it. Some part of me felt like an idiot for even thinking it, but this thing was what had yelled out to us. I lifted my arm and slowly brought my finger up until it was right in front of it and, after taking a deep breath, poked it. I wasn't sure what I was expecting, for my finger to bounce off it, move through it like normal water, or even be completely disintegrated. All I could hope for was one of the first two options.

I broke the surface like normal water, but felt a slight resistance as I pushed farther, like sticking your finger in gelatin. Except that this was living gelatin. I couldn't quite explain how I knew, but I felt it. I felt the magic resonating inside it. I felt its life force. I sensed its intelligence. And then it chuckled.

That human sound it made, even though it sounded gurgling, shook me up more for some reason than its earlier movement had done, and I quickly pulled my finger back, which came out of its watery body completely dry.

"I'm ever so sorry to have startled you." The water grew, or, more precisely, it divided its mass, slinking a little on the bottom, so another blob could grow from the top. If you used your imagination, it looked like a faceless, naked snowman made of flowing water.

"What are you?" Fionn had gathered the courage to step out from behind me and was now curiously staring at the creature before us.

"Fionn, you're being rude." The words escaped my mouth before I could stop them.

I shook my head. "Answer him, though, if you can understand us."

The upper blob of water moved up and down in an upbeat motion, which, for lack of a better option, I took as nodding.

"My name is Aeric," I wasn't sure how I was able to make the distinction, but somehow, I knew he turned his head towards me, "and I am a special being, such as yourself."

I froze. He just came out and said it, out loud, in front of Fionn and Mori. How did they react to it? I was too scared to turn my head and see what kind of expression they were showing.

"I'm not like you." The threatening tone of my voice shocked even myself, and it clearly shocked the creature in front of me. His upper blob almost completely disappeared into his lower blob for a moment, and even after it came out again, it seemed to lean back more than it had done before, farther away from me.

"It was not my intention to insult you. However, that is what my master thinks, and so it seems does the young human beside you." He had no fingers to point, but I somehow knew who he was aiming his words at.

I turned around and stared at Fionn, unsure if I should look shocked or worried or apologetic. "Fionn…" I started but immediately stopped. I didn't know what to say, how to explain it.

He got a defensive look on his face. "I didn't mean to, but what was I supposed to think?"

I cringed. Of course, he'd realized something.

I forced myself to give him a reassuring smile. "It's okay, Fionn, you're never wrong for being smart."

I turned back to the water creature in front of us. He had cleverly reverted all my attention towards Fionn for a moment, so the other half of what he'd said only now got through to me.

"You have a master?"

Its face lit up. At least, it seemed to me like it did. "Yes, master Raven. He is the one who approached the human boy as soon as he sensed your presence."

I narrowed my eyes. "How? Why Fionn? What does he want from us?"

The water special quietly stared at me in confusion. Had I asked too much all at once? Or did he not want to tell me?

"Through magic. Because he was the only one dreaming at the moment. And I want nothing from you. I only want to offer my help." A warm, pleasant voice reached us from behind, and all four of us spun around.

I blinked my eyes a few times, not fully able to take in what was in front of me. I'd never seen such an attractive person before in my life, not even in my imagination. A tall man, at least a head taller than me, stood in front of us, at the edge of the water of the small lake. A short, dark grey horn curved up from the right side of his head. His sleek, black hair which didn't reach beyond his ears softly flowed around it in the warm summer breeze. His skin seemed so flawless it made me wonder if he even had pores at all, and his bright green eyes deeply pierced into mine, sending a shiver down my spine, one that I wanted to feel again and keep feeling for the rest of my life. He was clothed in a set of loose, green robes that almost matched the magical vibrance of his eyes, but that, to my subconscious disappointment, hid most of his body from us. Although I had no doubt it was slender but muscular. I suspected he was older than me, but not by much. I wondered if he was even thirty yet.

Next to me, I heard Mom and Mori, and even Fionn quietly gasp, which pulled me back to reality. I knew from the mask I'd been keeping with me and the crystal in Alaexia that objects that had magic in them somehow possessed a certain attraction, something that pulled me in, but until now, I hadn't felt that in a person. There was no doubt that this man would've been extremely handsome even if he had been a normal human. Still, the amount of magic that somehow came from him or whirled around him blew all of us away, without any of us really able to understand what we were beholding. At least now I understood how Fionn had been so willing to trust this person. It honestly took me quite some restrain not to leap forward and throw myself in his arms.

I shook my head slightly, trying to gather myself, and forced myself to look at him as nonchalantly as I could.

"Why would you want to help us? Who are you? What do you even know about us?"

He smiled a bewitching, pearly white smile, and my heart almost jumped out of my chest. "I know that Mori over there is confused about everything that is happening and longing to go back to your old home, back to the last time she felt safe." He moved his eyes from Mori to Fionn. "I know Fionn misses his father but is too frightened to mention it."

He suddenly looked me in the eye with a piercing look that could see straight into the depths of my soul. "I know you are frightened, as well. Frightened to long for the life you left behind, frightened for the answers you will find as you move forward, frightened of what you will lose next, frightened to stand still."

He released me from his staring eyes and turned towards Mom. "And I know that Nayana is trying with all her might to keep your family together, no matter what, even if it means coming to this place that terrifies her so much because she is frightened that if she lets you go alone, she will lose you for good."

He looked back at me with a warm expression. "As for why I wish to help you, most people here will likely tell you it is because I have a weak spot for humans. I find them interesting. And what could be more interesting than an untouched special raised by humans? A special with a human heart?"

I narrowed my eyes. "Who are you?"

He kept smiling. My lack of interest didn't seem to bother him. "My name is Raven Ravenous, of the line of Ravenous." He coughed slightly to cover up his slight blush. "I suppose you could consider my parents jokesters."

I wasn't sure how to react to that, so I didn't.

He moved to the side, moving his hand in the direction of the lake in an inviting motion. "Will you not let me take you back to my home? I will answer every question you have."

I scoffed in such a condescending way I was sure it made Mori proud. "Do I look stupid to you?"

His eyes widened for a moment, and he pressed his hand against his chest. "Of course not, Thera. I would never think something so horrible." He let his arm fall back at his side. "I understand you cannot trust me immediately, and I cannot blame you for that, of course, but by now even you, who has no magic, must have realized that I am not out to hurt you," his look darkened, "unlike most of the other specials you will find both in this place and as you progress farther north."

His expression brightened. "I understand you are tired. Even if you do not let me help you with anything else, at least let me offer you the safety of my home for a good night's rest, and I will help you on your way in the morning with clean clothes and supplies."

He stepped aside again, making the same inviting gesture I'd ignored before. I looked at Mom. I tried so hard to fight the attraction his magic had on me that I wasn't sure if that was the reason I couldn't allow myself to trust him or if he couldn't be trusted for real, but the truth was that he'd already won me over.

Mom's eyes kept shooting from me to him and from him to the kids and back again, but eventually, she gave a nod.

Both Fionn and Mori let out a sigh of relief, which was immediately followed by a sigh of relief from Raven.

I looked at him in surprise, and he nodded apologetically as a response. "Well then, please follow me. It is not far."

With that, he turned around, and all four of us followed him at a safe distance while Aeric closed the line behind us.

I kept my eyes on Raven's back as we walked. A slight summer breeze made the robes he was dressed in flow elegantly behind him and carried his scent to me. Only at that moment did I realize it was part of the intoxication I'd been feeling. More than a scent, I was smelling an experience, that of opening a new book for the first time. I smelled the scent of the fresh parchment, but I could also feel the excitement that came with it, wondering what I would discover, what new things I would learn. But at the same time, there was something else mixed in there, something sweet. If I closed my eyes and breathed in deeply, it was like I was laying on my back in a field full of flowers in bloom, reading my new book. It made me feel calm and peaceful.

I opened my eyes to find him staring at me over his shoulder with a delighted expression. I had to blink a few times. After not seeing him for a moment, looking at him immediately had that same enchanting effect again.

Wait, I broke our eye contact. How long had I been walking around with my eyes closed? I looked past him to the building in the distance. Had he mentioned the size of his home when he had invited us to it? I couldn't remember, but if he had, he had undersold it. It wasn't a house; it probably didn't even qualify as a mansion. This was more like a palace, only without towers.

We walked for another half hour after that, and his 'house' only got bigger, until we eventually stopped at the entrance of the enormous yard in front of it, so we could take in its full majesty.

The house was made of stone but painted in a light color. Not exactly white, but close enough to reflect the sunlight, making it hard for me to look at it directly.

It was a long building, from left to right, although I couldn't see how far it would go to the back. Some part of me expected an enormous gate in the middle, but the front door wasn't all that different than our front door had been, except that the wood it was made from looked smoother, even a little shiny, and it was a double door. Both sides of the building were covered in big windows that were all open, so light green curtains could flow outside of them freely while the summer breeze would enter and leave the building as it pleased. Despite being attached to it, both the left and right wings of the building were placed more to the front, as if those two parts had needed to be even bigger than the rest. It seemed overkill to me, but it did give it a nicer appearance; it would've been too boring if it had been just one long block. Not that it would've been any less impressive, thanks to its sheer size.

In front of it, all the way from the front door to where we were standing, a big, beautiful yard spread out. I literally had to move my head from left to right to see the whole thing. A paved path with small, light but uneven stones that led from us to the door divided the yard two halves. Four huge flowerbeds with flowers in every color imaginable surrounded that path. The numerous flowers gave off an intoxicating smell that I immediately recognized as part of Raven's own scent. The beds were surrounded by low, green hedges and in the middle of each flower bed stood a strange statue that flowed water up from a modest basin at the bottom, through the stone statues that reminded me of elegantly flowing water, where it came out of the top and softly sprayed in the air, just to fall back into the basin below it again.

I stared at it in awe as we started walking towards it over the path. Was this magic as well? I looked at Aeric from the corner of my eye, or did he have something to do with it?

Fionn grabbed my sleeve and pulled it while keeping his eyes on the flowing waterwork in front of us.

I nodded, just as impressed. I could barely stop myself from jumping into that shallow but amazingly blue and inviting water.

Mori rolled her eyes, seeing both of us stare at it so mesmerized and passed us, apparently too grown up to be impressed. Although I could clearly see her look at it from the corner of her eye with a concerned expression on her face.

I tore my eyes away from it after noticing a part of the main path diverting to the right. It led between the two flowerbeds into a small park with several trees. All of them had a wooden bench built around it in a circle. Did that mean Raven had a lot of visitors, people that would come here to enjoy the sun and each other's company in that little park?

I narrowed my eyes. The path split up in several directions at the park entrance, but they all ended somewhere in or at the end of it. One of them led all the way to a simple field of grass behind the park. The only strange thing about that field was several poles that stood up straight in seemingly random places. Some of them even had a net tied between them.

That sight didn't sit well with me at all. What was he trying to catch there? And with such pathetic traps?

I turned back towards the enormous house, curious what it would look like on the inside, but instead of going straight, we turned left. We walked between the two flowerbeds and entered a small forest, or perhaps I should call it a collection of trees, denser than the park on the other side but not quite dense enough to be called an actual forest.

We followed the path we were on, which was the only path that went through that forest, and stopped in front of a second, much smaller, house. Smaller relative to the enormous building beside it, though, as even this second house was still at least five times as big as the home that we had to leave behind, maybe even more.

This one looked more like a normal house, though. It was built from light red bricks but had a similar, light grey, slanted roof. It was also covered in big, open windows, but it seemed to consist of more, smaller rooms instead of what had seemed like big, open spaces.

"What part of all of this is yours?" Fionn asked.

Part of me wanted to lecture him about being rude again, but another part of me, the confused part, was glad someone asked it.

Raven laughed. "I suppose you could technically say that all of it is mine, but this is the only part I live in. The bigger building over there is actually my school."

Fionn lifted an eyebrow. "Aren't you a little too old to still go to school?"

Mori immediately slapped her hand against her face in embarrassment, and both Mom and Raven hid a small chuckle.

"It is not a school I attend," he kindly explained, "it is a school I founded for children to learn all kinds of things."

That piqued Mori's interest. "Like magic?"

Raven nodded. "Yes, magic is one example. Reading is another one, and writing, science, biology, art, humanology. There is a class for most subjects you can think of."

I stared at him. Humanology? He had listed it next to writing and biology as if they were equally normal to learn for children. What was he teaching them about us?

"Let us go inside, and I will have some food and clean clothes prepared for you." Raven didn't wait for us to agree. He simply walked towards the front door, only a single door in this house, opened it and disappeared into the hallway.

For some reason, I started to have my doubts, but neither Mom nor the kids seemed bothered, and they hastily followed Raven inside, leaving me no choice but to follow them as well.

Raven led us through a relatively small but cozy, wooden hallway to a big dining room. The room was tiled with big, grayish-white tiles that seemed like they had just been mopped squeaky clean. One side of the dining room consisted completely of big glass doors, giving us a view of a patio with a swinging chair at the beginning of an enormous garden with a small lake, similar to the one we had been laying next to earlier that day. This lake was surrounded by big willow trees, whose leaves were slowly dancing in the warm summer breeze, sometimes gently touching the surface of the water, creating expanding rings that continuously kept the water in motion. A path made of light-colored wooden planks led from the patio to the lake and was surrounded by light, almost sparkling pebbles.

Somehow the garden gave me the feeling that the first half was meant for warm summer days like the one we were having at that moment. At the same time, the latter half could be better enjoyed during a rainy fall day or even in mid-winter when snow would cover the willows and their surroundings.

Despite these conclusions, we didn't go outside at all. Raven gestured us to sit down at a long, dark wooden table. It wasn't only polished until it shone, but the legs and the corners of the top were also covered in beautiful, intricate carvings. I sat down beside Mom and slowly moved my fingers over one of the carvings. Even though I couldn't quite make out what they were, they were clearly the work of a master woodcarver.

Raven walked to the glass doors and opened them wide, one by one, letting in that warm summer breeze I enjoyed so much. After that, he sat down as well, not at the head of the table, as I'd expected, but next to me, across from Fionn and Mori. The moment he sat down, several people, none of them as humanoid as Raven or me, walked into the room with plates full of incredible smelling food.

Any doubt or distrust that any of us might have still had completely disappeared as the servants put the serving plates, which were all made of glass, in the middle of the table. Both Mori and Fionn didn't waste even one second. They jumped forward, grabbing food with their hands, not giving the servants any time to put down a plate in front of them.

I saw Mom stare at them in shock from the corner of my eye, but after everything that had happened, I think she just couldn't get herself to punish them for their bad manners. I sighed relieved, she couldn't be more right, and as I looked to my right, I saw that Raven agreed since he seemed to have some trouble hiding an amused grin.

I looked at the food in front of us. I recognized some chicken, or what seemed like chicken, as well as tomatoes and onions, but the rest was pretty much all new to me.

Although deep inside I didn't want anything more than to follow Fionn and Mori's example and dig in, I managed to find the patience to wait for one of the servants to place a plate and cutlery before me. I thanked her with the politest smile I could muster up while trying to ignore her tusks, which were too big to completely fit inside her mouth and the small horns growing out of her forehead. She smiled back at me, laying her tusks even barer, and walked away. I let out a small sigh of relief, turned back to the table and picked up my fork, which was also made out of glass.

I lifted up an eyebrow. I hadn't noticed until now because I'd been too distracted trying not to stare at the strange-looking servants, but everything that was used for both the food and drinks was made out of glass.

"No need to worry. It is not dangerous."

I turned to my right to find Raven looking at me and my fork with an amused expression. He picked up his own fork and held it above the ground, attracting the attention of Mom and even Fionn and Mori, who had both stuffed their mouths as full as they possibly could.

After a look around the table to make sure everybody was watching, Raven threw the fork to the ground.

Mom, Mori and Fionn instinctively jumped up as if to get ready to avoid possible shards of glass flying around. I didn't react because I'd noticed the strange attraction that I recognized all too well by now coming from the cutlery, even before he threw it to the ground. As expected, the fork didn't break; it just bounced a few times and then lay motionless on the ground.

Raven bent over and picked it up, holding it up for all of us to see. Mom and the kids looked at it with big eyes, clearly giving him the reaction he'd hoped for.

He grinned proudly. "It is amazing what happens when you pour a little magic in everyday objects, is it not?"

Those words didn't quite seem to hit their target the way he'd clearly thought they would. Although there was no denying they were pleasantly surprised by what they saw, their experiences with magic hadn't been all that great the past few days. Having it shown to them as some kind of performance seemed to both excite and scare them at the same time.

Raven put the fork back next to his plate and lowered his head. "I apologize. I did not mean to frighten you."

Mom shook her head. "No, it's not your fault, it's just that…" She stopped.

Fionn finally swallowed the big bite he'd taken and frowned at Raven. "It's because magic is dangerous. You shouldn't use it for things like that. You should only use it when you have no other choice."

I hid a small laugh. Somehow, he'd taken the words that I hadn't had the courage to say right out of my mouth.

Raven didn't seem offended. Quite the opposite, he gave Fionn an understanding look. "You know, magic is not entirely as dangerous as you seem to think," suddenly, his expression darkened, "but it can be used by dangerous people."

Fionn lifted his head in the air. "And then it becomes dangerous." He said those words in a tone that clearly showed he didn't understand how Raven could not get that.

Raven chuckled. "I suppose you are right."

7

Despite how tired I was, despite being pleasantly full I was after eating the most amazing meal I'd ever had, despite laying in the softest bed I'd ever felt, it was hard for me to fall asleep. Raven had been right. It was pretty impressive what happened to even the most common objects when you infused them with a little magic, which is probably why I felt it in almost everything I passed or touched in this house.

I was shocked to see how much specials used magic in their day-to-day life, not that I'd ever really thought about it much. From stories and legends, I'd always assumed that all specials were like those that attacked our village, brutal creatures who'd rather fight wars and kill their opponents than talk to them, even the humanoid ones. Somehow, I'd always thought that they only used magic for that kind of grand-scale occasion.

Although I agreed with Fionn's view on magic, I also understood what Raven meant. I mean, it must be handy to have glasses that never break, and it felt pretty good to lay on a bed that made me feel like I was laying on a cloud. I breathed in deeply. The bed even smelled like a fresh summer night.

I breathed in again, the scent calmed me more than the softness did, and somehow, I must've fallen asleep because the next thing I knew, I was awoken by the sound of singing birds in the distance and sunlight sneaking in from under the thick curtains.

I kept laying on the bed, looking at the padded top of my canopy bed. It had a warm, olive green color. I turned my head to the curtains that had the same color, contemplating a way for me to open them and let the sunlight in without getting out of bed when they suddenly moved to the side all by themselves. I bolted up and stared at them. Somehow, I felt it wasn't magic that did that.

"You look well-rested, but you should really take a proper bath if they give you a chance for it today."

I didn't have to look to the left side of the curtains to make out a vague silhouette that was mostly hidden behind the bright sunlight anyway, nor did I have to see his mask to know who was talking to me.

I pulled my blankets up to my chin. One of Raven's servants had given me a nightgown yesterday that I wouldn't call skimpy, but I did feel a little exposed in it.

He stepped into the light, so I could see him grin at the way I was holding up my blankets.

I scowled, even though part of me somehow felt reassured to see that mocking grin again. "Are you a part of this school? Is that why you told me to go here?"

"When exactly did I tell you to go here?"

I thought about it for a second but realized he hadn't. "But you knew this was here, so close to us, and you didn't tell us to leave."

He shrugged. "I guess that's true."

"So…" I hated myself for trusting him enough to ask him this, but for whatever reason, I did. "Are we safe here?"

He leaned against the glass of the big window in my room that covered half of the wall and looked outside to the small forest surrounding Raven's home. "I don't think you have much to worry about here, but you shouldn't stay for too long."

I felt my eyes get big as panic started to spread through my body. "Why? What's wrong with this place? What's wrong with Raven?"

It was barely noticeable, but I saw him cringe when hearing that name. "I wouldn't say there's something really *wrong* with him. I just think he's a jerk."

I relaxed a little more. "So, you have a personal problem with him, but it has nothing to do with us?"

He smiled a completely fake smile at me. "Very good recap, thank you."

"Why do you think he's a jerk?" I ignored his mocking.

"I don't know, every word out of his mouth just annoys me, you know how that sometimes goes."

I did know how that sometimes went, although I had trouble imagining anyone feeling that way about Raven. Even if I wouldn't be affected by his magical attraction, I would still find him a very pleasant person.

"How come I don't feel that same strange attraction to you?" I blurted out the question before I even realized it.

He folded his arms and lifted his head slightly. "How come you're so rude to me?"

I didn't answer, I couldn't blame him for not wanting to answer a question like that, and I honestly didn't want to get into it any further.

"What's your name? You seem to know mine; do we know each other somehow?"

He tilted his head slightly as if he had to think about that. "We don't know each other. And for now, the less you know, the better."

I swallowed my anger. "Why shouldn't we stay for too long if nothing's wrong with Raven?"

He pressed his lips together and stayed silent.

I clenched my fists. Was he just going to ignore me every time I asked something he didn't want to answer? Or that he didn't know the answer to?

"Okay, then where should we go if we shouldn't stay here? We don't know anything about this place, or the creatures in it, except that a bunch of them tried to kill us."

He lowered his head slightly. "I… don't know. Yet. Right now, I'm going out of my way to fade you all, so I have some time to figure out what to do."

I wanted to jump out of bed, grab him, and shake him until he would give me a clear answer that made sense, but I was scared he'd disappear again if I even moved an inch. "What does that mean, fading us?"

He lifted his head to look at me but didn't answer again.

I took a slow, steadying breath. "Who sent those monsters after me? What do they want? How can I protect us?"

He shook his head and effortlessly jumped up, so he was standing on the windowsill. "It's better if you don't know, for now, Thera. Just trust me and hide here for as long as you can."

Without waiting for my response, he let himself fall backward, out of the window.

I jumped up, half tripping over my blankets, and ran towards it, staring outside, scanning the surroundings, but he'd disappeared.

I let out a deep sigh and turned around. He might have saved our lives, but I was starting to not like him very much.

What kind of magic did he have that he could disappear like that? It seemed so useless in any other situation than this. Plus, that mask. Why was he hiding his face? It's not like every other part of him didn't stand out in the moments he wasn't invisible.

I sighed again and walked towards the door. Was trusting him really the right thing to do? I didn't like it, but what other choice did I have? I couldn't go back out there where it was so dangerous with Mom, Fionn, and Mori, and I couldn't go by myself and leave them behind in this strange place after everything that had just happened. Dad had told me to stay together, to keep them safe. That was the most important thing I had to right now. Even if it meant putting my own questions aside, even if it meant trusting in that guy that I'd only seen three times.

I opened the door and nearly bumped into Raven, who was standing in front of it, his fist raised in the air as if he'd been about to knock.

He moved his eyes up and down over my body, and at the sight of me in my relatively short and low-cut nightgown, his cheeks and even his ears turned red, and he quickly turned around, showing me his back.

"I deeply apologize. I did not intend to stare. I came to ask if you would like to join us for breakfast. Your mother and younger siblings are already downstairs." His voice's tone was slightly higher than it was before, and I hid a pleased grin after seeing how uncomfortable he was. This, this was how you were supposed to react when seeing a woman when she isn't properly dressed. I couldn't help but hope that the masked guy was still somewhere nearby watching what just happened. Maybe he would learn a thing or two.

"I'll join you. Please give me a moment to get dressed."

He nodded, still with his back to me. "Please, take your time. I will wait for you here."

I closed the door and waited for a second to hear him lean his back against it, then I turned around and walked into the little bathroom attached to my room.

I suspiciously looked at the bent, silver spout attached to the wall above the glass sink. I leaned closer to inspect it, but the second I came within about ten inches of it, water started coming out in a neat little stream.

I instinctively jumped back, and the water stopped. I moved my hand closer to it again, and water instantly started streaming down. I stared at it in shock. This was incredible. Was it Raven's magic? Or did it maybe belong to Aeric? That last one seemed more likely to me, but at this point, I really started to believe that anything was possible here.

Now that I had figured out how to make this small spout work, I turned to look at the bigger spout that came from the ceiling of a second, smaller room, separated from me by a glass door. I opened the door and, without entering the room that was so small only one or maybe two people would fit into it, I stuck my hand inside and moved it upwards to the spout coming from the ceiling. I didn't have to get as close as I had to the smaller spout above the sink for the water to come streaming out. A big, hard jet of water. Warm water.

I let it splash on my hand for a bit while staring at it with a baffled look on my face. Warm water was coming out of the ceiling. I didn't have to boil it and mix it with cold water or do anything else to prepare it. It simply came streaming out as if it was nothing.

I hastily took my clothes off and stepped into the small room. The warm water that had stopped streaming the second I'd taken back my hand started raining down again. It hit my head with a pleasant weight, and I closed my eyes as it streamed down my hair and over my body.

I wasn't sure how long I stood there with my eyes closed, just enjoying the water, but eventually, I somehow managed to force myself to open my eyes and step out of that little room, immediately hearing the water stop behind me.

I put on my old clothes which were exactly where I'd left them the night before, on the dress chest at the end of my bed, but they didn't feel like the same clothes I'd worn before. The fabric seemed softer somehow. I stroked my hand over it. It was as if the fibers had changed into something else overnight, something much more pleasant. I brought them to my nose. They smelled amazing, like green apples; sweet, but refreshing. I put them on and looked in the mirror that was attached to the bathroom door. They might've felt and smelled completely different, but they looked exactly the same. That disappointed me a little.

I opened the door to the hallway to see Raven stand next to the tall window placed about every fifty inches over the entire hallway. I felt myself blush with embarrassment as I closed the door behind me. I'd completely forgotten that he was there. How long had he been standing there waiting while I was wasting all that time under the water?

As soon as he heard me, he turned around with a warm look on his face, as if he didn't even want to tell me off, and I followed him through the house to the same room where we'd eaten dinner the day before. I sat down next to Mom, who was already smearing some butter on a piece of bread. It surprised me to breathe in the scent of that bread. It smelled normal, like the ones we used to eat at home. Did the specials feel there was no way, or no need, to improve on it, even with magic?

"Good morning sweetie, did you sleep well?" Mom kindly pinched my shoulder, clearly happy to have all her three kids close to her again. I could still see dark circles under her eyes though, I wondered how she slept her first night alone. It made me want to hug her, but I knew she wouldn't be happy with me doing that in front of everyone.

"Ther!" Fionn leaned towards me over the table to hand me a piece of bread. "Did you see the water that comes out of the wall?"

"Yeah, I saw, it was amazing."

Mori snorted. "I thought you said magic shouldn't be used so frivolously?" She didn't look at Fionn when she sneered at him like that but kept smearing a sticky-looking brown substance on her bread that smelled suspiciously close to chocolate. My mouth started to water. There was no way I wasn't trying that.

Fionn's excitement disappeared from his face, and he quickly sat down on his chair again. "Well, it shouldn't, but that doesn't mean it can't feel nice when it's there." He mumbled it under his breath, and I saw Raven hide a grin from the corner of my eye. He clearly seemed to enjoy slowly winning Fionn over to his side. I ignored it for now and turned to Mom instead.

"I slept great almost the entire night, until this morning when I dreamt a masked person was standing next to my bed, trying to wake me up, and then I woke up." I narrowed my eyes and saw her slightly lift an eyebrow in response. "Isn't that strange?"

"That is strange," she nonchalantly turned towards her bread again, "maybe it was your subconscious telling you it was time to get up. You did sleep in longer than any of us after all."

I shrugged and took a serrated knife to cut open the piece of bread Fionn had handed me. It seemed Mom had understood what I meant. She would come to talk to me about it later when we were alone. I looked at Raven from the corner of my eye again. The masked guy had said he wasn't a bad person, even though he didn't exactly like him. Did that mean we could trust him?

"Raven," I spoke his name softly, and the second he turned to me and looked deeply into my eyes, I lost myself for a moment again.

He seemed amused, clearly realizing what had happened.

I blinked quickly and tried my best to focus. "Thank you for helping us and being so kind. If there's anything I can do to repay you, please let me know." I tried to match the warmth that he always seemed to have in his voice and expressions.

He thought about it for a second. "There is something, actually."

I stopped myself from showing any expression. There it was. What was he going to ask of us? What was he going to make us do? I looked at Fionn and Mori from the corner of my eyes. Whatever it was, I would find a way to do it by myself, so they could stay out of it.

He coughed slightly after seeing the look on my face. "Do not worry, it is nothing big, and you do not have to do it at all if you do not want to."

He sat up straighter as if to prepare himself for what he was about to say. "The thing is, even though I told my servants not to inform the students, it seems that *somehow* some of them caught wind of several humans staying here and well…" he scratched his neck awkwardly, "they are extremely curious. After everything they have learned about humans, I think they would greatly appreciate the chance to meet you and perhaps ask you some questions."

I froze. Meeting an entire school full of specials? The fact that there were so many walking around in this house alone unsettled me enough already, but to be in a classroom full of them, being questioned about what it was to be a human? I didn't like that idea one bit, not for me, not for Mom and especially not for Fionn and Mori. I turned my head to the left to look at them. They both stared back at me with a terrified look on their faces. Obviously, they felt the exact same way I did, although they seemed to have some qualm about saying no.

"I apologize," Raven spoke before I'd even answered him in any way.

"You do not have to do it if you do not feel comfortable with it. I should not even have asked you." He smiled reassuringly at all three of us, and somehow, I believed that he meant what he said.

"It's okay. We'd love to meet with your students."

Fionn, Mori and I turned around simultaneously to stare at our mom in shock. I could see from the corner of my eyes that even Raven raised his eyebrows in surprise.

"Are you absolutely sure? I do not want you to feel like I am pressuring you in any way. I simply thought it would be a good way for both us specials and you humans to meet and learn about each other."

106

Mom nodded. "I agree. I think we'll all learn a lot from it, and I don't feel pressured, but I do feel like it's the least we could do after all you've done for us." She smiled at him, effortlessly matching his warmth in her smile, much better than I'd done.

I absolutely didn't agree with anything she said, but I did feel like she was pretty amazing for taking on Raven's challenge so fearlessly.

I turned back to Raven. Judging from the delighted look on his face, he probably didn't see it as a challenge, but I refused to be taken in by that amazing face.

"Thank you, Nayana. My students will be delighted. And I promise you to carefully oversee the entire class and personally make sure they do not ask you anything inappropriate." He turned back to his own plate with a bright look on his face. "Well then, let us all enjoy a big breakfast and then head for the school!"

I looked down at my own plate, which had half of a piece of bread on it, covered in a thick layer of what indeed seemed to be a creamy kind of chocolate. Only a second ago, I'd nearly entered a state of trance after tasting that sweet substance that worked so well with the crunchy white bread, but right now, the thought of taking another bite made my stomach turn.

If Mom decided we had to do it, I would, no matter how much I didn't like it. Besides, she was right. We owed Raven. This seemed like a relatively small thing to do in return for what he did for us. So, I obediently ate the rest of my bread, and I noticed that Fionn and Mori forced themselves to do the same.

It didn't take long before we were all done, and we followed Raven outside, over the cobbled path towards the school. That day was as bright and beautiful as the day before, but that only seemed to make the shadow that the school building cast over us even darker and more ominous. If I grabbed Fionn and Mori and Mom right now and ran away as fast as possible, would that make me a smart or a bad person?

We followed Raven into the building and through several tiled hallways. Somehow, the temperature in this building was a little lower than outside, which would normally make it a safe haven away from the heat of the summer sun, but at that moment, it just made me shiver.

I tried not to breathe in too deeply. Overwhelming scents rolled over me like waves, some amazing, some repulsive, most of them unknown. I'd thought there was a lot of magic in Raven's house, but I hadn't really felt anything yet. The walls of this school were vibrating with it. Was every single student in here able to use it?

"How many students do you have?" My voice cracked.

Raven put his finger against his chin to think about it. "At this moment, it should be around two hundred and fifty."

I felt my blood turn into ice. Two hundred and fifty specials, all who were much stronger than humans, who could all use magic. If even one of them decided to turn against us, we would be in severe trouble.

Raven stopped in front of the last door on the left and opened it. I took a deep breath to calm myself down and then followed him inside, to immediately be intensely stared at by about thirty sets of eyes.

I tried really hard not to show my inner panic and stared back. The room was big, about three times Raven's dining room. The floor was a slope, probably almost a yard higher

108

in the back than in the front, making sure that even the students in the back would have a good sight of the teacher. Aside from that, the classroom wasn't all that different from the schools in human territory, especially the bigger ones. There were two rows of big wooden desks, making sure every student had enough room to place their books and utensils. A small stairway in the middle of the room led up to the end, between the two rows of desks.

The right side of the room was covered in big windows, and next to the window closest to us was another wooden desk, slightly bigger than the others, probably the teacher's desk. A big black board with some chalk drawings on it hung from the wall behind that desk. I wasn't sure what kind of lesson we were interrupting, but it definitely wasn't humanology.

Raven walked towards the stairway, where Aeric was smoothly flowing down from. That surprised me. I'd completely overlooked him as I was taking in the room. My suspicion immediately grew. Raven had insinuated that one of the servants had leaked the information about our stay here, but as of now, Aeric was my number one suspect.

"Thank you so much for coming here." Aeric smiled at both Raven and us through, what I was sure at that point, could only be telepathy.

Raven politely smiled back. "Thank you for having us."

Aeric moved to his desk, where he flopped down to land on his chair that was far too big. "Well then, I will leave the rest to you, master."

Raven smiled politely again. "Thank you, Aeric."

He turned to us. "Nayana, Thera, Fionn, Mori," he gestured to the thirty students before us, "this is our advanced class, which means that they have all had at least one field trip to human territory. Some of them have even briefly met humans before."

I looked at the students that were gawking at us. There were so many more different specials than I could've even imagined. I mean, there were different kinds of humans too, different heights, different weights, different skin colors, different hair- and eye colors, but it was nothing in comparison to what I saw before me at that moment. Some specials were at least twice as tall as me, and I hadn't noticed it earlier, but there were smaller desks, like the ones you would find in dollhouses, on the regular desks for specials that resembled the tiny fire creatures we'd encountered in Alaexia. I saw skins in literally every color of the rainbow, horns, fangs, water like Aeric, fire and rocks, too many limbs, not enough limbs, things that only looked like limbs, extra eyes, single eyes, eyes that lit up. I could've gone on endlessly. Describing every child in here would've probably taken me more than a day.

Raven had given us a few seconds to take it all in but now turned to his class. "Class, these are Nayana, Fionn and Mori, humans." He paused and gestured to me. "And this is Thera, an untouched special who was raised by and amongst humans."

My heart stopped. All thirty students collectively gasped and stared at me as if I were some sort of unbelievable sight to behold. I felt panic rise up from inside me. How could he tell them that so casually?

One of the students, a light blue-skinned, short kid with big tusks sticking out of his mouth that reminded me of the servant that had given me my plate yesterday, stuck his hand up in the air, his arm stretched as far up as he could reach.

Raven turned to him. "Yes, Mokan, you can respectfully ask your question," he turned to us, "it is up to the four of you, of course, if you choose to answer it. Do not feel pressured, and if you are not comfortable, please inform me, and we will stop immediately."

Mom nodded and then turned to the special kid that still had his hand raised in the air. "It's okay, Mokan, please ask your question."

Mokan lowered his hand and stared at Mom with big eyes as if he couldn't believe she could actually speak. "D-do you know Herold?"

"Herold?" She had a pensive look on her face, probably going through a list of all the people she knew in her head.

"Herold, the current king of Herodia?" The question had surprised me, but this felt like the safest bet after giving it some thought as well. After all, there was no way this kid was talking about some random human named Herold somewhere in human territory.

Mokan's eyes became big with excitement, and he nodded his head excessively. "So, you know him? What kind of a person is he?"

I frowned. What kind of a person was the king of a country that I'd never even been to, or would ever have a chance of going to? Did this kid think that just because we were human, we somehow knew every other human out there? I thought this was the advanced class. Better not answer him like that, though.

"I haven't met him personally," I looked at the three standing next to me. Only at that moment did I noticed that I'd subconsciously moved to the left, hiding Fionn and Mori behind me. "None of us have, he lives in Herodia, which is across the ocean, and none of us have ever left our homeland."

I felt guilty about my defensive response after seeing Mokan's disappointed expression.

"But I've met some travelers who've been there, and they told me he was a good king. A little moody at times apparently, and strict, but fair."

Mokan's face lit up, although it creeped me out to see his tusks as he smiled. "That's amazing. Our textbook says he comes from a long line of kings and queens that were known for their fair judgment!"

That surprised me. I'd expected their questions to be more like, 'what do humans eat', or 'where do they live', but nothing as in-depth as this. What kind of class was humanology? Did they even learn about our history, our leaders? I narrowed my eyes. Were they learning about us, or were they learning how to conquer us?

Another hand rose up in the air, and Raven pointed in their direction. A tall girl with long green hair that almost had a plantlike texture stood up, holding her hands up flat in front of her, supporting a much smaller creature, about the size of my index finger. If I hadn't been looking closely, I would've mistaken it for a rock. It was similar to how the creatures that had attacked Alaexia had seemed like normal flames until you took a closer look.

The tiny rock creature stood up on two little pebbles, which I took to be his legs, and opened his mouth, producing a much deeper voice than I expected.

"How do humans procreate?"

I stared at him with a shocked expression and, honestly, a blush on my face.

"Kero!" Raven reprimanded him, which surprised me as well. Even when he was angry, he was still a masterpiece to behold. "I warned you to be respectful!"

I couldn't see the look on Kero's small face, but the plant girl behind him seemed reluctant.

"But sir, you said we should take this opportunity to learn as much from these humans as possible. Doesn't that mean we should ask them everything there is to know?" Kero's voice boomed through the room. Part of me understood his logic, but the way he called us 'these humans' annoyed me. I opened my mouth to give him a piece of my mind, but Raven beat me to it.

"Just because I told you to learn from them does not mean you can be rude to them, Kero. They are not animals you can freely observe how- and whenever you want. They are living beings with feelings, like you and me."

I looked at him. How much more did he plan on pulling at my heartstrings?

"Except they don't have magic."

A young, humanoid-looking boy that sat slumped in the front almost spit those words out at me. "And they're weak."

I stared him straight in the eye, all my fear instantly gone. Why had I been afraid of a bunch of snot-nosed brats in the first place?

Fionn put his hand against my arm to push me aside and took a step forward. "You don't need magic to be strong." He stuck out his chest. "I bet Thera is stronger than any of you specials in this classroom."

The boy, who had sleek blond hair that had been braided to the back of his head, grinned condescendingly. "I'm sure she is. She's a special after all, just like us, except she's an adult already, while we're still children."

Fionn's proud expression disappeared. Had he forgotten for a moment? It didn't matter if the kid in front of us was right or not. I honestly wanted to slap him in the face.

"Being a special doesn't automatically make you stronger," I tried to keep my tone as calm as I could, "nor does having magic. I've seen humans take down specials like Kero with my own eyes."

Shit. Instant silence fell over the entire room. Even Raven stared at me with a shocked look in his eyes. This didn't go the way I'd hoped it would at all. Why couldn't I have kept my mouth shut?

"Why?"

I turned to the right. I hadn't seen his mouth move, but that deep voice definitely belonged to Kero. "Why did they do that to them? Because they were so much smaller than them that they knew they could win?"

I quickly shook my head. "No, of course not! Those specials were the ones who-" I stopped, was I really going to accuse those fire creatures of attacking us in front of a class full of specials, even though back then I'd already been pretty sure that those specials hadn't been trying to hurt us on purpose?

"It wasn't like that," my voice had become softer, and it seemed like the entire class leaned forward to be able to hear me, "those specials, they seemed scared and confused, but they were setting the city on fire, and the humans were trying to protect themselves and each other. I'm pretty sure they couldn't even see those specials for what they were. All they seemed to be able to see were small flames raining down on their city."

The class stayed silent, and I turned to Raven, desperately thinking of a way to apologize to him, but he stared at me with a cold look in his eyes.

"Was that what *all* people there saw when they looked at those specials?" His voice hadn't changed, but somehow it felt so icy cold that I was scared to move.

"I…" I started but didn't finish. What was I supposed to say? Yes, I knew what they were, and I tried to convince the others to see it as well, but they chased me out? Yes, I knew what they were, that's why I didn't kill any myself? Those were just excuses. No matter what I said, I'd known what they were, but I'd still left the city, leaving those specials to die by human hands. I lowered my head. What did that make me, a coward? The bad guy?

I glanced up at him again. People had been cold towards me before. As someone who had always been considered 'strange' and 'an outsider' in the village I grew up in, I was no stranger to being treated like that, but it had never felt as horrible as it did right now. It took me at least a few seconds to realize why.

It was his magic. His magic that kept attracting me, that felt warm and welcoming, had suddenly turned cold, as if it had completely closed itself off from me and everything around us. I guess someone's magic didn't exist in one constant state. It seemed to change along with a person and their emotions. Or at least Raven's magic did.

I straightened my shoulders and forced myself to stare back into Ravens eyes as bravely as I could. Only after gathering the courage to do that, did I realize that Raven wasn't looking at me at all. His gaze seemed to be focused on something far off in the distance that nobody else in that room could see. Was he even still paying attention to what was happening around him?

From the corner of my eye, I could see another student raising their hand to ask a question. My heart jumped, only a few moments before I'd been so worried about these questions, but now I was happy there was still a student brave enough to ask one.

I turned towards the girl that had raised her hand. She had scaly skin and very thin eyes and lips that were barely more than slits in her face. I couldn't even find a nose at all. Her whole appearance seemed very snake-like to me, but she still managed to show me a polite smile.

I hesitantly smiled back at her. "Yes, you."

Those words seemed to break Raven's focus on whatever it was he'd been looking at, and from the corner of my eye, I saw him blink a few times with a confused look on his face and then turn to the snake girl. The cold that had surrounded him a moment ago disappeared, and his usual warmth instantly replaced it again. It was like an enormous weight got lifted off my shoulders, and only at that moment, when I subconsciously relaxed, did I notice how much I'd tensed up because of Raven's reaction.

The snake girl got up, looking understandably nervous. "Are you…" she hesitated for a moment but then forced herself to continue, "are you untouched because you grew up with humans?" She pulled up her shoulders as if she expected a scolding like Kero had gotten.

I lowered my voice slightly, worried I'd scare her off even more if I didn't. "I think so since until a few days ago, I didn't even know what it meant to be untouched. I thought I was just a type of special that doesn't have any magic."

She opened one eye wider than the other. "Does that mean humans don't know about magic?"

I thought about it. "It's a little difficult to explain. Humans think of specials as myths and legends. In those legends, specials have magic, so in that aspect, they are aware of it, yes. Although lore tells us that specials are born with it."

I heard a gasp behind me, and I looked over my shoulder to see Mori's shocked face. I hadn't told them about that part of my conversation with the masked guy, but it seemed she instantly reached the same conclusion I had.

"Does that mean you will eventually get magic as well?" She looked me straight in the eyes, no sneering, no mocking, just an honest question, accompanied by some worry.

Part of me wished she hadn't asked that in front of all these specials, but if she hadn't, one of them probably would have. I completely turned around to face her and took a step closer to her, trying to block the thirty students behind me from her view to create a moment between only her and me.

"I know that sounds scary, Mori, but I will if that's what it takes to protect you and Fionn and Mom. Are you okay with that?" I didn't whisper those words, but I spoke them softly enough that only those close to us could hear them.

She took a step back, and the words Raven had spoken the first time we met, about how Mori was confused about everything that was happening and how badly she wanted to go back home where she felt safe, echoed through my mind. This information probably didn't help her feel less confused. I could only hope that my words and the intention behind them at least made her feel a little safer.

"Will you do it even if I tell you not to?" Her voice was barely more than a whisper, and I was sure that none of the students had heard her.

I stared at the insecure look on her small face. Mom had always told me that when raising kids, there were times you had to be strict and do what you think is best, even if it would make them hate you for a while because in the end, it was all for their sake. Was this one of those moments? I loved Mori with all my heart, and I knew she loved me too, but part of me wasn't sure how much more I could push her before she'd come to hate me for real. Was it better for me to lie to her and give her some time to get used to the idea? I was scared that if I told her 'yes' at that moment, I would estrange her from me to the point of no return.

I slowly shook my head. What Mori needed most was to be able to believe that I would listen to her about something this important.

8

Three weeks passed in the blink of an eye, and no matter how many times I asked Raven, he reassured me that we were welcome to stay as long as we wanted, and so far, the decision seemed to have been made to stay indefinitely. Raven had offered to enroll both Fionn and Mori in his school, and although they both refused, they would often follow him and sit in on several classes, but only the ones that Raven or Aeric taught.

I wasn't all that crazy about going there. After everything we had been through, part of me was happy that the three of them were able to trust specials that fast, but part of me also couldn't believe they were so gullible. Yes, these students were just kids, like Fionn and Mori, but where did they come from? I'd seen the same kind of creatures as the ones that had attacked our village. Where were their families? If they lived this close to the border, were their fathers or mothers or cousins some of the specials that killed Dad? I was too scared to ask them what they knew about it directly, too scared to discuss it with Fionn or Mori or even Mom.

So, I mostly steered away from the school and instead walked the grounds, which were many times bigger than I'd even imagined. Raven did not only have a successful school, but he also had many fields full of all kinds of vegetables and grains, some of which I recognized, most of which I didn't. The farmers that worked these lands were specials who lived on his land. Rather than saying Raven was the master of the Ravenous household, he was more like the king of his own little kingdom. A kingdom that he let me explore freely.

I hadn't walked through any of the small villages that were scattered all over the grounds. I knew the rumor of an untouched special, raised by humans, had spread like wildfire and every special I came across instantly seemed to know it was me. I managed to get away from them before I ever had to talk to any of them, but the thought that they all knew unnerved me.

Was that what the masked guy had meant when he'd said that it wasn't that hard to track an untouched at all?

I rounded the village that I knew was somewhere to my left and kept following the edge of the barley field I was walking next to. I knew there were paved roads between every so many fields, but I avoided those as well. So far, none of them had tried to hurt or chase me or even been unpleasant to me, but they were still specials. I didn't know anything about them. I had no idea which one of them was friendly, and which one was like the ones that had destroyed our home.

I left the fields and walked up a grassy hill, which meant I'd almost reached my destination. I stopped on top of the hill, in the shade of a single, fully blooming tree, and looked out over the fields and villages that made up Raven's kingdom, with the school as his shining castle in the center.

Even from here, I could see the bustling going on around the school. Kids taking a break in the trees' shadow or

120

playing with balls on the grass field with the strange poles with nets around them, which I learned served as goals. Fionn and Mori were probably somewhere among those kids.

I sighed, slightly melancholic. It was like nothing had changed at all like we were still back home. Even among specials, the kids would still go out and make friends. And even among specials, even among my own species, I was still an outsider.

I turned my back to the school and started walking again.

"Wait! Miss Moralis!" A small wave that kept breaking and rolling over itself moved in my direction. I stopped and waited for Aeric to come to a wobbly standstill in front of me. Without a nose or mouth or any kind of features whatsoever, he somehow breathed in heavily.

That interested me. "Do you need air to breathe?"

He wobbled up and down. "Water consists of one-third out of oxygen, so even though I do not breathe like you do, I do need air to survive."

I thought about it. "But you're not just water. Not normal water, at least."

He nodded again. At least, that's what I thought the wobbling was supposed to be. "That is true, in the same way, that there is more to you than blood and muscle and bone and skin. There is more to me than just water."

I tilted my head. "But you can't see through me. I can see through you."

Aeric laughed. It was a strange sound, bubbling, gurgling almost, but very contagious. "And how can you be sure that I cannot see through you?"

He got me there. There was no telling what Aeric was capable of.

"Do not worry, miss, this is my magic, the fact that you can hear me speaking to you, the fact that you can see me smile, even though I do not have a mouth." He affirmed it by brightly smiling at me.

I leaned closer to him; my curiosity piqued. "You mean telepathy? That's what you received?"

He nodded again. "That is what I felt I needed most, and it seems the Source agreed with me."

I leaned even closer. "The Source?"

He stopped, not only with talking or smiling, but he also completely stopped moving. I was literally looking at a still body of water.

I hesitated but then softly pricked him with my finger. "A-Aeric?"

Suddenly his bright smile appeared again, and he looked up at me. I unconsciously moved back.

"I humbly apologize. I lost myself in my thoughts for a moment."

That was the worst excuse I'd ever heard, but I made sure he wouldn't see that on my face. "So, about what you were saying? The Source?"

He shook his head a bit too fast, and some drops of water flew off him and landed on the ground, where they disappeared into the earth. "Let us not talk about it anymore. It is not very interesting."

"It's very interesting to me."

The lower of the two blobs that made up his body grew a little thinner and taller. "I apologize again, miss. It is simply that master Raven does not prefer for me to talk to you about it."

I clenched my teeth. "Why?"

He stared at me in silence for a moment. "Were you perhaps on your way to the stables?"

I frowned. What kind of distraction was that? Did he really think I would forget about it now? I opened my mouth to pry further but stopped as I saw his entire body literally shrink a bit in anticipation. I had to remind myself that this was not a bad guy, simply someone who was following orders.

"How come you call Raven 'master'? I haven't heard any of the other teachers do that." If he wasn't going to talk to me about magic, he might as well tell me some more about Raven.

His face instantly lit up by the thought of telling me his story. "None of the other teachers indeed call him master, but that is because the other teachers are different from me." He wobbled back and forth a bit as he seemed to think about it. "Or I suppose I should say I am different from them."

A little lump grew out of his lower body, like a tiny hand. He used it to gesture to a rock underneath the tree we were next to. Somehow it seemed really adorable, and I quickly sat down on the rock that he climbed onto and sort of sat down on next to me.

"You see, there are different kinds of specials. There are the ones like master Raven and many of the teachers and students, higher specials. And there are specials like me. We are sentient like you, but we are not quite the same. We are a lower level of beings."

I grimaced. "That's a messed-up thing to say… Does Raven really agree with that?"

Aeric stayed silent for a moment. "I suppose he does; it is how many have thought for many generations. But I should say that master Raven is not like most."

He stared off in the distance. "I was a body of water. I could not move like this before. All I could do was be still and perceive the world around me. I felt happy when the sun shone on me, or when a new fish was born in me, or when other creatures drank from me and stayed alive because of me. I felt sorrow when people spilled parts of me or threw their garbage in me. But that was all there was to it. You could say I was not quite like normal water, I was not like the animals walking around or swimming in me, and I was a far cry from the normal kind of specials that are gathered here, the ones that talk and think until I met master Raven."

Even though I couldn't see his face, it was clear he thought very fondly of that memory.

"Master Raven was traveling at that moment and coincidentally decided to set up camp next to me. To this day, I am not completely sure what it was that changed me. I suspect my longtime exposure to master Raven's magic, but one thing I was certain of was that I started to change. After only a few days, I was able to move parts of myself. I was so happy that I started moving nonstop, which master Raven immediately noticed, of course. After realizing that I was not just any body of normal water, he started talking to me. Nothing grand, he complimented me on my clearness and freshness and how healthy the plants looked that grew in me. After seeing my elated reactions to his words, he started telling me stories. Stories about things he had seen while traveling, stories about the school he wanted to build, stories about all the things he had managed to accomplish with his magic."

The water on the lower half of his body sloshed up and down against the stone we were sitting on as if he were joyfully swinging his legs back and forth. "His stories made me want more. I wanted to be free from that place I had been stuck in. I wanted to be able to walk around and have adventures like master Raven. It took me an entire night of trial and error, but right before the first morning light, I managed to separate a part of me and step out of the water."

He grew taller, and two little arms wriggled out of his lower blob. He spread them widely as if he were proudly presenting himself to me. "That is how I came to be."

I applauded his theatrics. "That must've been an amazing experience."

He lowered again with a warm expression. "It was. But I still was not content. I wanted to speak to master Raven the same way he had spoken to me. I wanted to be able to think as deeply as he did. I wanted to feel as many emotions as he did. I wanted to be of use to him, to the person who had helped me become more."

I tried not to show any kind of excitement. "And that's how you received your magic?"

He wobbled his upper blob up and down. "Master Raven makes dreams come true, and even without me being able to tell him my dream, he knew what it was, and helped me achieve it. After I became what I am today, he took me along with him and taught me many new things until he eventually brought me here."

He tilted his head. "It is not strange for stronger specials to have underlings like me, like the old me, who cannot think for themselves, but who can follow orders." The look on his face suddenly darkened. "The flames you spoke of, the ones you saw in Alaexia, I think they were like the old me as well. They possess their own feelings, their own sense of existence, but they are bound to a master."

I looked at him, at his small figure, at his lowered upper blob. "Are you bound to Raven as well?"

He nodded slowly but then stopped. "I was bound like them at first. It was the only way for me to move about freely. Without master Raven's magic inside me, I would have never been able to move or ask for my own magic." He shrugged. "I know master Raven does not think of himself as my master in that sense, but he is the reason I became what I am. He has taken care of me from beginning to end. When I finally dared to tell him I wanted to teach others the way he had taught me, he made me a teacher in his school, and when parents and the other teachers and even the students expressed their concerns, he defended me. That is why, even though master Raven would never ask me to call him master, I do it because I prefer to, to show him the great amount of respect I have for him."

I stared off into the distance the same way he did. His way of thinking made sense to me, and his words had moved me deeply, but I hadn't really learned anything new about Raven at all. All that story had told me was that he was kind and that his magic was strong. Pretty much the two things I'd first noticed about him when I'd met him. Well… aside from his dazzling looks.

"What did Raven gain from doing that for you?"

I instantly got the frown from Aeric that I'd expected.

"He did not gain anything from it."

His tone was defensive, but I couldn't stop myself from pushing further. "Then why do you think he did it?"

The front of Aeric's lower blob moved in a resolute motion, his version of angrily folding his arms, I figured. "He did it because he is a kind person."

I sighed. "But doesn't even a small part of you think that's hard to believe?"

He immediately shook his head, splattering small drops of water.

"So, then I just have to believe that that's the only reason he is helping us right now? Just to help us, because he's so kind? There's nothing he wants from us eventually?" I'd decided to come right out and ask it.

He shook his head again.

I leaned back and looked at the grain at the bottom of the hill that slowly swayed back and forth on the warm summer breeze. "Then what is his plan for us? To stay here for the rest of our lives? Let the kids go to school, find a job, build a life here for themselves?"

Aeric looked at me. I think we both realized what all my questions were really about at that moment.

"If that is what you and your family wish for, I know master Raven will permanently welcome you here." He gave me a comforting pat on my leg. "But you are not a prisoner, miss Moralis. You are safe here, and I believe you would enjoy life with us once you get used to being with your own kind, but if you think there is more for you out there, then you are, of course, free to go and explore all possibilities."

He turned to the right and looked off into the distance, where we could hear the school-bells ring, indicating the end of the lunch break. "My advice is that you think about it carefully, however. As someone who was equally new to this world as you are, I can assure you there is a lot out there that I wish I had not seen, that I wish I did not even know of. It is not only your life you would be risking, after all."

He moved up and then rolled off the stone. "You have only been here for a short time, and as long as you remain within the borders of master Raven's land, you are safe. So, take as long as you need and think everything over before you make a final decision." He turned around. "I better head back before I am late for my next class."

He started flowing away, but I got up and ran after him. "Wait!"

As expected, he immediately stopped and popped up into his usual form again. "Yes, miss?"

I gave him a doubting look. "Did Raven ask you to come and talk to me?"

The second of silence told me everything I needed to know. He sighed slightly, bubbly, realizing he gave himself away. "Master Raven was concerned. He is concerned that you are having trouble fitting in, and he thought you would perhaps find it easier to talk to me about it than to him."

"Because you've had some experience not fitting in?"

He nodded happily.

"Will you tell him about everything we talked about?" I tried not to sound like a little kid who'd told someone a secret and regretted it afterward.

He thought about it for a second. "If master Raven asks me, I will not lie to him."

Exactly the answer I expected. "But as long as he won't ask?"

He gave me an almost mischievous smile. "As long as master Raven does not ask, I see no reason to bother him with a random conversation you and I had together."

I chuckled. "Thank you."

He hesitated. "I should warn you not to get your hopes up too much, though. Since it is about you, miss Moralis, I am convinced he will ask."

I stared at him. Was it because I was the untouched human special, or was there another reason Raven was so interested in me? I shook my head, stopping myself from wishful thinking. There was no way someone like Raven would be interested in me for any other reason than that and I knew I would make a fool out of myself if I asked, so instead I stayed quiet and waved to Aeric as he flowed away.

I turned into the opposite reaction and started walking towards the stables, where I'd been heading before Aeric stopped me. There were two reasons I liked going here. One was that, although they looked a little different, the horses here were very close to the ones at home and I not only liked horse riding, but it also made it easier to get around. The second was a nest of little kittens.

I entered the stables and, under loud neighing, walked straight to the back, where I knew they were hiding in the hay. It was nothing strange, no different from any other kittens we had at home, just four adorable little balls of fur.

I sat down on the lowest bale of hay next to them and picked one up. It let out a cute meow that caused his three brothers and sister to wildly start crawling around in every direction, although they were still too young to be able to walk properly, and they kept falling over.

I giggled and pressed the one I was holding against my chest as I softly petted his cute little head. "Don't worry, little buddy, I'm not going to hurt you. We've met before, don't you remember?"

I kept it warmly pressed against my chest for a moment but then put it back with its kin and got up to saddle one of the horses. Raven had generously told me to use whatever horse I wanted, and so I'd chosen one that somewhat reminded me of the big, old horse we had when I was a little kid. It was so big that I couldn't even see over its back. It had a very light, almost blond shade of fur, surprisingly small, delicate hooves, and a beautiful, flowing mane. The only difference with our old horse back home, or any horse back home, was the little barbs that grew out of its hind legs, above his hooves, and the two small horns that grew out of its head, in front of his ears. After every kind of special I'd seen in Raven's school, a pair of horns on a horse hadn't surprised me in the least. All it meant was that instead of only carrying you into battle, this horse could actually fight with you if necessary. But despite its outer appearance, it still had the personality of a normal horse; as long as I treated it calmly and friendly, it repaid me in kind.

I took my time to brush it and clean its hooves before I finally saddled it and led it out of the barn. The second we stepped outside, and it smelled the fresh air, I saw its ears point up straighter, and he started to pull at the reins; it was rearing to go. I grinned. No need to keep it waiting then. I put my foot in the stirrup and hopped on his back with ease. I loosely held the reins in my hands and gave him a little notch with my heels. He snorted excitedly and then broke into a run. I gave him as much freedom as he wanted for a while. Not only did he seem to enjoy himself galloping around however he wanted, but this fiery guy knew these surroundings much better than me, so I just trusted him to stay within the borders of Raven's land.

Which turned out to be a mistake.

I'd let my guard down, and I wasn't paying as much attention as I should have been. Maybe that's why it took me so long to realize that the strange scent I smelled wasn't something I recognized from anything or anyone on Raven's land, even though I did recognize it. It was a mixture of dried-up blood and ash. The exact same smell that had drenched the air that night I lost my dad and my home.

The horse stopped the second we reached them and whinnied nervously. I stared at them in shock, completely paralyzed, my mind blank. Or maybe the opposite of blank, I wasn't sure. What were they doing here? Were they looking for me? Did they recognize me?

There were five of them. Five blue, long-limbed monsters. They were sitting around a fire, cooking something I didn't want to know of what it was. All five of them turned their head to us and stared at me in confusion. So, they hadn't noticed I'd been coming their way. Were they here by coincidence? If that were the case, shouldn't I just get out of here as fast as I could, back to Raven's land, where I should be safe?

I lifted up my hand to try and steer my horse away from them, but the moment I moved, it was like I broke a spell that had been keeping them motionless. The one that was closest to us jumped up and, without even grabbing his weapon, ran towards us while letting out a loud, wild battle cry.

That scared my horse so much it flew off and kept running straight ahead, not caring about where it was going or how both our skins got slashed open by the branches that hit us.

I leaned forward, put my arms around its neck so I wouldn't fall off and trusted it would take us far away enough from those monsters that we could shake them off and find our way back home. But somehow, the screams that followed us didn't get any softer or more distant, and I started to panic. What if they could somehow keep up with us or, even worse, catch up to us? My horse had been running for a long time, even before we ran into those bastards. What if it got too tired to keep going?

I somehow gathered the courage to look over my shoulder. I didn't see them, but I could feel how close they were.

I would be able to take on one or maybe even two of them at the same time, but five was too much, nobody would survive that. I closed my eyes and clenched my fists around the reins. We weren't going to outrun them, I was sure of that no matter how I looked at it, and the only way to survive fighting them was if I wouldn't have to fight all five of them at the same time. I had to separate them somehow.

I took my feet out of the stirrups and climbed on top of the saddle in a squatted position. If I could jump in one of these trees we were passing, would at least one of them follow my horse? I had no choice but to take that gamble. As soon as I was on top of one of these branches, I would figure out a way to separate the others. That way, I might be able to buy some time, and I was fairly sure they wouldn't hurt my horse if they didn't need to try and get me off it.

I looked up at the branches above that rushed by, trying to find a good spot to jump in, just in time to see a noticeably light-skinned hand reach down. It grabbed me by the back of my shirt and pulled me up with some effort. I felt how I flew up in the air, my body still moving forward, as if it was trying to match the direction my horse was still going in, just to be pulled back and painfully land on the thick branch beneath me.

I looked up at the dark mask in front of me, but the man wearing it didn't give me any chance to talk. Instead, he pushed me hard-handedly, so I fell backward, bumping the back of my head against the actual tree. He immediately followed and pressed his own back against me, carefully keeping his eyes pointed at the ground beneath us.

"Don't talk, don't move, don't even breathe. Just make sure you're covered by me as much as possible." His words came out fast and softer than whispers. I made myself as small as possible behind him, pressing myself as flatly against the tree as I could while anxiously keeping my own eyes glued to the ground beneath us.

We waited there as the sounds of those monsters' footsteps came closer until they passed right under us and kept running forward. My heart had been about to explode, but the second they passed and disappeared from our view, I couldn't stop myself from letting out a relieved sigh and relaxing my body, which had been painfully tensed up the whole time.

The masked guy in front of me relaxed as well, although not as much as me. Honestly, the only reason I even noticed it was because of how close he still was to me, which I hadn't paid much attention to until then. I looked at him from the back while he scanned our surroundings. He was wearing a thin, loose, black shirt that covered both his arms but, thanks to its wide neck opening, showed me a bit of his back. It didn't seem very broad but was more muscular than I'd thought, now that I could look at it closely. Although his skin was as white as milk here as well. I leaned to the side, wondering if his shirt would show me as much of his skin in the front as well.

Noticing that my attention had moved somewhere else, he turned halfway towards me with his lips pressed tightly together, clearly annoyed, but I ignored it. I couldn't see much, but his sharp clavicle and the upper part of his chest were clearly visible. I hid a slight grin. His chest seemed to be as smooth and hairless as his face.

"You smell like a barn."

Those few words were all it took to snap me back to reality and focus on his face again, of which I could only see half as usual.

"And you smell like nothing. Why is that?" Two weeks ago, I'd asked him something similar, and he had avoided my question. But in the past few weeks, I'd learned two sure things about magic. One, it attracted and entranced me. Two, I could smell it.

I didn't feel that kind of paralyzing attraction to this guy, though, and he didn't seem to have any scent at all, as far as I could tell. In other words, why couldn't I sense any magic from him?

He stared at me without saying anything for a second but then nodded to my coat. "But that thing in your inner pocket does smell like something, doesn't it?" He looked up at me again. "Isn't that enough?"

Enough to make you believe I do have magic? Was that what he was asking me?

"Thera!"

I looked down. Raven road underneath our branch on one of the horses from the stable. Whatever the guy in front of me had done to fool those blue monsters before didn't have the slightest effect on Raven. Or maybe he had stopped doing it, giving Raven a chance to find us.

"Urgh," the guy in front of me let out an annoyed sigh, "this guy."

"Thera!" Raven jumped off his horse, and at the same time, the guy in front of me put his arms around my waist and simply let both of us fall off the branch. I screamed as we headed towards the ground, but halfway, in mid-air, he spun both of us around, which must've looked pretty amazing from the sidelines, and somehow quietly landed on his feet, lifting me up with his arm, so I landed next to him a second later. Nothing about my landing was gracious the way his had been, but at least I didn't get hurt.

Raven grabbed my upper arm and pulled me away from him. He took a step to the left in the same movement, blocking me from the guy's view.

I didn't like that. And I didn't like the way Raven had pulled me away from the person who'd clearly been helping me, as if he thought he had to save me from him.

"What are you doing here? Why are you after her?" His voice was low, and the magic around him had gone cold again, the same way it had done that day in the classroom. He wasn't holding up a weapon, he wasn't even moving or standing aggressively or defensively, but all three of us instinctively felt that it would only take mere seconds for him to rip the guy in front of us to shreds. Not that my masked savior seemed impressed or intimidated in the least.

"Calm down, Rav. I was clearly only helping her since you can't seem to keep up." An obvious provocation, that seemed to have some effect, because the change in Raven's magic gave me chills.

"She is safe within the borders."

The guy laughed. "And how much longer will you force her to stay there, playing house with you?"

That seemed to surprise Raven. "I'm not forcing her. She's staying with me because she wants to, because she feels *safe* with me." The way he emphasized that word made me feel it was meant for the both of us as if he wanted to reassure me that he really wasn't trying to keep me with him against my will.

The guy snorted. "Is that so, Thera?" He leaned to the side so he was able to see me. "Do you feel 'safe' with this guy?"

I started to get annoyed, in how many more different ways were they going to emphasize that word? But then I relaxed again and nodded, to his clear disappointment.

He suddenly grinned. "Ah, I see, well then, I guess there's no need for me to stay anymore." He stuck his hand up in the air and waved shortly, only once. "Bye."

After that, he simply turned around and walked away. I followed him with shocked eyes. That was the first time I'd seen him leave in such a normal way. It felt strange and disarming. Was he really leaving, just like that? I'd nodded to his question because it was the truth. I believed that we were safe with Raven, but why did that somehow feel like I'd chosen to trust Raven over him?

Raven turned to me, and I cringed, but he didn't yell at me. He didn't even say anything. He just took a step closer to me, put his arms around me and pulled me close.

"Oh, thank the gods, I was so worried." He mumbled the words in my hair, and they sounded so sincere that I felt guilty.

As fast as he had embraced me, he let me go and took a step back, with a little blush on his cheeks. "I-I apologize, it is just that… I thought I had lost you."

I slowly shook my head, relieved that the icy cold surrounding him a second ago had disappeared again. "No, it's okay. I'm sorry for going outside the borders. I didn't mean to, but I was riding one of the horses and-" I stopped and looked around me in a panic.

"I'm so sorry, Raven! I thought they might not hurt him if he wasn't carrying me, and then that guy pulled me off him, and I didn't see where he went…" I stopped and looked at Raven, who had quietly waited for me to finish rambling.

"It is alright, Thera. It knows the way home, and, in the meantime, you can ride with me." He walked over to his horse that had calmly been waiting by the tree and took the reins in his left hand while holding out his right hand to me.

I hesitated for a second. I knew that he was trying to get me home safe as fast as possible, but for some reason, even though I used to do it with Fionn a lot back home, riding together suddenly felt far too intimate. Even if the front of the saddle, which went up a little, would be between us, he'd still have to press his chest against my back to hold onto the reins. Or, if I held the reins, he'd have to hold onto me to make sure he wouldn't fall off. I trembled; I honestly wasn't sure which I'd prefer.

9

The ride home was as tense as I'd thought it would be, but not in the way I'd thought. Raven's chest was pressed closely against my back, and I could feel the warmth that came from it burn in my stomach excitedly. He held his arms next to mine to hold the reins as our horse slowly walked us back to safe premises. Raven seemed to put in the effort to not let his arms lean against mine, as if he were trying to at least avoid the physical contact he could. I kept my eyes down as I worried about why. After that first hug he'd given me, his attitude had become much colder again. Not in the same way as before, or in a way that scared me, but more in a cool, distant way, and I wasn't completely sure why. Was it because I crossed the border of his land? But hadn't he forgiven me for that a few moments ago?

I quietly took a deep breath to gather my courage. "Raven-"

"So, that is the man you have been dreaming of night after night?"

The second I'd opened my mouth, it seemed he had no longer been able to contain himself.

I wasn't exactly sure what he was talking about, but I didn't like it. "No, I haven't."

"You probably do not remember; a lot of people forget what they dreamt about the second they wake up." His voice was very monotone, as if he weren't indirectly telling me that he could somehow see my dreams. I stopped trying to look over my shoulder. Wait, didn't I know that from the beginning? Hadn't he somehow inserted himself into Fionn's dream in order to reach out to us?

So, had he been going into my dreams every night? Not inserting himself or talking to me like he'd done to Fionn, but just watching every little thing that happened in my unconscious mind. I didn't like that.

He immediately seemed to notice the change in my attitude. "I apologize for making you feel uncomfortable, Thera. It is not something I do purposely. I cannot even control it."

I wasn't going to let myself be convinced that easily. "So, when you appeared into Fionn's dream and told him to come to you, that was an accident as well?"

He scraped his throat, uncomfortable under my cold tone. "Not exactly. I suppose you could say there are two facets to my chosen magic."

I lifted an eyebrow. Why did he emphasize chosen like that? But I decided not to ask, not before I had a satisfying explanation for his invasion in my dreams.

"One facet, the one Fionn experienced firsthand, consists of me putting myself in the dreams of other people while I am awake, and without me knowing what those dreams are about." He shook his head. "Believe me, I sometimes end up in the most incredible places, seeing things I could not possibly imagine."

He paused for a moment before he continued his story. "The second facet is one that I have no control over, as it happens while I am asleep as well. Rather than dreaming my own dreams, my mind gets pulled into dreams that surround me. There is no satisfying logic to it. Often, I see the dreams of people who are experiencing extreme emotions. When they desperately long for something, for example, or when they are really hurt or extremely happy. But there are also times that I spend an entire night watching someone take a stroll through a park or have a drink with friends, things that do not seem to hold any real meaning."

I couldn't see his face, but I noticed how he tightened his grip on the reins. "Ever since you entered special territory, Thera, I have been seeing your dreams every single night. I have seen some of your mother, plenty of Fionn, and only a few of Mori, but yours would come back every night, and they were almost always about him."

He snorted with disbelief. "I did not realize it was him until just now, though. You shroud him in so much mystery that there was no way of telling who or what he was. The only thing I could ever see clearly were those accursed masks, but he never used to wear those before, so I could not have known."

He laughed bitterly. "A smart move on his side, I suppose, but he was always like that, using whatever he could to hide from the world like a coward."

"He's not a coward." That came out angrier and more defensive than I'd meant it to.

I composed myself. "He saved my family and me. If he hadn't warned us to run when our village was about to be attacked, none of us would be alive right now."

Raven stayed quiet for a while. "But if he would have remained and fought with you, maybe you would all still be alive right now."

I fell quiet. That thought had never crossed my mind, not even for a second. Why? Was it because that guy looked so light and frail that I'd automatically assumed he wouldn't stand a chance against those monsters? But even if he was weak, there must've been something he would've been able to do. Why hadn't he stayed with us? Why did he keep disappearing after giving us only the smallest sliver of help?

"Trust me, Thera, that person does not even deserve half of the mystery and gratefulness you allocate him." Raven's voice sounded soft. He clearly felt reluctant to tell me the harsh truth.

I wasn't sure what to say. I couldn't do much about the mystery, I mean, the more I spoke to him, the less I felt like I understood him, but gratefulness… It was true that he'd left us to fend for ourselves after warning us, but it was also true that he *had* warned us. Should I not be thankful for that? Raven was right, if he'd stayed, Dad might have still been alive, but there was no way of telling what would've happened.

I sighed. I might've been too quick to trust the masked guy. I mean, by the gods, I didn't even know his name.

I lifted my head, suddenly realizing that Raven did. "What's his name? How do you know him?" If he was going to say all that stuff about him, he should at least give me a reason to listen to him.

"It is best if you do not know. You should forget about him." Raven's voice was resolute. He was clearly done talking about him. "Just, whatever you do, even if you decide to see him again, do not trust him, please."

I frowned. "But I should trust you? Even though I know about as much about you as I know about him?"

That seemed to hit the spot. His arms flinched. "You are right. To you, there must not be much difference between us, as we have both been trying to keep you safe in our own way while also keeping you in the dark in our own way."

We finally reached the stable, and Raven jumped off the horse. I immediately missed the heat of his chest against my back, to my own annoyance. He held out his hand to me, but no matter how much I wanted to hold it, I ignored it and got off the horse by myself.

He grinned at my stubbornness. "Thera, before we discuss anything further, I want you to know that I am not keeping things from you because I want to or with ill intent. I am simply trying to protect you. No matter how brightly the sun shines everywhere here, the world outside these safe borders is darker than you could possibly imagine."

I didn't say anything back and watched as the master of these safe borders saddled down, fed, and started brushing his own horse.

"This magic of yours, what do you use it for? Why did you ask for this kind of magic?"

He didn't say anything back at first but calmly kept brushing his horse, an image that under any other circumstance would've made me melt completely. How was it even possible to look this entrancing while standing in a dusty stable that smelled like hay and cleaning salts and horse poop?

"The Ravenous line was a clan of warlords, every single one of them known and feared for their power and their hunger for blood."

His voice was soft, and he refused to look me in the eye.

"I was not like them. I was a weak and sickly child, and the sight of blood made me gag. Strangely enough, my mother was the one who was deeply disappointed in me, but my father, the fearsome warlord, was always kind to me. He would always tell me that it was okay to have different dreams than my parents and that if I did not want to fight, I should find out for myself what it was I wanted."

He laughed slightly, shaking his head. "Unfortunately, it is not that easy to find a dream for yourself, especially not when you are surrounded by warmongering monsters who could speak of nothing but blood and fighting and brag about their kill-count."

I swallowed, trying not to look too horrified, not to interrupt him.

"But since I chose to go against their beliefs, I felt pressured to have something to show them that was worth betraying my family for. So, under my father's occasional guidance, I started trying out all manner of things."

He stroked the manes of his horse before moving his brush over them. "My father's worldview was small, so we started with all kinds of weaponry and fighting styles, like sports, not to kill with, which obviously was not successful. After that, I started reading books about people who had their dreams come true, such as famous painters, or musicians, or people who had found and united with their true loves."

He glanced at me, fast, barely noticeable.

"I tried all of it, but painting frustrated me, and I enjoyed listening to music a lot more than creating it, and I was only a little kid back then, so I was not even interested in girls and true love, or any kind of love, yet."

He grinned. "I became so desperate that finding a dream for myself became my dream, which is rather pathetic and not something I could use as an excuse to turn away from my family's customs and beliefs."

His grin turned into a distant smile. "I was too weak to fight with them, but I did not have anything of my own that I wanted to do, so instead, I started helping our troops wherever I could. I would take care of their horses, I sharpened their weapons, I took care of their wounds, I simply did whatever I could to be helpful in any way, to my mother's great shame."

He shook his head. "The great warlord's son running around between the foot-soldiers, tending to their needs like a mere servant."

He leaned over to the left side of the stable, exchanging the brush he had been using for a softer one.

"One night, I was taking care of one of my father's lieutenants. He had been cut deeply; the wound had started to get infected, and he had fever dreams. He would talk in his sleep, saying the name of one of the female soldiers who had been helping me. I might not have known much about love, but by then, I had read more than enough stories about it to know what was going on. Since that lieutenant was about to die from his infection, I decided to at least help him make that last dream come true, so I wrote a long letter to her, telling her everything the lieutenant had been mumbling about her in his sleep. As soon as she read it, she ran over to him and embraced him."

He smiled warmly. "I have never seen such a frightening man have such an incredible look on his face. He did not have the slightest notion as to what was going on but was extremely happy nonetheless."

He stroked his hand over the rough hairs of his horse's long, shining mane again. "That lieutenant miraculously

144

recovered, and those two got married not long after that. I had never felt so good about anything I had done in my life. It had been frustrating to be so weak, to be a disappointment, it had been even more frustrating trying to find a dream for myself to prove that there was more to me than that, but it was strangely easy and satisfying to make somebody else happy."

He smiled fondly. "When I told my father, he took me to th- He took me to receive my magic."

I stared at him, but he avoided my eyes just as carefully as he'd avoided slipping up on a vital piece of information about receiving my magic.

"Anyway, most children receive their magic when they are eight, I received it when I was ten, which is why nobody seemed to have high expectations when I departed to go ask for it, but somehow, not only did I get it, I got…" he seemed to think about it for a second, "I got so much more."

He turned to look me in the eye for the first time since he'd started telling his story. "It might sound rather cliché, but you could say I received the power to make dreams come true." He tilted his head. "Well, I have the power to know people's dreams, and I use the power and fortune I inherited from my family and any other magic I can muster to make those dreams come true."

"Because that makes you happy?"

He confirmed that with a bright look on his face and I didn't have the heart to say anything else about it, like how it must be nice to have that many people owe you. Somehow, I really believed that he didn't do it for such a tainted reason.

"Is that why you were so pissed that the masked guy is my dream, even though you don't trust him?"

His look darkened. "That man is not your dream, Thera. You just dream about him." He corrected me with a stern voice, the kind of voice only teachers used.

I folded my arms. "Then what is my dream?"

"I cannot tell you that, Thera."

It was like a slap in my face. "You can't, or you won't?" I knew he was hurt by my cold tone, but I couldn't stop myself.

He lifted his shoulders. "I cannot. I do not know what ought to do because you do not seem to know yourself. That is why your dreams are so vague and confusing. All I know is that your dream is not that man. It is something he represents for you. You have to figure out for yourself what that is."

He finally stopped brushing his horse and put the brush back in the little basket that hung outside the box. He closed the door behind him and walked closer to me, putting his hand on my shoulder, and looking me deep in the eye, sending a shiver of excitement through my body that I desperately tried to hide from him. "There is no need for you to figure it out right away, Thera. Take your time to give it some careful thought. The answer will come to you eventually. For now, let us go home and get something to eat, okay?"

I nodded instantly. Only the thought of that amazing food was capable of tearing me away from Raven's hypnotizing stare.

We left the barn and followed the same path home I had taken there, through the fields, to my surprise.

He looked at me over his shoulder with a knowing expression. "I noticed that you do not like to pass through the villages, so I thought you would prefer this route." He answered my unasked question as he looked forward again. "But I do hope you will give them a chance someday. I know they are the ones being rude for staring at you, but they do it because you are something exceedingly rare around these parts. I am convinced they will forget about it and go on with their daily lives once they get used to seeing you here and you have become a part of those daily lives."

I didn't answer him. As someone who was an outsider even to his own family, he should know better than anyone that that was not how things worked. Yes, seeing me would become normal at some point, and they'd probably stop staring, but I would never be 'one of them'. I'd tried that many times back in our village, but it never worked. People never fully accepted someone who was so fundamentally different from them. The only way to truly be a part of other people's daily life was to find people who were either the same as you or just as different as you.

It was already dark outside by the time we reached the house. Raven opened the front door for me and told me to take a seat in the dining room, after which he disappeared. I assumed to ask one of his servants to prepare us some food, but instead, he came back with his arms full of plates and bowls with as much food as he could carry. He put it all down in front of me, handed me a fork and started to eat straight from the serving plates with his own fork without any decorum.

He looked at me with his mouth full and covered it with his hand. "Are you not going to eat?"

Talking with his mouth full was so unexpected from him that I could only laugh about it. Just for a moment, after that, I shamelessly dug in myself too. How on earth did he still look this attractive even with his mouth full of food?

I don't want to say we silently ate like a pair of hungry animals, but that was pretty much how that dinner went down. Whether it was Dad's slimy mashed potatoes, as Fionn called them, or the godlike meals we got served here, food always brightened my mood.

Afterward, I helped him stack the empty plates and bring them to the kitchen, full of servants who immediately took them out of our hands to clean them. So, Raven hadn't been trying to be thoughtful towards his kitchen staff, who I'd assumed had already left for the day. He'd served us all that food himself because he wanted to? Why did that move me a little bit?

He walked me up the stairs towards my bedroom.

"Raven?" We quietly walked side by side, and I stared out of one of the many windows in every hallway.

"Yes?"

"Your parents, what happened to them?"

He thought about it. "After I received my magic and proved to be much more powerful than even my father's best warriors, my father was truly proud of me. Even my mother seemed pleased when she saw it with her own eyes."

His fingers uncomfortably played with the fabric of his robes. "It was a strange feeling. For as long as I could remember, I wished for that very thing to happen, but when it finally did, I did not need it anymore because I had found something that fulfilled me and made me much happier than her approval ever could. We tried to find a way to live together for a while, but in the end, it was not a good fit, so I decided to leave."

He relaxed his hand, letting go of his robes. "My father let me go to figure things out for myself, and for a while, I traveled around, met all kinds of people, made all kinds of

148

dreams come true. My parents remained the way they were, fighting whenever they could. But the climate in special territory changed a lot during that time. Most specials were done with the fighting and the wars. They were done being scared, so a lot of clan leaders and line holders came together and brokered a fragile peace.

After that, going out and taking over other clans the way my clan had always done was not something you could do anymore, and little by little, our clan fell apart. The ones who could not say goodbye to the fighting life left and became mercenaries or likewise. My father decided to switch tactics like most clan leaders had done and immersed himself into the political war."

He shook his head. "Looking back on it, I actually think that lifestyle fitted my father a lot better. I always thought I was the only one who was different from everybody else, but my father was a lot more kindhearted than I had always thought. He preferred winning wars with words, and not with bloodshed."

His look darkened. "Not everybody agreed with that, unfortunately. The fact that everybody was forced to stop killing each other in wars did not mean they stopped killing each other altogether, and when I was fourteen, my father was poisoned by a man he thought he had an understanding with."

He laughed bitterly. "Is that not almost ridiculous? He survived over forty years on a nearly constant battlefield, just to be killed by a few drops of liquid mixed into his wine."

I lowered my head. "I'm sorry. Despite all the bloodshed, your father sounds like a kind person."

I cursed myself, despite the bloodshed? What kind of stupid thing was that to say?

Raven smiled. "Thank you, coming from someone who understands, that means a lot."

"So, your mother also…" It wasn't exactly changing the subject, but it felt safer to talk about.

His face instantly became cold, and part of me cringed, waiting for the entire magic around him to turn cold as well, but it didn't.

"My mother remarried a man who…" he snorted, "well, let us say I do not like him very much, and I do not keep in contact with her." His coldness disappeared. "Or she with me. As she was married into the Ravenous clan, she did not become the new head after my father died. I did, which meant I also got all the power and riches my parents had gathered. And to her utter disappointment, I used it to settle in this land and build this school, trying to turn the meaning of Ravenous into a hunger for knowledge and kindness, not for blood."

He looked at me as we came to a stop in front of my door. "What did you think when you first set foot in this land? Am I coming at least a little closer to my goal?"

I looked him straight into the eyes without getting lost this time. "Honestly, the first time I set foot in this place, I was too distracted by all the magic that surrounded me from every corner all of a sudden, but I can say this. You don't smell anything like those monsters in the forest today. Their magic smelled like blood, and…" I didn't finish because I didn't want to spend any more time thinking about them. Instead, I gathered every ounce of courage I had and took his hand. "Your magic smells like wildflowers and new books. I like it a lot."

He looked down at our hands and then stared up at me with a baffled expression while his entire face turned red. He seemed to notice it and quickly turned it away from me. "I…" He coughed softly and showed me his face again, which was already back to its old self. "Thank you."

I let go of his hand and opened the door to my room. "Goodnight, Raven."

I tried to close the door behind me, but he put his hand against it to stop me, and I turned around, simultaneously worried and hopeful about what would happen next.

He took his hand off the door. "I-I apologize. I just… I want you to know that I will find those Boreans and punish them for what they did today." He frowned. "And as for *that man*," he clearly tried as hard as he could to put as much disdain in those two words as possible, "nobody can enter these lands without my knowledge, and if he even tries to take a single step across the border, I promise that I will make him regret it. So, you can feel safe and sleep calmly tonight."

Without saying anything else, he turned around and walked away. I closed the door behind me and sighed deeply, leaning against it.

"Urgh, tell me about it. I'm regretting it already."

My heart jumped and I instantly looked at the window, knowing he would be on the exact same spot he was before. And I was right. He was sitting on the windowpane, one leg dangling lightly over the edge in my room, the other pulled up, so he could lean his arm on his knee.

He put his forefinger against his chin. "Although I'm not sure what I regret more. Having to, very easily, by the way, sneak into this place again, or having to listen to that nauseating conversation."

"Nobody asked you to listen to it, and if you don't like it, then get out," I snapped.

He raised an amused eyebrow. "Is that any way to talk to the person who saved your life today?"

I walked towards my bathroom and left the door open slightly so I'd still be able to hear him while I changed clothes, not that I expected him to still be there when I'd come out.

"You really shouldn't open your door for guys like this all the time, you know? Not all men are as gallant as me or as pathetic as Raven." He opened the door widely and shamelessly walked in at the very moment I put on my nightgown. I quickly let go of it so it would fall down my body, covering my bare stomach, which had been right in the open for him to see.

"Why are you here again?"

He leaned against the doorpost, and even though I couldn't see the rest of his face because of the mask he was still wearing around me, his mocking smile had disappeared.

"Are you okay?"

Hearing him say anything sincere made me have to swallow for no reason whatsoever and very much against my own will.

"What are you talking about?" I avoided looking him in the face and walked past him back to my bedroom. My arm very slightly touched his, and I felt myself getting goosebumps.

"What am I talking about?" He repeated, already in his usual mocking tone again. "Well, for starters, you were attacked by a gang of murderous monsters." He gave me a mean grin. "Also, you had to spend the rest of the day with that stick in the mud, so…"

Almost, he almost had me fooled. "Well, I'm fine. You saved me from those murderous monsters, as you came here to remind me so gallantly, and I actually like spending time with that stick in the mud, so…"

He laughed. "Well, if you're not too shaken up to be mad at me for some reason, I guess you're fine."

He walked past me to the window and graciously jumped onto the windowpane again. "If that's the case, I bid you goodnight, my lady." He stuck out his arm to the right side while making a circling motion with his hand and then took a deep bow. After that, he turned around and had already stuck one leg in the air when he froze and turned back to me.

I waited, preparing myself for what was about to come.

"About what I said earlier, about me sneaking into this place, I am the only person in this entire land who's capable of doing that, so you really can go to sleep tonight safely."

After those surprising but incredibly reassuring words, he turned around to jump out of the window, but I grabbed his arm.

He lifted up his head and looked at me through the dark gauze in front of his eyes. "Aren't you being aggressive all of a sudden? What is it? Do you want me to stay here tonight?"

I let go of his arm and took a step back, covering myself with my arms. "Why won't you even tell me your name?"

He pressed his lips together for a moment but then turned back to me completely. "I thought it would be best if Raven didn't know you were connected to me somehow."

"But he knows now." I pulled up my shoulders.

He jumped off the windowpane and walked over to me, stopping far too close to me. "What will I get in return for telling you?"

I turned my head away from him. Had he said that in any other way, it would have made me angry, but he was too close. I could almost feel his body against mine. My mind went completely blank. "F-fine. Then don't tell me."

I tried to sound as convincing as possible, but I could die from embarrassment hearing the weak tone of my voice.

He snickered softly and walked back to the window. "It's Dayn."

I snapped my head up, but he had already jumped out of the window. I ran towards it and looked over the edge. We were on the third floor, and a fall from here would hurt even me, or worse, but I didn't see him lying on the ground. I didn't even see him running away. He'd disappeared into thin air as usual.

I sighed, closed the window, and crawled into bed. What was it with these guys? What gave them the right to meddle in my life, put my stomach into knots, set my body afire, and then leave me alone like this?

10

I was nervous. I kept staring at Raven from the corner of my eye but didn't have the courage to start a conversation in the middle of breakfast, especially with everyone there. After Dayn had assured me we were safe within Raven's borders, and since hearing Raven's story, I actually believed that he was only helping us because he kind of got off on helping people. So, I'd decided to take both his and Aeric's advice and stay for a while, to think about what I wanted to do from here on out. What was the safest thing to do for my family. And in order to do that, I had to find a place for myself within this community. Maybe I could get some sort of job and buy or build a house for Mom and the kids to live in when the time came that I had to go. At least until I would come back for them.

Fionn and Mori didn't have any magic, but most subjects in Raven's school didn't even seem to have anything to do with magic, so maybe they could enroll permanently and start following all of the classes. They would be safe, they would learn a lot, and when they were a little older, they would be able to decide for themselves what they wanted to do.

I looked at Raven from the corner of my eye again. Would he somehow be able to help me board one of those ships, so I could leave with Mom and the kids if that was what they wanted to do? I shook my head. No use to think about it now. First, I somehow had to ask him if there was a job in this place that I could do.

"Raven."

I turned my head; Mori had pulled up her shoulders and stared Raven straight in the eye with the most intense look I'd ever seen her wear. She looked as if she was going to war, not asking Raven a question, but somehow, I understood how she felt. I leaned in a bit. This was the first time Mori had spoken to Raven directly, and I couldn't wait to hear what she wanted to ask him.

"Is it alright if Sarena comes to visit today after school?" She cringed. "We'll stay in my room and won't bother anyone." She added that last part as quickly as she could as if she needed to say something like that to convince Raven to agree.

It bothered me a little. Was she scared of him? Or was she intimidated by speaking to him directly, like I was most of the time? And how come she asked Raven if she was allowed to hang out with some special I didn't even know?

I think Raven noticed how annoyed I was by that before I was even aware of it myself. He smiled uncomfortably. "Of course, it is alright with me, as long as your mother agrees."

Mom forced herself to nod, although I saw the same hesitation in her eyes that I felt. "Of course, you can sweetie, it'll be fun having Sarena over."

So, my mother knew this special too? Even worse, she knew Mori had gotten close to her? Why didn't I know any of this?

156

I swallowed my last piece of bread and resolutely got up, making everybody turn their heads to me in surprise.

"Give me a second to grab a bag. I'm coming to school with you guys." I didn't wait for them to answer me but turned around and ran upstairs, where I quickly filled a leather bag with some papers and a pen I had laying around the room.

It was the second time I'd set foot in that school, but it was still as overwhelming, maybe even more. I stopped myself from gagging and tried not to breathe too deeply, so I wouldn't get any more nauseated from the thousands of heavy scents that surrounded me.

Mom put her hand on my shoulder, and I looked up at her. She pinched me comfortingly and pointed to a door behind her. "Aeric and I have to go to that classroom. Will you be okay going with Mori?"

There was no hiding what I thought from her. I forced myself not to look like I was about to get sick and nodded confidently. "Of course it's okay, Mom. I'm fine. You have a good class."

Fionn, Mori and I waved at her and Aeric and then walked into the opposite reaction. We were late thanks to me, so only a few other students were still in the hallways.

Fionn suddenly turned to the right and stopped in front of a light green door, where he looked at us over his shoulder. "I'll see you later."

Mori waved at him. "Have fun, Fionn."

He walked into the classroom and closed the door behind him. I watched it happen with a despondent look on my face. I knew they were here every day doing this. I'd known that the whole time, but somehow seeing each one of them go off on their own as if it was nothing scared me. Was this how much they had gotten used to their new lives here already?

I turned to look at Mori, who was walking to the end of the hallway. She'd told Fionn to have fun so sincerely, like a sweet older sister. Could it be that she only acted like such a teenager in front of Mom and me? Although I felt a little hurt by that thought, I was happy that she was at least supportive of Fionn, especially since I'd been so distracted ever since we got here.

At the end of the hallway, she opened a dark green door on our right. I suppressed a sigh of relief. We'd been walking in the direction of the classroom where all four of us had been answering questions from a bunch of students only three weeks earlier, and I hadn't been looking forward to going back into that class again.

I followed Mori as she took a seat close to the front, in the right sight of the room, without even looking around first. I guess she already had her own seat here, and there was no open seat next to it for me. I think that until she looked up at me in surprise, she hadn't realized how lost I felt in this place or how hurt I was that she'd just sat down and left me standing. She looked around the room until she found an empty seat almost all the way to the back, on the left side of the room. She pointed to it with an apologetic smile.

"There's a seat over there. Most people sit in the same seat every time, but you can sit wherever you want, and you'll be able to overlook almost the whole classroom from over there." She'd tried to use her kindest voice. I obediently walked up the stairs, wriggled myself behind all the chairs to reach the empty spot Mori had pointed towards and awkwardly sat down on it.

As soon as I sat, I looked down to watch what Mori was doing. Since she'd walked to that seat so quickly, I'd assumed she sat down next to her friend, but she didn't pay any attention to either of the specials next to her, which probably meant that neither of them was Sarena.

"Wow, I've never met an untouched before. This is crazy!"

A high-pitched voice came from my right side, far too close near my ear. I turned around to see the source of it and instantly felt my blood turn into ice.

"But then again, I've never actually seen humans before either. That's only for the humanoid-looking specials of the advanced class. Not that I'm in the advanced class, though, so it wouldn't matter even if I did look humanoid. Although now that Fionn and Mori are here every day, I guess everyone gets to see humans. It doesn't seem all that weird anymore now. Will you be coming every day from now on too?"

I stared back into those big, round, slightly bulging, eyes and I wanted to throw up. Three small, short horns stuck out of the left side of his bald head, his ears were eerily small, his limbs were unnaturally long, his torso too short, his mouth too broad, his skin had that light blueish beige color that became a much darker blue around his horns and the upper side of his arms. Even as a child, he still looked like a monster.

His look of excitement slowly changed into one of insecurity. "Can you… not speak like Fionn and Mori? Or do you not understand me?"

I scowled. Seeing one of these monsters up close had paralyzed me for a second, but hearing it insult me brought me right back to reality.

"Of course I can speak, *borean*." I nearly spit the word, the word Raven had used to describe those monsters in the forest yesterday, in his face, but instead of him being scared or insulted, like I'd intended, he sighed with relief.

"Oh good, it would've been hard to communicate if you wouldn't have been able to talk. And I would love to communicate with you more. There's so much for us to learn from you. I've never met someone so interesting before." He smiled and stuck his hand out to me, a hand that was eerily similar to my own but with much longer fingers. "I'm Corean, by the way. Nice to meet you."

Was he insane? I stared at that hand in front of me. A hand that didn't need a weapon to be deadly. A hand I'd seen wrapped around the necks of people I grew up with. A hand that had set my village on fire. A hand that wounded Dad so badly he…

I was about to vomit up blood. I didn't want to think about any of that. I didn't want to see all those images appear before my eyes again.

I turned and looked at Mori, who was listening to the teacher in an almost relaxed manner. Had she calmly been sitting in the same room as this monster this whole time?

As if she felt my staring eyes, she looked at me over her shoulder, quickly smiled and turned back to her book. Part of me was grateful that she hadn't waited for me to smile back, because I didn't have it in me to even force a smile at that moment, although I suddenly realized why *she* could. She didn't know. She and Mom and Fionn had left the village before those monsters attacked, and they hadn't gone back with me. They hadn't seen those strange creatures killing people left and right. People that we'd known our entire

160

lives. They hadn't seen Dad laying on the ground, bleeding out.

I turned back to the young monster sitting next to me, awkwardly pulling his hand back. There was no way I could tell her, or Fionn, not when the only person they could point their hate at was a child that had never even seen humans before he met us.

"I see you're not into physical contact. That's okay, I'm a bit of a hugger myself, but I'll try to respect your wishes. As long as we all respect each other's wishes, no one has to feel uncomfortable after all, right? Although I read in a book once, the best way to make friends sometimes is to break through social barriers. Don't worry, I'm not the type to do that. But you can let me know when you feel comfortable enough to shake hands."

He showed me a surprisingly white grin. Was that how those other monsters had grinned too? Why couldn't I remember clearly? Somehow this kid's grin kept popping up in my head instead when I tried.

I desperately searched my mind for something to say, a way to get the hell out of there, but he suddenly leaned in closer to me, and I instinctively moved as far back as I possibly could.

He stopped moving, his already bulging eyes getting even bigger, but then he slowly leaned back and chuckled awkwardly. "Sorry about that. I guess you like your personal space as well. Don't worry, I won't come too close then. It's not like we need to sit close to each other to talk. That's all I want. I've been dying to meet you. After all, I have so many questions. For example, as an untouched, can you-"

"Corean!"

Both of us jumped and turned our heads to the front of the class, where the teacher, the tallest woman I'd ever seen, with dark red skin and bright orange hair that almost reached her knees, threw us a strict look. "Save it for recess."

Corean obediently nodded and lowered his head, focusing on the open book in front of him.

With his head still lowered, he turned to me, barely noticeable. "I can't wait for recess. Let's have lunch together!"

Corean shared his textbook with me, but aside from that, he left me alone for the rest of the morning. The second the bell rang, though, he seemed very set on keeping his promise to have lunch with me. Mori had left the classroom as one of the first people, and since I couldn't find her among the many students that flooded the hallway, I was forced to reluctantly follow Corean to the cafeteria. Although I tried my best to keep as much distance between us as possible. Something he seemed to respect like he'd said he would.

I followed him to a long bar where adults were scooping up food for the people in line and got a plate of food that, even though it looked less than appetizing, still smelled insanely good.

I left the line we'd been in, while he was still waiting for his food, and stood there with my plate in my hand, looking around the enormous room, filled with rows of long, rectangular tables with even more chairs, which in turn were all filled with students. I was literally looking at a sea of people. If I wanted to get rid of the borean, I had to do it now.

"Thera, over here! There was a free spot!"

I looked to my left. Corean had walked past me without my noticing and had sat down at the last table in the row, the one closest to the line of people waiting for food. He was

162

right. There really was a free spot, several of them, all around him. Some other students were sitting a few chairs away from him. They had sort of looked up at the sound of Corean yelling, but they didn't pay any attention to him. Somehow, he seemed very lonely sitting there, surrounded by empty chairs in this room chock full of people, but that didn't mean I should go sit with him, did it?

I looked around me. The longer he kept waving at me, the more people started looking at me, all of them clearly curious about what I was going to do. I hesitated, I didn't want to spend any second longer with that monster, but I was also worried about what kind of rumors I'd start if I'd just walk away from him now. I didn't want to ruin the fragile bonds Fionn and Mori were starting to build, so I and sat down on the other side of the table from him.

He sighed with relief. "Thank the gods, for a second there, I thought that maybe you didn't want to sit with me. Not that I'm trying to say you should. I would understand, of course. You're free to sit wherever you want. I was just really looking forward to finally being able to talk to you."

He leaned in closer to me, a piece of bread in his hands. "How come you decided to come to school today? You've never come by yourself before. Do you not like it here? Are you too old to follow the classes? Are you doing something else? Did you go to school in human territory? What did they teach you there?"

Even though I was listening to him and not talking, I still felt like I needed to catch my breath. Did he always speak like that?

I thought about his questions and decided to focus on the first one. Although I could hardly tell him I only came to see for myself if we were able to trust this Sarena, if she was worthy of being Mori's friend. "Since Mori and Fionn go a lot, I wanted to see what it was like."

It was strange talking to this creature so normally, but at least I didn't have to feel guilty about lying to him.

He nodded. "That makes sense. But then, shouldn't you be having lunch with them?"

I tried not to make a face. "I couldn't find them." At least that was the truth.

To my surprise, he politely chewed and swallowed the small bite he'd just taken before answering me again. "Well, Fionn usually goes outside for lunch, and Mori apparently doesn't like to eat in the cafeteria, so she usually eats somewhere else with Sarena, although I don't know where."

I stared at him. How did he know that? Was he following them?

The light blue color of his cheeks turned slightly green, and he chuckled awkwardly. "It's because they're the humans. Everyone always knows where they are and what they're doing. Everyone always talks about them. Not to me, but I hear it sometimes when I sit nearby. It was even worse at first, now that they've been here for a while and they keep coming more often, the talk is starting to die down."

I didn't react. I was trying too hard not to show how much that worried me.

"Wait, so you know Sarena as well?" I hadn't realized it right away, but this could be an opportunity.

He shrugged. "I tend to remember a lot of things; I can't really help it. Besides, there's not really that many students in the entire school, so it's easy to remember names."

"So, you don't actually know her. You just know who she is?" I tried to sound as nonchalant as possible.

"I guess I know her a little. She's really nice."

I waited, but that was all. I hid my frustration. "What makes you think that? Have you talked to her before?"

He suddenly lowered his eyes, pricking his fork in the mysterious, red-colored substance that was our food. "We haven't had any long conversations or something like that, but she stands up for me when the others bully me, even though she's actually really shy herself."

"The others bully you?" Even though you're a monster strong enough to break someone in two without even trying? I couldn't say it, but I'm sure my surprise told him what he needed to know.

He cringed, barely noticeable, but enough to tell me that this was actually pretty unpleasant for him to talk about.

"It's nothing too bad. It's just that boreans don't have a very good reputation, so the others don't want to hang out with me." He slowed down his usual high pace of talking. "And they think I'm annoying, so they tell me to get lost or say mean things to me when I talk too much."

Feelings of guilt rolled over me, but I stopped myself from giving in to them. Unlike those horrible kids, I actually had a good reason to not like boreans.

"Why?" If he was such a talker, I might be able to learn something about them from him.

"I don't know, I guess I can be kind of nosy," he chuckled disarming, "I like to learn new things and sometimes I can't control my excitement, and I ask too many questions."

I grinned. I couldn't stop myself; he answered me so innocently. "Not why do they think you're annoying, why do boreans not have a very good reputation?"

"Oh…" his cheeks turned green again as he blushed. "Well, you probably don't know this since you grew up with humans, but the boreans are kind of known as… bloodthirsty."

He averted his eyes from me, and his voice softened as if he were worried anyone else than me would hear. "In the past, there weren't a lot of rules or politics. Every argument or disagreement between clans was decided by wars and fighting. The ones who survived were the right ones. But there were many specials who didn't like to live that way, intelligent specials, who could think more than two steps ahead and debate when they didn't agree with something.

Those specials would often get more magic somehow, and little by little, they started to take over and implement rules." He slowly shook his head. "No, that isn't exactly right. Those specials didn't *get* more magic. I think it's more correct to say they could use the magic they got more completely, on a higher level."

He scoffed. "So, people started to think of them as higher beings, while the clans that didn't have those capabilities that kept up with their old ways were considered lower beings, obsolete beings."

He suddenly looked up. "The boreans are considered as such, even to this day, even though there are many of us who don't live like that anymore, who can use magic just as plentiful as other specials."

He looked down at the bread in his hand. "Although there are still many boreans left who live like they did back then. Small groups work as mercenaries and do whatever they're told, without caring about what it is, without thinking for themselves."

He slammed his hand, with the piece of bread still in it, down on the table and looked me straight in the eye. "But I'm not like them!"

I flinched back and stared at that intense look in his eyes. "Yeah… I can see that."

I really did. This kid, he looked exactly like those monsters, but somehow, I truly believed he was different.

I leaned closer to him until I was completely hanging over the table and breathed in his scent. "You smell like a library."

He leaned back, uncomfortably staring at me with wide eyes. "I'm… sorry? I showered this morning." He lifted his arm and smelled the back of his hand. "I used rose-scented soap. Just like everyone else here. Did it fade too much already? Do I smell musty? But I haven't even been in the library yet today."

I laughed and sat back. "No, sorry, that's not what I meant. You know how everyone's magic has a certain kind of scent? Yours smells like a library. Which is a good thing." Because if you were like those other monsters, you would smell like dried-up blood, I thought to myself.

He leaned closer to me, giving me a fascinated look. "Everyone's magic has a scent to you? I've never heard of that before..."

He finally put the crushed piece of bread in his hand back on his plate and folded his arms as he stared at me in thought. "I guess even as an untouched, you have a certain sensibility to magic. That makes sense. Maybe all specials have. If we didn't, how would we be able to receive and control magic after all? I wonder if it would express itself in every untouched in the same way? If you're able to smell magic, would another untouched be able to see it, for example? What would that look like? Are children too young to notice something like that before they get their magic?"

He rambled on, but I didn't really hear the rest of it. How was it possible he'd never heard of something like that? I folded my arms as well. I had told Raven what he smelled like, but I hadn't specified it was the scent of his magic rather than his own. I knew for sure I'd mentioned it to Dayn, and he didn't seem to think it was weird, but he never reacted the way I thought he would. Like a normal person. Plus, he seemed to know a lot more about a lot of things than he would tell me.

I glanced at Corean, who was wiping up the crumbs of bread that he had spilled all over the table. This kid was the first person here who spoke openly and honestly to me. Let's see what else he would tell me before Raven or anyone else could stop him.

"Corean, where did you get your magic?"

He looked up, the crumbs still in his hands. "From the Magic's Source, where else?"

He leaned closer to me. "Did you know there's a legend about a human who received magic from the Source? The legend is kind of vague, and everybody always laughs it off when you start about it, but wouldn't that be incredible?"

I tried not to look too surprised. He'd answered me so quickly, clearly unable to believe I even had to ask it, like it was the most normal thing in the world.

"Yeah, that would be pretty incredible. So… about the Source, where is it?"

I held my breath.

"What do you mean where is it? Nobody knows."

I unfolded my arms and put my hands on the table, trying not to slam them in frustration. "Nobody knows? Then how did you get your magic from it?"

He looked at me strangely, almost as if he were pitying me. "You really don't know a lot about magic, do you?"

For some reason, it felt as if he was asking me if I wasn't very intelligent, and it annoyed me, but I swallowed my defensive reaction. "I guess that's what happens when you're not raised here. Or have ever been here before."

He gasped. "I forgot about that! I'm sorry."

He emptied his hand full of crumbs on his plate and put it back on his tray. "I don't know where the Source is because only the Keepers know. You're taken there without being allowed to see the way, and it's protected by magic, so it can't be found by anyone who doesn't already know the way. But if there are other things you want to learn about magic or anything else, you can go to the library. It has thousands of books about magic, and it stays open even after the school closes. I go there all the time."

I excitedly jumped up, surprising Corean, who moved back so fast that he almost fell off his chair. "Let's go now."

He hesitated and quickly glanced around in every direction. "We can't go now; classes are starting again in a few minutes."

I shrugged. "Who cares?"

He breathed in shallowly as he stared at me, but then he slowly got up as well, moving close enough to me so I would be able to hear him whisper. "Are you saying we should skip class?"

He had a worried look on his face, but somewhere in those big eyes, I could also see an exhilarated twinkle.

I hid my grin behind my hand. As someone teased by her classmates a lot as a kid, I was no stranger to skipping classes, so I was surprised to find out Corean had never done it before.

"That's exactly what I'm talking about. You don't have to if you don't want to, though. I'm pretty sure I'll be able to find the library by myself." I felt cruel, manipulating him so obviously, but Corean was clearly a smart kid; it's not like it would have hurt him to skip one or two classes. Especially not if it were to hang out in a library.

He nodded his head quickly, but only very slightly, and I patted his shoulder despite myself. "Great, let's go."

I picked up my own tray, put it back on the kitchen counter and left the cafeteria, followed closely by Corean, who seemed to be copying my every move while looking over his shoulder every few seconds.

I glanced at him. "You're just walking through the hallway. Nobody's going to find that suspicious unless you act suspicious."

He looked at me in shock, as if he couldn't believe I'd called his behavior suspicious.

I turned back to hide my grin from him again. "Also, at some point, you're going to have to walk in front, because I don't know where to go."

He didn't say anything, clearly too nervous to talk, but obediently started walking in front of me.

He took me through half of the hallway, then up a staircase, and then back through half a hallway again, only a floor higher, meaning the library was exactly above the cafeteria. Not only did it feel very illogical to only have one stairway go up, halfway down the hall at that, but it also didn't make a lot of sense to me to place a library, the most silent room in a building, above a cafeteria, the loudest room in a building, at least until we walked into the library and Corean closed the door behind us.

For a moment, I thought I'd gone deaf. A silence fell over us and surrounded us, mixed in with a pleasantly fresh temperature and the smell of wood and old books.

The library was almost as big as the cafeteria. There was enough room to fit about three hundred people, but it was almost completely filled with bookcases. All filled to the nook with books. Even the open second floor that stretched from the wall to about three or four meters to the middle of the room, secured with a dark wooden railing, was covered in bookcases. Plenty of tables with chairs and stools were placed close to that railing so people could read without being bothered.

The first floor also had several large wooden tables placed in the middle of the room and a few more on the other side of the room from where we were standing, near the left corner, underneath one of three enormous windows. But even between those windows, the walls were covered with bookcases, although these were a little narrower, so they would fit right in between.

I gave Corean an exhilarated look as I walked through the room, passing several big, heavy bookcases. They were standing in a long row between the tables in the middle of the room and the walls. "This is amazing."

He followed me around with a pleased expression on his face. "I know. Not a lot of people come here because technically you can pass all your classes with the books you get at the start of the year, but some people like to come here and read up on more than just what they teach in class."

He looked around, suddenly nervous again, but there was obviously nobody here but the two of us. Even if more kids had decided to cut class, they wouldn't come to the library.

I took a green book out of one of the bookcases I passed and looked at the cover. It had a silver drawing of some sort of big cat on it. I put it back, cringing at every sound I made while doing so.

"It almost feels wrong to talk in here," I whispered as softly as I could.

He laughed out loud. "That's because the room is spelled to not let any sound in, so when there's not a lot of people, it becomes really quiet, but it's okay to talk normally."

Spelled? I wondered. Not infused, like most of the stuff in Raven's house?

"How did he do that?" For some reason, I felt it was still safe to assume that it had been Raven's doing.

Corean shrugged. "I'm not really sure. Because he's so much stronger than all of us, he can do a lot more with his magic than any of us. Sometimes he can even use a completely different kind of magic if that's what it takes to make someone's dream come true." He folded his arms, something he seemed to do when he was deep in thought. "It's entirely possible that someone dreamed of a quiet room to read in and that mister Raven was somehow able to silence this room because of that, even if he normally wouldn't be able to use that kind of magic."

"Hm…" I turned back to the bookcase, taking as many interesting-looking books out I could carry, and sat down at one of the big tables underneath a window. What kind of ridiculously convenient magic was that? Did that even exist? Raven had told me that he used his family's wealth and power to make people's dreams come true but looking back, I couldn't deny that that sounded like a vague concept. Besides, he didn't say he used magic to make dreams come true, but he also didn't say he did not use magic, so part of me had to wonder if what Corean had said could be true.

He sat down opposite of me, with his own pile of books. He took the first one, opened it, and quickly flipped through it. Only a few seconds later, he closed the book, closed his eyes for a moment, opened them, put the book away and took the second book off the pile, starting the process all over again.

"So… what's your magic?" Although after that, I was pretty sure I knew the answer to that question.

He looked up and blushed as if he'd been caught doing something embarrassing.

"I uhm… take in knowledge." He uncomfortably flipped the cover of the book he was holding open and closed. "I know that doesn't really sound very magical, I mean, everybody can take in knowledge, but it's more than that. Most of the time, I only have to touch something to learn about it. The longer I touch something, the more I get to know about it."

He put his hand on the table we were sitting at. "Take this table. I know when it was built, who built it, what they were saying and doing while they were building it, how many trees were cut down to build it, how old those trees were, who planted them."

He stopped and held up the book he'd been nervously playing with. "With books, it's like double information. When I touch them, I learn about the book itself. When I flip through them and see the words, I learn the content of the book." He showed me a surprisingly warm look. "It's why I love them."

He put the book down again and stroked the cover lovingly, then he suddenly seemed to remember he was talking to me and looked up with bright green cheeks. "That's probably the lamest magic you've ever heard of, isn't it?"

I resolutely shook my head. "It's not lame. Knowledge is power. You know, it helps you understand things. Why did you think I wanted to come here?"

His face instantly lit up. "Really?"

"Really. Raven told me that most specials ask for magic when they're about eight years old, so you must've been a smart kid to realize something so important so early on in your life."

His bright look turned dark, and he averted his eyes. "I wasn't. More like the opposite."

I uncomfortably moved in my chair. "Are you saying you were, like… slow?"

He nodded regretfully. "Boreans aren't exactly known for their bright intellect, and even for their standards, I wasn't a very bright child. It was so bad that the other kids would tease me for it, even at that age, and I hated it. I wanted nothing more than to be smart, to prove to all of them that I could do it, but no matter how much I studied, it was really hard for me to retain a lot of information. And even if I remembered any, I still didn't understand it, so it wasn't of any use to me. That's why, when I was taken to the Magic's Source, I asked it for the magic that would make me smarter than anybody else, that would enable me to possess all the knowledge in the world."

He giggled softly. "In the end, magic doesn't exactly work like that. At first, I wasn't even sure if anything had happened at all, and I cried for days, thinking that even the Magic's Source thought I was too stupid to have magic."

He turned to face me again, a clear look in his eyes. "But then, one night, I couldn't fall asleep anymore because I kept thinking about the goose that had been killed to fill my pillow with feathers, and I realized I'd learned that just by laying on it. The Source hadn't given me all the knowledge in the world. It had given me the capability to learn and retain and understand it all. It's up to me now to gather as much as I can."

He smiled at the book in front of him. "I wanted to be smart to prove to everybody that I was just as good as they were, but at some point, I really came to love learning, even when people make fun of me for being boring, or asking too many questions, or only thinking about books and stuff." He looked up at me. "That's how I eventually ended up here."

Suddenly, his eyes filled with excitement. "That must be why my magic smells like a library to you!"

I laughed. "I think so too, yeah."

He opened the book in front of him and looked up at me again. "Alright! Let me know everything you want to learn, and I will help you!"

11

"Aaaah…" I let out a deep sigh and lifted up the book I was reading just to slam it down on the desk, startling Corean, who'd been immersed in his own book. I leaned back in my chair and let my arms dangle next to my body.

"Did that book say something you didn't like?" Corean gave me a strict look. "It's not the book's fault, you know? If you want to slam anything into the table…" He stopped and folded his arms, tilting his head slightly, as if he had to think about how to finish that sentence.

"I should slam the writer into the desk?" I did it for him, and he stared at me in shock.

I laughed. "Why are you looking at me like that? You're the one who started that thought."

He fidgeted with the edge of the page he'd been about to turn. "I know, but that's why I stopped it in time."

I rolled my eyes and leaned over my book again, glancing at Corean. How was it fair that this sweet kid had to be stamped with the name 'Borean'? Or with their appearance?

We'd spent a big part of almost every day of the week in the library for more than a month already, reading so many books and scrolls that the lines sometimes seemed to float off the page and followed me home to haunt me in my dreams.

The library door creaked open, and we both turned to see who it was. I leaned so far to my right I almost fell off my chair. This was the first time that anyone else had joined us here in the middle of the day, right before lunch break.

"Ther?" Fionn stood in the door opening, staring just as surprised at us as we were staring at him.

"Fionn?" I got up. "What are you doing here?"

He held up his hand to stop me from walking over to him and approached us instead. He sighed and let himself fall in the chair next to mine. "I… I didn't sleep well last night, so I was looking for a quiet place during the break."

I stared at him, trying not to look too judgmental. I knew for a fact Fionn had slept well because I'd taken up the habit to check both his and Mori's bedroom before I went to sleep myself. But Fionn didn't often lie to me, and I couldn't imagine he wouldn't have a good reason for doing it. Not that that didn't just make me more curious.

"Well," I slit my book over to him, "I can borrow you this one to use as a pillow if you want. Corean and I are just reading, so we won't make much noise if you want to sleep for a bit."

He rolled his eyes at me with a slight grin but still took the book and rested his head on it. His face in my direction.

I lifted my hand and softly patted his hair; glad he didn't push it away.

Suddenly, he lifted his head slightly and sniffed the book. "That's weird; this book smells like flowers."

I nodded; I'd noticed that as well. "Some of the books here do. I'm not really sure how, but I think it has something to do with Raven's magic making this place soundproof."

He put his arm on the book and lay his head back on it again. "So, you're saying Raven's magic smells like flowers? That's strange."

I took another book from the stack next to me and opened it. "Is it? Maybe it just means he really likes flowers?"

He didn't respond for a while, but then he suddenly switched arms and lay back down with his face turned away from me. "Like Dad?"

My hand froze on the page of my book. "…Y-yeah."

I waited, but I think Fionn was weighing his words just as carefully as I was.

"Dad always smelled like flowers too. Is that why you trusted Raven so quickly, even though you told me we shouldn't? Because he made you think of Dad?"

I stared at the back of his head, at his soft, dark hair, at his tensed-up shoulders, at the way he was clutching the book so hard his knuckles had turned white. "I'm not sure. That might've been part of it."

I could feel my heart beating in my throat. I didn't want to cry in front of him, I wanted him to think I was strong, but every thought of Dad made my eyes burn.

None of us spoke about Dad much at all. Mom was trying to be strong, just like me, even though I knew how much she was hurting inside. I think Mori tried just as much as me not to think about it, scared that she'd start crying whenever she did. Neither of them had dealt with it by distancing themselves from me, though, unlike Fionn.

Slowly, sometimes barely even noticeably, he'd been moving away from me. He didn't talk to me the way he used to do. He didn't laugh as much as before. He didn't crack a lot of jokes or tease me, and the moment I tried to have any kind of serious conversation with him, he would casually change the subject and then leave quickly afterward.

But now he'd come to me first, now he had brought it up. Did that mean he was ready to talk about it? Did that mean he wanted to talk about it? That he'd wanted to talk about it all this time?

I clenched my fist, accidentally crinkling the page in my hand. I didn't know what to say. "What about you?"

He shrugged. "I don't know. I guess I like Raven. He's nice to me."

I shook my head, even though he couldn't see it. "I mean, do you like flowers as well, like Dad?"

He didn't answer, and I chuckled to fill that silence. "Do you remember how we used to tease him about it? Because it looked so funny for such a big, strong guy to like cute, little flowers."

He still didn't respond, and I put the page down, gently flattening it with my hand to undo the creasing. "I like them. Flowers. And I liked that Dad liked them too. I liked how happy he looked when he was working in the garden."

I suppressed a sudden sob and gave myself a second to calm down. "I liked how easy it was to see what a kindhearted person he really was that way."

He suddenly slammed his hands on the table next to the book and got up so fast that his chair fell backward.

The loud clanging filled the entire library, and I stared with big eyes as Fionn walked away without saying anything.

I jumped up as well but couldn't bring myself to follow him for some reason as he slammed the door behind him.

That was the first time Fionn had ever done something like that. I didn't know how to react. Even though I was supposed to be his big sister, even though I loved him so much, I didn't know what to do.

I walked over to his chair to pick it up. What had set him off like that?

I stopped with the chair still in my hands. Was that it? Was he too angry to want to hear anything positive? I shook my head and put the chair down. Or was it the fact that I'd been too airy about it? That I even laughed? Did he think I wasn't serious enough? That I wasn't hurting enough?

I lowered my head and let myself fall back on my own chair, staring at the book in front of me without being able to read a single word.

"I-I didn't know you lost your father. I'm sorry." Corean awkwardly tried to gain my attention. "H-how did it happen?"

I didn't look at him. It was hard enough for me to talk to Fionn about it; I didn't really want to start talking to Corean about this. "Our village was attacked. He died fighting."

It was a curt answer, and I saw Corean cringe hearing it. I knew that wasn't very fair of me. I knew by now that he wasn't good at this kind of stuff. He talked a lot, *a lot*, but mostly about shallow stuff and things he'd learned or wanted to learn.

"I'm sorry." He lowered his eyes and rubbed his finger against the edge of the cover of the book he was reading. "I-it must be hard to be a big sister."

He lifted his head slightly but kept his eyes on his book, clearly determined to have this conversation with me. "Sometimes, it almost seems like you're more like their mother than their sister."

180

He finally looked up. "I-I think they're really happy to have you, even if it's hard for them to show that at times."

I covered my eyes with my hand to hide the tears that I could barely fight back anymore. "Thanks, Corean."

I blinked a few times and took a deep breath before I dared to show my face to him again.

"What about you? What's your family like?" I had to change the subject before he would make me cry for real.

He shrugged. "It's just my parents and me." He chuckled. "My family isn't really complicated. My parents weren't really happy with me wanting to go here, but in the end, they supported me."

He suddenly closed the book in front of him, and his eyes started to twinkle. "They couldn't afford to pay for it, though. So, for a while, I thought that was the end of it, but then my mother packed my bags one day and told me that I just had to go and find a way to make it happen if I really wanted this. That if I was smart enough to be able to go here, I should have no trouble finding a way to actually go here."

He chuckled as he put the book on his 'read' pile. "So, I traveled here, knocked on Raven's door out of the blue and begged him to let me join his school, saying I'd do anything in order to pay for it."

He took the next book and stroked his fingers over the leatherbound cover. "I think Raven was so fascinated with someone like me wanting to go to a school like this so badly that he agreed right away."

I smiled as I leaned on my hand. "Making dreams come true is what he does after all."

Corean nodded and opened the book. "It didn't feel really right to me to accept it for free, though, so I often do odd jobs around here whenever it's needed, and I help work the fields on the weekends."

I grinned and he lifted an eyebrow. "What?"

I shook my head and flipped a page, even though I hadn't read a single word. "No, it's just… I think you're a good kid, Corean."

He breathed in, staring at me with a mixture of surprise and happiness.

I forced myself to keep smiling, even though it made me a little sad. I guess not many people had ever said that to him.

"Thera…"

I looked up at him. He was fidgeting with the page again.

"About Fionn…" His eyes narrowed.

I felt my shoulders tense up for some reason. "What about Fionn?"

He hesitated, his eyes glancing back and forth. Eventually, he seemed to give up. "It's nothing."

I leaned closer towards him. "It's okay if you want to say something."

He quickly shook his head. "No, it's nothing. I shouldn't have mentioned it." He lifted up his book and put it upright on the desk, hiding half of his face behind it.

"Do you think I should've followed him?" I blurted out the words that I'd wanted to ask him this whole time.

He lifted his head from behind the book a little. "I-it didn't look like he wanted you to."

I sighed and leaned back. I agreed. "What about Mori?"

He gave me a confused look. "Well, I didn't hear your conversation with her, so I'm not really sure…"

I grinned and shook my head. "No, I mean, do you think I should go talk to her as well? Fionn ran away like that, but

182

he did start to talk about Dad first. Do you think Mori is waiting for me to talk to her about it too?"

He lowered his eyes, hiding his face behind the book again. "I don't know. I talk to Fionn sometimes, but…" He hesitated. "Mori doesn't like to talk to me, so I'm not sure."

He looked up. "Not that I know either of them very well; it's only been a month, after all."

I flipped another page without reading a word. A month didn't sound like much, but it had felt like an eternity to me. So much had changed, so much was happening, there was so much to get used to, I still had so many questions. And all the while, I was constantly scared. I was scared that I'd lose my family if I tried too hard to find the answers to my questions. Scared that any moment the boreans that had attacked our village would attack here too. Scared of what else was out there. Raven seemed to be able to hold the boreans off so far, but would he be able to do the same thing for the person who'd sent them? How long before that person would come for me themselves? Should I get away from here before they did? Leaving my family behind here where they were supposed to be safe?

I shook my head, pushing those thoughts down deep. "Why doesn't Mori like to talk to you? That doesn't sound like her."

Mori was direct, to the point that she sometimes seemed mean, but she wasn't someone to exclude others or treat them badly for no reason.

He rubbed the edge of the cover with his finger again. "I-I don't know. It's not like she really has a reason to talk to me. She doesn't know me very well. I don't think she knows you and I became friends. And there are so many other people here. And I'm not a girl, and…" he quickly glanced at me over the edge of his book before lowering his eyes again, "and despite her scaly skin, Sarena still looks a lot more human than I do."

I looked at him, at the pale blue color of his skin, the horns on his head, the out of proportion length of his limbs, his bulging eyes. He was right. I'd gotten used to it at this point, mostly. But at first, I would've much rather spent time with Sarena than with him.

"Well, I guess I can't argue much about appearances, but on the inside at least, you look more than human enough to m-" I bit my tongue. "Sorry… I'm not really sure if that sounds bad or good to you."

His light blue cheeks turned slightly green again as he hid even further behind his book. "Well, the main image I have of what a human is, is you, so if that's what you meant, then it sounds pretty good to me."

I quietly stared at his bald head peeking out above his book. If anyone had told me just a few weeks ago that I'd one day feel the urge to hug a borean, I probably would've hit them. But here I was.

My head was still spinning from the amount of reading I'd done that day when I left the library and went back home. For now, I'd focused on finding more information on the Magic's Source, since no one seemed to want or be able to tell me much about it. But apparently, specials didn't like to write about it either.

I walked up the stairs towards my room. Normally, we stayed in the library until after school, but today had felt extra draining, and I'd given up not that long after lunch break ended.

184

I stopped as I passed Mori's room and moved closer to her door. She was talking to someone. I didn't recognize the voice, but it sounded like a young girl too. Probably Sarena. Those two had become almost eerily close very fast.

I leaned against the wall next to the door and tilted my head so I could hear them.

"So, you had to fill your bath bucket by bucket? Humans really are behind, aren't they?"

I frowned, already annoyed, but I had nothing to worry about, not with Mori. "That's rich coming from someone who comes from the Realm of Progress. Not to mention that you can all use magic. I mean, if it weren't for Aeric, this realm wouldn't have showers and fountains either."

I lifted my fist slightly. That was my girl.

The room turned silent, and I leaned closer to the door.

"Are you still worried your sister is trying to get magic as well? I hear she's been spending a lot of time in the library with Corean."

That surprised me. Even though they'd gotten close, I'd always imagined their conversations to be more like the one before, nothing serious like this.

"It doesn't matter what she's doing with… with that guy. Thera said she wouldn't do it if I asked her not to." Mori sounded resolute.

"And you believe her?"

I clenched my fists. It didn't sound like she was egging her on. It sounded like an honest question, but it still made me so angry I could barely stop myself from storming into the room to set her straight.

I didn't, though. I was ashamed to admit it, and I was ashamed that I stayed there eavesdropping on my own little sister, but I wanted to hear Mori's answer.

"…No."

It was like I felt the ground disappear beneath my feet. I closed my eyes and clenched my fists so tightly that my nails cut into my palm to stop myself from running in there. Instead, I decided to leave before breaking her trust any more than I already had.

"But…"

I stopped. I couldn't help myself. I was desperate to hear what would follow that 'but'.

"It's not like she would do it to hurt me or something like that. It's just that, if that's what she thinks she has to do to protect us, then she'll do it, even if it makes us hate her. She's always been like that." She chuckled softly. "It used to always really annoy me, but now I'm a little relie-"

I was distracted by a warm hand on my shoulder. I turned around in shock, staring into Raven's mesmerizing, green eyes.

"One sister is playing hooky, and the other one is eavesdropping on her. How do you suggest I react?"

He whispered the words softly, close to my ear, sending a wave of longing throughout my body that surprised me and probably turned my face beet red.

He grinned, seeing it, and gestured to me to follow him as he walked away from Mori's room.

"I'm sorry." I caught up to him. "She shouldn't be skipping classes after you let her join so kindly."

He shook his head. "And she especially should not bring other students with her when she does."

That irked me a little, even though I knew he was right.

"I'm not going to get mad at her for it, Raven." I figured it was best to be clear. "I can't get angry at her for not going to a school I personally didn't really want her to go to in the first place."

I sighed. "But I guess she did choose to make a commitment, so I won't stop you if you want to lecture her."

I stuck my head in the air. "And I especially won't stop you if you choose to lecture the student skipping classes who's actually, officially enrolled in your school."

Raven chuckled. "I suppose I understand your point. I did not mean to sound like I was blaming Mori. I am not. And I will not lecture her."

He stopped when we reached the door to my room and turned to me. "I know the situation is not ideal, so I understand that she prefers to be in her room where she feels safest." He gave me a warm smile. "But in time, that will change. For both of you."

I lowered my face. He was wrong, but I didn't have the courage to say it out loud.

He suddenly took my hand in his. I felt my face burn up but didn't pull my hand back. Instead, I softly squeezed his, drinking in his warmth, even though it wasn't nearly enough. I wanted more.

I'm not sure if he noticed or if he just felt the same way, but he slowly leaned in to kiss me. I lifted my head and closed my eyes as he pressed his lips against mine.

He kissed me gently, almost carefully, sending my stomach in complete disarray. I'd been kissed before, but I never knew it could be like this.

Suddenly, to my great disappointment, he stopped and stepped back from me. "I-I apologize, I…"

I melted as I watch him fidgety look for the right words to say.

"No, it's okay. You don't have to apologize. I..." I brought my hand to my lips to feel the place he kissed but realized what I was doing at the last moment and stopped myself, feeling my cheeks turn even redder. "I-I'm glad you did."

His face lit up. His nervousness quickly made a place for confidence. "Good, then I will do it again soon."

He grinned and walked away before I could answer.

12

Two more months slowly passed like that. By the end of those two months, I'd read enough books from the library to fit one whole bookcase, while Corean had nearly finished the rest of the books in the library altogether. I'd learned a lot in that time, too much to remember all of it, but in the end, I still hadn't found what I was looking for. I could tell you that the specials divided their territory up in realms, not in countries like we humans did. I knew all those different realms, and I knew who ruled them, what they believed in, and who their followers were. I learned about more different kinds of specials than I ever wanted to know. I knew the most common types of magic and how they worked. I knew all about the flora and fauna of the realm we were in at that moment, the Realm of Dreams, but none of that had helped me figure out what I wanted to do. What I should do.

The only useful thing I'd learned was what Dayn had already told me the second time we met, which was that there were only very few records of people asking for magic as late in life as me. And among the very few specials who had tried, even fewer had survived. Because their bodies hadn't developed and grown up with the magic, they couldn't take it and eventually broke down. In rare cases, their bodies managed to adapt, but their minds couldn't take it, so they would completely break mentally and end up as adult babies. Only less than one percent managed to completely adjust and come out of it unchanged, with magic.

I stopped walking, feeling a tingling in my back as if someone were watching me. I looked up and turned around, shocked to realize I'd walked into one of the villages close to Raven's home. Had I been too deep in thought? I'd decided to take a different route to the stables as a change of pace, but somehow, I must've taken the wrong path somewhere. I couldn't even see the stables from where I was.

I looked around in every direction. Which way did I have to go?

I turned back in the direction where I'd felt that gaze coming from. A woman around the same age as Mom stood in front of one of the houses, a young boy on her arm, and another clinging to her leg. All three of them had five completely black eyes scattered over their forehead, which was much bigger than mine to accommodate them. Their skin was a deep red and covered in scales. Not like Sarena, not snake scales, something bigger, rougher.

Something about the look in those eyes warned me to stay away from them, but she was the only person I saw in this village, and I needed someone to tell me where to go. Besides, wasn't this what Raven wanted? Me talking to the people in his realm, getting along with them?

I gathered my courage and walked up to her, but the moment I came closer, she pushed the boy that was clinging to her leg behind her while turning her entire body away from me to protect the boy she was holding.

I slowed down. "S-sorry, I didn't mean to scare you. I just…"

"Stay away!" She yelled the words without looking at me, but I could hear real fear in her voice.

I instantly stopped. Why? What reason could she even have to be scared of me? She didn't know anything about me. If anything, shouldn't I be the scared one?

"Okay." I spread out my arms a little to let her know I wasn't carrying anything I could hurt them with. Although I immediately realized that probably meant very little among specials with magic. "I won't come any closer. As a matter of fact, if you could just tell me which way the stables are, I'll leave right away."

She didn't answer, and I hesitated. "There really is no need to be scared of me." I could hear how small my voice sounded.

"We're not scared of you." A man that looked very similar to the three in front of me stepped out of the house. "We just don't want you here."

He walked forward, protectively placing himself between me and his wife and children. "Having an untouched and humans walking around here… it's wrong. Humans belong in the human realm, not here."

I stared at him, unable to find any words, any kind of useful comeback. Unwillingly, I took a step back, my heart beating in my throat. These people were supposed to be like me, they were supposed to be my kind, but how was this any different from how it had been at home?

I turned around and ran away. It didn't matter. They could think whatever they wanted. I never asked them to accept me. I just asked for directions. If they were too small-minded to at least give me those, then that was their fault, not mine.

I stopped suddenly and held my breath. Two of them, Boreans. They were leisurely walking there, talking in a language I didn't recognize, even though I'd heard them speak in my language back in our village.

They noticed me less than a second after I'd noticed them, and unlike me, who had completely frozen at their sight, they came running towards me.

I reset myself and turned around, running away from them as fast as I could, but two loud thuds stopped me. I looked over my shoulder to see both of them lying on the ground.

I hesitated. I had no idea what had happened, but they were quickly crawling up again, and if I waited too long, they'd catch up to me.

I looked ahead towards the village I'd just left. I'd automatically started running in that direction, but who knew what would happen if I lured these two monsters there. I couldn't put them in danger.

Running had been my first instinct. It's what we'd been doing this whole time. But there were just two of them. I slightly bent through my knees and lifted my arms, even though they were shaking. I was going to take them out before they could hurt anyone.

The one on the right had gotten to his feet and now reached his hand in my direction to have it stopped by nothing. He and I both raised our eyebrows, seeing it.

He made a fist and hit it against that invisible wall a few times, so hard that I was afraid it would go through at any second.

The other one had jumped up too and followed his friend's example. "This damn thing!" He kicked it and then suddenly looked up at me.

"You look like you're ready to face us. Come over here where we can reach you!"

I lowered my arms slightly. Even though I knew they could, even though I heard Corean do it all the time, it felt so strange to hear them speak just like me. Like normal people.

I took a step forward. "Why are you following me? What do you want from me? Who sent you?"

The Borean just growled and hit his fist against the barrier again, even harder than before. "If you want to talk, then come fight us!"

I narrowed my eyes. "Answer my questions first, and I'll come out there!"

That seemed to pique his interest. He stopped ramming against the barrier and stared at me with his bulging, yellow eyes for a moment. He opened his mouth to say something, but then suddenly stopped and blinked a few times. He looked around him, confused as if he were looking for something. The other one followed his example, asking his friend something in their own language.

I took a step forward. "Wh-"

I was stopped by a cold hand that covered my mouth from behind. I quickly looked over my shoulder to see Dayn standing behind me, his chest pressed against my back.

He put his finger against his lips to shush me and then let go. Without taking his eyes off the Boreans, he bent over to pick up a piece of rock and threw it somewhere in the distance.

They turned around to the sound of the rock falling and immediately ran towards it.

He let out a sigh of relief and walked towards the barrier.

"How did you do that?" I followed him, but he held up his hand to stop me, making sure I wouldn't step outside of it.

"It's called magic. You know, the thing you've been researching this whole time." He ignored his own warning and stepped out of the barrier.

I narrowed my eyes. "Those two couldn't get through it. Why can you?"

He shrugged. "It's because I'm so much better than them. Than anybody, really."

Then he disappeared. Just like that. He didn't even try to divert my attention or pretend to go behind something like he usually did.

I looked around for him just like those two Boreans had done a moment ago, but just like them, I didn't see him. Was he still here? Probably not. He'd been moving into the direction the Boreans had disappeared into. Was he going to follow them? Even though he clearly wasn't strong enough to take them on?

Was this how he'd been keeping my family and me safe here this whole time?

I shook my head. He might've kept us hidden like that, but the one who'd been keeping us safe was definitely Raven and his barrier.

I walked away from that barrier. It didn't do me much good to think about it too much.

I opened the door to the stables after finally finding it and stepped inside. My horse, or the one that Raven had lent to me indefinitely, started neighing. I patted it on the nose for a bit but didn't saddle it. Today, I'd just come to hang out with the kittens, who were almost full-grown cats by now.

I sat down on the bale of hay and made a tch tch tch sound to lure the kittens, who were probably playing around somewhere in the stable.

One of them, with fur as black as Raven's hair and that I'd therefore called Raven Two came running towards me, already purring. I picked it up from the ground and put it on my lap, where it immediately curled up against me and fell asleep.

I breathed out deeply and felt myself relax. The past few days had been stressful. After we were done going through the entire library, I felt like I'd hit a dead end, which worried me. After the first month here, Raven had given us our own house. It wasn't nearly as big as his own house, but still bigger than I would ever be able to pay for, even if I worked till the day I died. Nonetheless, I promised him I would find a job to at least pay him back a part of it. He refused, saying that it was a gift and that he was happy to have humans living on his grounds, getting along with his people. In the end, I accepted it, more so that Mom and the kids didn't always have to live in some else's house than because I wanted it. In exchange, I would often help out at the school and teach humanology classes with Mom. Although Raven still asked us to have dinner with him almost every day. He still found enough moments here and there to steal a kiss from me.

The kids both seemed to have adapted to life here. Sarena came over most of the time, and she and Mori would hang out in Mori's room. Fionn didn't seem to be that close to anyone in particular, but he would sometimes go out to play on the field or in the park.

Both of them liked to spend most of their time at home, though, a lot more than they used to do back in the village. Not that I could blame them, obviously. After everything they'd seen and how unsafe they must've felt while we were on the run, being in a house that was protected by the magic of someone they trusted must've felt like a safe haven for them, a place where they could feel at ease. So, I let them be, even though it meant that they spent a lot less time with me now. Especially Fionn, who had always tried to drag me along wherever he went before all this but who kept avoiding me more and more now.

Not that Raven gave me a lot of time to feel lonely. When I wasn't in school, in the library or with Mom or the kids, I was with him. He would take me for walks past the fields, or we'd go horseback riding together. We ate together, a few times we even drank together. We talked a lot, although not about anything important. After opening up to me about his childhood, he would sometimes talk about that, more often, he told me about all the kinds of dreams he had helped come true and how he'd managed to do that, sometimes with the help of magic that he could only specifically use at that moment, for that particular dream, like Corean had speculated.

He asked me many things about my 'life among humans', as he called it. He hadn't lied when he said he found humans interesting, and it seemed that it wasn't a coincidence that he had built his school so close to human territory.

At one point, after I told him what I'd learned about the Magic's Source, he confessed that he'd tried to keep that from me because I'd seemed so desperate when we first met that he'd been afraid I would try to go and ask for magic even after learning about the risks.

In what had become kind of a humdrum life without purpose but full of insecurities, those moments with Raven really brightened up my day. Talking to him was always interesting, and looking at him couldn't bore me in a million years. And the way he would suddenly kiss me sometimes was so…

I leaned back against the hay bale behind me. At the very moment that I allowed myself to think about it, Raven opened the door and stepped into the stable. His face lit up when he saw me, and he walked towards me, almost tripping over one of the cats that had run up to him.

He bent over and picked it up, although it immediately started to struggle. He stopped in front of me, trying to calm down the struggling kitten by awkwardly petting its back.

I laughed and picked up the little black kitten that was still sleeping on my lap. "Here. Furcoat doesn't like to be picked up, but Raven Two loves it. He falls asleep as soon as you put him down."

Raven obediently put Furcoat on the ground and carefully took Raven Two out of my hands. He sat down next to me, so close that our sides touched, and I immediately drank in his bodily warmth.

"Did you just call this cat Raven Two?" He could barely complete his sentence without laughing as he carefully put Raven Two on his lap, who immediately crawled into a little black ball and fell asleep.

I felt all the blood in my body rush to my face.

He grinned. "Because of his black fur?"

I nodded, unable to look him in the eyes.

He patted the cat, his grin broadening. "I will take that as a compliment. What about Furcoat?"

I scratched Furcoat's head as it rubbed against my leg. "She's a calico, so she has really pretty fur, the kind that people would love to have coats of."

He grimaced. "That is frighteningly dark. Please do not turn my cats into coats."

I laughed. "So, what are you doing here?"

His expression immediately turned serious. "Well, you seemed a little blue yesterday during dinner, and I have not seen you, so I thought that you might be here."

I patted Furcoat, who jumped onto the bale next to me. Even though I came here to be alone with my thoughts, it made me happy he was worried about me.

"So…" He awkwardly looked at the sleeping cat on his lap. "Are you a little blue?"

I almost started laughing. "Yes, I am," I said, deciding I might as well be honest.

He stared at me, clearly not sure how to respond. Should I have lied and said I was fine? I would've done that with anybody else, but I thought it was alright to tell the truth since it was Raven.

"I know this sounds ungrateful and selfish, but I can't stop thinking we shouldn't be staying here the way we are. I know Mom and the kids are happy, as happy as they could be in this situation, but…" I averted my eyes, "shouldn't I at least go out there and find out where I came from, who my biological parents are, who I am? Who sent those monsters after me? And why?"

Raven picked up Raven Two and put him on the ground, under loud protest. He watched as the cat ran away and then took my hand in his.

He looked me deep in my eyes, and it took me all the concentration I could muster up not to get lost in them. "If that is something you need to know, then I will help you find the answers to those questions." He narrowed his eyes. "If you feel you have to leave here to do that, I cannot stop you, of course, but Thera," he leaned closer to me, "I do not want you to go."

"…what?" My mouth felt dry. I had no idea how to react; all I could think about was how close he was to me.

"I want you to stay with me." He smiled seductively. "Not indefinitely, but forever."

He placed one hand on the hay behind me and leaned in even closer so that our faces were only a few inches apart from each other. "You will be safe with me, even if you want to go out there and see more of the world. You can do anything you want, as long as you are with me. Please," he brought his face closer to mine, his lips so close I could feel his breath against my skin, "stay with me."

Finally, after what felt like an eternity, he pressed his lips against mine. I was very aware that this wasn't our first kiss, but he'd never kissed me like that before. So tender, yet so hungry. He wrapped his arms around me and tightly pulled me against him as if it bothered him that I couldn't come closer than physically possible. His tongue moved against mine, and he stroked his hand through my hair, clutching it gently.

He caressed my neck with his other hand and slowly moved lower, over my shoulder, my chest, firmly grasping one of my breasts, as he softly used his own weight to push me back. I immediately gave in and lay with my back on the hay, moving my hands over his sculpted body.

As if I wasn't entranced enough, he suddenly sat up straight, took off his jacket and undershirt and leaned back down to kiss me again with a mischievous look on his face. He kissed my neck and pushed up my sweater to lay my chest bare. He moved down, and I closed my eyes and stroked my hands over the toned muscles on his back as he slowly, carefully kissed a trail down from my neck.

Was this really going to happen? Part of me wanted nothing more than to pull him even closer and do anything I wanted with him, let him do whatever he wanted to me, but another part of me was panicking. He asked me to stay with him, he honestly told me how he felt, did letting this happen mean that I agreed to that? Was this moment of weakness, this moment of ecstasy, going to determine my future, the rest of my life?

"Ahum, cough cough." A dry tone reached us from not that far away, and we both turned around in shock.

I crossed my arms in front of my bare chest and looked around in a panic, ready to explain myself in case Mom or, even worse, Fionn or Mori had come in, until my brain finally registered the voice we'd heard, and I felt myself relax subconsciously. Without knowing why, I immediately looked up.

Dayn was sitting on one of the big, horizontal wooden beams that supported the roof of the stables. He'd pulled one leg up, leaning his chin on his knee, while the other leg loosely hung over the edge of the beam, carelessly swinging back and forth.

Even though I'd just seen him, it felt like a long time ago that I'd seen him sitting somewhere up that high, looking down on me with a mocking look on his face.

I hadn't paid any attention to it before, but for some reason, I suddenly noticed he was wearing that same black shirt as before. Despite being in the most embarrassing situation I'd ever been in, I couldn't stop myself from thinking how beautiful he looked in all black. Raven had told me that he didn't deserve even half the mystery I allocated him, but how could I help but think I was staring at the very epitome of mystery itself?

"Before you guys go any further, there's some trouble near the school that probably requires your attention." That was all. No jokes, no words about what he'd witnessed us doing, just that one warning.

"What-" Raven jumped up. "How are you here?"

Dayn snorted. "Oh right… that barrier you're so proud of… Yeah, turns out it's not really that big of a deal. Not for me, at least. Of course, Thera already knew that."

Raven grabbed his undershirt from the ground and pulled it over his head in an angry motion, after which he started taking big, furious steps towards Dayn, stopping almost right beneath him and looking up at him as if he were about to fly up there and rip his throat out.

Dayn tilted his head. "I don't mind you coming up here, and I'm okay with coming down there too if you want, but are you sure that's what you should be doing right now?"

At the very moment, he asked that a loud scream that I recognized as Aeric's reached us from outside, and both Raven and I turned to the stable door in shock. Without wasting another second, without saying anything else, without even giving me a last look, Raven turned around and ran out of the stables.

I got off the bale of hay as well and pulled down my shirt, ready to follow him to see if there was something I could help with.

"Are you serious, Thera?"

I stopped but didn't turn around. Somehow, I couldn't bring myself to. I could feel his eyes burning into my back, making me feel even more naked than I'd been a second ago.

"I thought you were looking for some meaning here, a place to fit in, but instead, this is how you've been wasting the time I've given you?" There was no sign of the usual teasing tone in his voice.

I swallowed, although it hurt my throat for some reason. "This was the first time." I could barely get the words out, and after I did, I didn't get a reaction for so long. I started to think he hadn't even heard me at all.

"So, is this what you've decided to do? To stay here with that boring dud for the rest of your boring life, maybe have some boring kids that can run around in your boring house, so they can continue your boring line, after your no doubt boring deat-"

"That's enough!" I turned around, no longer ashamed, just seething with anger.

He got up and jumped off the wooden beam, softly and gracefully landing on his feet as always, even from that terrifying height.

"If that's what you've decided, Thera," he walked towards me with a few big steps and stopped right in front of me, looking down on me even though we were both standing on the ground, "then tell me now, because I don't have to hang around here trying to protect you if you're not going to do anything with the life I-"

He stopped and averted his face for a second before letting out a big sigh and looking back at me.

"So?" He stared right at me, and for a moment, I could swear I could almost see his eyes through the black cloth.

Normally, that would've piqued my interest, but I was too pissed off at that moment. "Then what am I supposed to do according to you, huh? What is it that you're so, apparently desperately, waiting for me to do?"

202

He scoffed. "Figure it out." After that, he walked past me and put his hand on the door handle, ready to walk away, but I wasn't going to just let him disappear this time.

"Figure it out?" I could barely suppress the anger in my voice, and he stopped, with his hand still on the handle, his back still turned towards me, which pissed me off even more.

"You have got some guts, you bastard. I *have* figured it out, I've been figuring it out this whole time, and I might not have found what I'm looking for, but I'm sure about one thing; I'm not the only person I have to think of, and I can't protect my family by running and hiding and looking for danger just to figure out who I am. And I sure as hell can't rely on someone who keeps disappearing every time I speak to him for more than two minutes!"

He started to turn to me but stopped and turned back to the door. I wasn't sure what was happening exactly, but it almost seemed as if he didn't know what to say, although I couldn't imagine that to be true.

I waited for what felt like an eternity, and right before I couldn't take it anymore, he slid the door open and stepped outside. "Raven won't be able to keep protecting you like this, no matter what he thinks. And I won't be able to keep buying you time." He closed the door behind him.

Normally, I might've run after him, and part of me wanted to, but I knew a whole lot better by now. He would be nowhere to be found the second he'd closed that door. I took two calm steps towards it and opened it, immediately having my suspicion confirmed, and then started running.

I ran all the way back to the school, where a group of people had gathered outside on the grass field. I pushed my way through the crowd to the open circle in the middle, where Raven was already standing. Opposite of him stood

Corean, looking incredibly uncomfortable, his big, light blue hands covered in red. I turned back to Raven and felt time slow down. Fionn was sitting on his knees behind him, his hand pressed against his left eye, although I could see blood drip out from under his fingers.

The world around me faded, and all I could see was Fionn until I slowly turned around to Corean.

"You." I'd started walking towards him with big, purposeful steps before I even realized it. I should've known. I should've never let myself be deceived by him. I should've never allowed myself to see him as anything other than a Borean. I wasn't going to let this happen, not again.

I reached out my hand to him. It would literally take me only that one hand to snap his neck. Was this what you call blind rage?

I stopped less than a yard away from him, or I should say I was stopped. I looked over my shoulder, and it took me a few moments before Raven's hand around my upper arm became clear in my vision. He was clearly using his real strength, and as my rage faded slowly, I could feel how much his tight grip around my arm hurt.

"Calm down, Fionn is alright." Raven's green eyes burned into mine, waiting for me to come to my senses.

I ignored him and looked at Fionn. He'd gotten up and took a step closer to us, still covering his left eye.

"It wasn't Corean, Ther. He was helping me! What are you doing?" His voice cracked, and he looked as if he were about to cry as he pointed to the ground between us.

I looked down and took a step back, completely startled. Not only had I not noticed them until that very moment, but I'd almost stepped on two unconscious kids laying on the ground. One very humanoid kid, not even all that much bigger than Fionn, and one big, tall kid covered in fur from head to toe.

I slowly moved my eyes to Fionn again, who stared back at me in anticipation, and then I turned to Raven, slightly pulling on my arm that he was still holding.

He sighed with relief and let go. "It seems that these two," he pointed to the two unconscious students at our feet, "got into an argument with Fionn and when things turned physical, Corean apparently came to Fionn's aid, unfortunately knocking these two unconscious."

Shit… shit shit shit shit shit! I turned around, but I didn't need to look at Corean to know how hurt he looked. I hadn't even doubted it for a second. Without even taking a good look around or assessing the situation, I'd let my prejudice take over and completely lost control.

I took a step closer to him, but he immediately took one back, and I froze. Not knowing what else to do, I just stood there staring at him, pretending not to notice the tears he was desperately fighting back.

"Alright, that is enough excitement for today! Everybody return to class immediately!" Raven clapped in his hands twice and gestured for everybody to start moving. "Peitan, Karell, carry these two to the healer's office for me!"

Two kids, the biggest in the entire group, immediately ran towards us to pick up their schoolmates and carried them away with ease. The rest of the onlookers slowly followed them.

Raven turned to Fionn first. "I will take you to the healer at my house, so she can look at your eye. After that, you can go home for the day if you wish."

Then he turned to us. "Corean, I think it was really kind of you to protect Fionn, but you still hurt two other children, and you especially should know better than anyone that violence is not the answer."

He looked at me for a second and then back to Corean. "Fionn and I will head back first, but I want to see you in my office after school today to have a talk about this, understood?"

Raven had never seemed more like a teacher to me than at that moment, and even though I knew he was right, part of me wanted to slap him for talking to Corean like that after what I'd already done to him.

Corean didn't respond to Raven's words, but he kept standing still in the same place, even though he didn't seem happy at all that he was being left behind with me.

I stayed where I was, at a safe distance from Corean, until I'd watched Fionn and Raven disappear into Raven's house.

"So…" I looked at him, but he kept his eyes glued to the ground at his feet. "Corean, I'm going to come closer now, okay?"

"No." His voice was barely more than a whisper, and I wasn't sure what to do. He was scared and hurt, and I didn't want to aggravate that, but I also wasn't going to talk to him with this kind of distance between us. So, in the end, I decided to ignore his answer and walk closer to him anyway. To my great relief, he didn't back away this time. I stopped next to him and sat down in the grass, gesturing to him to sit down next to me.

I hid a smile when he immediately obeyed.

"I thought you really believed me when I said I was different." His voice was even smaller than before, now that I was so close to him.

"I did. I do."

He suddenly lifted his head and looked me straight in the eyes. "You wanted to kill me!"

I opened my mouth to say something, but his glare shut me up.

"Don't try to tell me you weren't actually trying to kill me. I could see it in your eyes. I know what it looks like!" Tears started streaming down his face, and I tried not to think about how he knew something like that.

"You're right." I pulled up my knees and wrapped my hands around them. "And I'm so sorry."

He didn't say anything back but instead turned his head away from me again.

I watched as he wiped the tears off his face with rough, angry movements.

"Corean, this is in no way an excuse for my horrible behavior towards you just now, but there's something I want to tell you about what happened to my family and me before we came here."

He didn't respond, but from the way he turned his head to me just slightly, I could tell that he was curious about what I was about to say. I took a deep breath and told him about that night the Boreans attacked our village. How they killed most of the villagers. How they set the village on fire. How they killed Dad, and how I killed several of them.

Corean stayed quiet while I talked and still didn't say anything after I was done, so we just sat there in silence for a while.

"So, that's why you looked like you were about to vomit the first time we met?" He asked it so nonchalantly that I almost burst out laughing.

"You noticed that, huh?" Guilt crashed down on me.

He nodded slightly. "A lot of people act like that, so I was kind of used to it, but you still talked to me, and you still spent time with me, so I was still happy."

I felt my stomach cramp up and cursed myself. How could I have ever thought, even for a second, that this vulnerable kid that was too kind for his own good was a horrible monster?

"I'm so sorry, Corean. I've spent all this time trying to protect what's left of my family, and when I saw Fionn on the ground, hurt, and your hands, hands like theirs, covered in blood, it was like I was back there, and I just…" I didn't finish my sentence. It was all just excuses.

"But I really do believe you're completely different from them, and I do like talking to you and spending time with you, so…" I plucked a blade of grass, unable to look him in the eye, "even if you never want to see me again, I hope you'll at least believe that."

I saw him look at me from the corner of my eye, and then he suddenly let out a big sigh. He quickly wiped away his tears, much calmer this time, and turned to me completely with his usual bright face. "I do believe that, and I don't never want to see you again."

He looked at his hands. "I guess I kind of understand what you must've felt just now, and, you know… with my hands like this, and Fionn hurt like that, I guess it was an honest mistake to make."

I exhaled, shaking my head. I couldn't help myself. Who else but this sweet, upbeat kid could forgive me for something so horrible so quickly? I could honestly hug him. No, you know what? I wrapped my arms around him and pressed his head against my shoulder. He tensed up but didn't move away from me.

"Thank you, Corean. And I promise you I'll never do something so cruel to you ever again."

He nodded and awkwardly waited for me to be done hugging him, which took me a while.

After I'd let go of him, I got up and wiped the grass off my pants. He followed my example, and I folded my arms.

"Now, I don't want to be 'that person', but you should really go back to class, after you've visited the healer's office as well, to let him have a look at your hands."

He grimaced but obediently turned around and walked back to the school building. I watched him for a moment and then quickly ran to Raven's house.

I stepped onto the patio in his garden at the same moment he walked out of the dining room it was attached to. He stopped and looked at me, clearly unsure what to say.

"Thera…" he started, but I didn't want to hear the rest at that moment. I had something more important to think about.

"Is Fionn okay? Where is he? Am I allowed to kill those two kids who hurt him?"

He looked shocked for a moment but then hid a chuckle as if he thought I hadn't honestly meant what I said.

"Yes, he is fine, he is in his old room, and no, you are not allowed to kill them." His look darkened. "But I will make sure they are punished for their actions."

I nodded reluctantly and walked past him. Punished, my hiney. He would just give them some extra homework or maybe expel them for a few days. None of that would teach those little bastards a real lesson, but I was going to have to let it go for now.

I walked up the stairs to Fionn's old room. 'Old room', I shook my head, as if we hadn't only been in this place for three months. I stopped in front of his door, took a deep breath, and knocked on the light wood.

"Ther?"

I smiled. "Yeah, it's me. Can I come in?"

"Yes." That was my Fionn. No 'whatever', of 'if you must', or any other way most kids would react. Just a clear, honest answer.

I entered the room, closed the door behind me and walked over to his bed, where he was sitting upright, leaning against a bunch of fluffed up pillows. He'd tied the curtains of his canopy bed to the side and opened the curtains of his windows, so he could enjoy the sun that was shining on his face.

I looked at him, and my smile disappeared the second I saw the big, white eyepatch that covered his left eye. "Is it bad? Does it hurt?"

He put his hand against the eyepatch. "Not at all. Raven was overreacting with this thing. One of those guys hit me, and it left a small cut next to my eye, that's all." He shrugged. "Although my eye will probably be black tomorrow."

I chuckled and sat down beside him. "Well, I'm pretty sure that's still nowhere near as bad as how those two guys will feel."

Fionn grinned halfheartedly. "Thanks to Corean. He helped me, even though he hates being in big crowds and fighting." He stared at me with an accusatory look on his face.

I sighed. "I know, and I cannot tell you how bad I feel about what I did, but I apologized to him, and I think he forgave me."

He pressed his finger against his cheek as he thought about it for a moment. "Well, if he forgave you, then I guess it's okay."

I suppressed a chuckle. My innocent little brother.

"Thera…" The tone of his voice had changed. "When are we ever going to leave this place again?"

He looked down at his hands that had tightly clutched the sheets draped over his legs.

"Fionn, I know that something bad happened today, but it's not always like that, right? I mean, you've made friends here that you have fun with, right? And I promise you that those two kids won't ever hurt you again, I'll personally see to that, so you don't have to b-"

"It's not like that!" Fionn interrupted me with a loud voice, and I stopped, shocked.

He sighed and lifted his head. "You're right. I mean, I haven't really made any friends, but this place isn't so bad, and I'm not worried about those two at all. It's just that," he looked down to his hands again, that had let go of the sheets and were now motionlessly laying on his lap, "I tried to fit in here, and that was fine for a while, but I can't keep pretending as if everything is normal. I'm tired of acting like everything is okay."

I stared at him. His words made my heart bleed. "Then… what do you want?"

"I don't know. I mean, when I think about going out there again, I get scared. And when I think about going back home, I get scared too, but…" He looked at me in desperation. "Don't you want to know who killed Dad? And why? Don't you want to know why they want to kill you?"

He shook his head and clenched his fists. "You and Mom and Mori act like it never happened, like everything is fine, but I can't stand it! I hate that no one ever talks about Dad! And even when you do, you all only talk about funny things he used to do or say, and you laugh about it." He pulled up his shoulders. "It's like none of you even miss him."

I swallowed, unable to find words. Instead, I just put my arms around him.

"Fionn…" I pressed my face against his hair. "I miss Dad so much. I miss everything about him. How he wouldn't talk much, but he would always pat me on my shoulder to show me he was proud of me. How he would use every opportunity he could to turn everything into a lesson. How he always made me feel safe, even though we both knew I was much stronger than him. How he would always reassure me I was his daughter, no matter what, and that he didn't want to hear anything else about it. How he was always on one line with Mori, secretly winking at her when she'd get into a fight with Mom. How he would carry you around on his shoulders, pretending to drop you to make you laugh."

I loosened my embrace so I could look at him, even though that meant he'd see the tears burning in my eyes. "Talking about silly stuff like funny things he used to do and say is just easier."

He silently wiped the back of his hands over his face. "I get that. Even though I really want to talk about it, it's hard. I don't want to say something wrong or make you cry." He looked up at me. "I'm sorry I ran away last time."

I shook my head, stopping myself from crying again. "That's okay. And you don't ever have to worry about making me cry. If there's something you want to talk about, you can. That's what big sisters are for."

I got off the bed, lifted up his blanket, and sat down next to him, leaning against the big pile of pillows against the backboard.

I put my arm around him, and he leaned against me.

"Then I want to talk about leaving."

I hesitated. "It's not really that easy Fionn, we have no idea where to go, and it's dangerous out there. Don't you remember how it was out there for only three days before we came here?"

He scoffed. "That was different. We didn't know anything back then, and you were always trying to pretend that you were human too. But we've learned a lot here, and you don't have to pretend to want to run away. You can fight to protect us if you have to."

I was glad he couldn't see my face at that moment. I hadn't exactly been pretending to want to run away, even though I had tried not to let them see what I really was.

"Fionn!" The door slammed open, and Mori walked in with big, hasty steps, even though she was already completely out of breath. "I heard… you got hurt!"

She put her hands on the mattress and took a deep breath before looking up at us and gasped even harder to see Fionn's eyepatch. She jumped on the bed and crawled over to us.

"Oh no! Fionn…" She didn't finish her sentence, but tears started welling up in her eyes.

Fionn rolled his eyes, embarrassed by the fuss she was making. "It's fine; it's just a scratch, nothing to cry over."

Mori frowned and averted her face. "I'm not crying, idiot." She sat down closely next to him and exhaled deeply.

Fionn pulled up his nose at her. "You're all sweaty."

She scoffed. "Yeah, our class was having a field day, so I had to run here all the way from the potato fields."

I lifted an eyebrow. "Those are all the way behind the first village." Since when was she able to run that long? Or that fast? We hadn't been sitting here for all that long yet.

Fionn laughed. "Didn't you know, Ther? Ever since Mori had such a hard time keeping up with us back then, she's been training a lot."

I stared at her in surprise. "You have?"

She looked away, annoyed. "Whatever, I just don't want to be a burden the next time." She lowered her head, and her voice softened. "And I didn't want you guys to leave me behind here when you leave again because I wasn't able to keep up with you."

Her words completely baffled me. I had no idea she'd felt that way or that she'd been preparing to leave soon, like Fionn. What on earth had I been doing this whole damn time?

"What about Sarena? Haven't you become friends with her? Don't you like living here?"

She shrugged. "This place will still be here later, and Sarena will still be my friend." A mean grin suddenly appeared on her face. "Besides, shouldn't I ask you that question about mister Raven?"

I felt my cheeks get red. "Raven will also still be my friend if we get back. If we decide to leave."

She snorted. "Yeah, right, your *friend*."

I decided to ignore that for now. I was confused enough as it was already about that.

"Mom is on her way here, too; she was with our class." She said it as if she only now remembered.

I gave her a teasingly judging look. "Did you run over here by yourself and leave Mom behind?"

She folded her arms. "Well, she wasn't as fast, and I didn't know how Fionn was doing."

I suppressed a laugh. "So, you've been training because you don't want to be left behind, and the second you get faster than her, you leave Mom behind?"

"That was only in here. It's not like I would do that out there!"

"I hope not, young lady." Mom stood in the doorway that Mori had left open, even more out of breath than Mori had been. She looked at Fionn's eyepatch.

"Since you're smiling like that, does that mean you're alright?"

Fionn quickly nodded, and Mom smiled at all three of us. "This is a nice sight I haven't seen for a while, all three of my babies having fun together."

She walked over and sat down in the middle of the bed, opposite the three of us. "So, what's going on here?"

I turned to Mom. "We want to leave." There, I said it, after three months of being afraid, of lying to myself about not knowing what I wanted, I finally said it out loud.

"Okay." That was all, no questions, no arguments.

"Okay?" I couldn't stop myself from repeating.

She shrugged. "Well, I can't say I'm happy about it, but it was going to happen eventually. We might be safe here for now, but I'm not so gullible to believe everything will be fine here forever, just because Raven says so, no matter how well he means." She sighed. "And since we can't just run and hide for the rest of our lives, we should go face whatever's after you head on."

That surprised me, but it also made me happy. "Yeah, I think so too."

"Yes!" Fionn smiled as brightly as he possibly could. "So, when are we leaving?"

Mom frowned. "Thera and I will be leaving as soon as possible. You and Mori are staying here."

His smile immediately disappeared. "What? Why?"

"Yeah, why?" Mori looked just as upset as I felt. For a second. Then I realized Mom was right. It would be dangerous enough for just her to come along, but it'd be a lot harder for me to protect three people at the same time. Besides, whoever it was that was after me. That much was clear, so Fionn and Mori would be safe if they stayed behind, within Raven's borders.

Both of them pouted as Mom explained that to them.

"Then what are we supposed to do here?" Fionn tightly clutched the sheets in his fists again. "What if something happens to you?"

Mom moved closer to him and put her hand on his hand. "Nothing is going to happen to us, you'll be fine in here, and we'll be fine out there."

He pushed her hand away. "How do you know that? What are you even going to do?"

"Well, for starters, I think we should get Thera some magic."

All three of them jumped. I seemed to be the only one who wasn't surprised to hear Dayn's voice.

I turned towards him. He was sitting on the windowpane, his legs crossed, his back leaning against the closed window. Even I was wondering how he got there this time.

"Who…" Mom didn't finish her question but just stared at him.

"Who are you?" Mori had no problem finishing her question instead.

"What are you?" Fionn had no problem asking a different kind of question.

Dayn snorted. "I'm not rude. That's what *I* am."

Mori lifted an eyebrow. "Not rude? You snuck into a young boy's bedroom somehow and inserted yourself into a private conversation."

I could barely keep in my laughter seeing him press his lips together in response.

"Why are you wearing a mask? It looks weird."

A part of me wanted to shut Fionn up, but a much, much bigger part wanted to burst out laughing even more.

"It looks better than your lame eyepatch."

My will to laugh disappeared. What was he, a little kid?

Fionn wasn't impressed by his blunt comeback. "Are your eyes hurt as well?"

Dayn shrugged slightly. "Yeah, something like that."

I wanted to roll my eyes. Something like that, yeah, right.

"Mom, Fionn, Mori," I looked at them and gestured to Dayn, "this is the guy-"

"Who saved our lives back then." Mom seemed to have finally gotten herself together again. She turned to him. "Why are you showing your face to us now all of a sudden?"

Mori snorted. "Half his face."

Dayn grinned, clearly appreciating Mori's sharp tongue, but his grin quickly disappeared, and he turned to Mom. "I'm here now because Thera yelled at me."

I frowned, instantly pissed off again, although I could see Mom's slightly amused expression from the corner of my eye.

He sighed and looked at me. "You were right. You haven't been able to rely on me. Only warning you for danger once and then hiding away, leaving you to deal with it yourself, isn't enough to protect you or earn your trust. So, if

you'll still have me, I'll be here for you from here on out."
He turned to Mom and the kids. "For all of you."

He opened the window and swung one leg over the windowpane. "I'll be waiting for you at the lake where we met before, so come find me when you're ready to leave."

After that, he gracefully jumped towards the ground. Mom, Fionn, and Mori all jumped up to look out the window and turned to me in shock when they found that he'd already disappeared.

I rolled my eyes. How were things any different now? He still disappeared after talking to us for a few minutes, he still hadn't actually told us anything, but somehow an enormous feeling of relief fell over me. Had I really been this upset about my 'fight' with him? That honestly worried me, but I decided to push it away and not think about it. All that mattered at that moment was that I'd finally made up my mind.

13

I picked one piece of clothing after the other out of my closet. I came here with only the clothes on my back, so it made sense I'd gotten some new ones at some point, but I hadn't realized how many clothes, beautiful ones of amazing quality, I'd gathered over these past three months. Many of them I couldn't even remember getting myself.

I pulled out a long, light blue shirt with a silklike ribbon that was a little tighter than the rest of the shirt, sewn along the waistline. I put it on and looked at myself in the mirror. It looked pretty, and it fit perfectly. Somehow, I felt like that shirt was making me look better than I really did. Did Raven have this made for me without my knowing? Was he the one who infused it with magic, or had that been the tailor?

I took the shirt off and looked at it. Part of me wanted to take something so pretty with me, but if I could feel the magic inside it, then wouldn't everybody else too? I reluctantly put the shirt back in the closet and put one of my own, magic-free shirts on again.

"So, you are really going to leave just like that?"

I jumped and spun to face the door, to see Raven looking at me with an expression I couldn't place very well. How long had he been standing there? I felt myself blush and turned away. Only a few days ago, I'd partially undressed for him, I'd let him touch me all over, but now, for some reason, I felt embarrassed by the thought that he'd seen me change shirts.

"Yeah." I focused on closing the clasps of my leather bag, avoiding making eye contact with him.

"Then I am coming too." He sounded resolute as if he'd already made this decision.

"What? No!" I looked up at him in shock, realizing too late how that must've sounded to him. The hurt look on his usually smiling face stung in my chest, but I'd unconsciously yelled out how I really felt. It's not that the thought hadn't crossed my mind, but I didn't want him to come.

He moved closer to me. "Even though I can protect you? Even though I can keep you safe?"

I finally let go of my backpack and turned to him completely, looking him straight into his beautiful eyes. "I don't need you to keep me safe, Raven. I need you to keep Fionn and Mori safe. I'm leaving them in your care."

He lifted an eyebrow. "Without asking me?"

I smiled at him. "I knew you would do it no matter what."

He sighed and studied me, noticing that I was clothed in my traveling outfit and clearly set to go. "Were you even going to say goodbye?"

"Of course, I was, I just…" I lowered my head. "I wasn't sure how."

"Well," he took my hand, "I could think of a hundred ways for you to say goodbye that I would like very much." He grinned playfully. "But for now, I would be content with a simple 'goodbye' and, perhaps, a promise you will come back to me after you have found what you are looking for?"

220

I quietly stared back at him. I couldn't. Raven was everything I could possibly ever want, but I didn't want to make a promise like that to him. I wasn't sure if I wanted to come back to him, not in that way, at least.

I took my hand out of his, and the happy expression on his face disappeared. "I see…"

Words couldn't possibly express the pain I felt in my chest, looking at that broken-hearted look on his face.

He shook his head. "No, it is quite alright. I am aware I have been asking a lot of you, perhaps too fast." He forced himself to smile, and I wanted to scream inside. "All you should do for now is focus on coming back safe, as a friend, and then I will find enough time to make you fall in love with me for real."

He said it with so much confidence, staring straight into my eyes, that my heart skipped a beat, and for a moment, I wondered if I'd made a horrible mistake, but I forced myself to stay silent.

I put the backpack on and looked at him one last time. "Please take care of Fionn and Mori."

I walked past him and left our home as fast as I could, meeting Mom outside the front door. She'd put on her old clothes as well, the ones she'd been wearing when we left the village.

She was looking around as if she was searching for something. I shook my head, we'd taken our time to talk to the kids yesterday and to say goodbye to them, but they'd mostly been angry that we were leaving them behind, so I doubted they would come to see us off now.

"They are watching from behind the curtains in Mori's room." Raven stood in the doorway, leaning against the frame with his arms folded, looking at me with that forced smile.

The fact that he chose to be the better person and come out to see Mom and me off made me feel even worse.

There had been no need for him to tell me where the kids were. I knew they'd be closely watching us from somewhere.

I turned to my mom. "Let's go."

She left, with me following right behind her. We walked to the edge of Raven's land in about twenty minutes, where I could see Dayn's silhouette waiting for us, sitting on a far too high branch of one of the trees. I walked up to it and stopped underneath him.

"I thought you would wait for us at the lake?"

He leaned forward, so he could look down on me from where he was sitting. "I got bored. Plus, I wasn't a hundred percent sure you would come, and I have a better view of your place from here."

"A better view of my place?" I made a face. "You do realize how creepy that sounds, right?"

He jumped off the branch and landed beside me, light as a feather. "Yeah, I know, but trust me, it's not for whatever dirty reason you came up with."

I folded my arms. There was no doubt in my mind that the road ahead with this guy was going to be a long one. "Then what is the reason?"

His usual grin disappeared. "Just… believe me, I have one."

He ended our conversation by taking a step past me towards my mother. "Miss Nayana, are you ready to go?"

Mom hid the amusement she felt about the look on my face after he'd brushed me off and nodded, so he turned around and started walking away from the border, heading north.

Mom and I followed not far behind him. I looked at his back. I was able to see the nape of his neck above the collar of his black shirt. It looked elegant and kissable. I immediately shook my head, annoyed. I didn't want to think something like that about him, especially not with Mom walking next to me.

Okay, I tried to cheer myself on, just try talking about something, anything. "So, now that we'll be traveling together, why don't you tell us something about yourself?"

He slightly shrugged his shoulders without looking at us. "No, thank you."

I immediately got frustrated again but swallowed all the insults that came to mind and instead forced myself to be kind and try that again. "Please?"

He chuckled softly. "My refusal wasn't really because of your rudeness, although I do like this tone a lot better."

I clenched my fists, worried I might hit him against his smug face if I didn't. I heard Mom chuckle softly, and I threw her an angry glare before I turned back to him.

"Fine, then don't tell me anything, as per usual. I'll just think whatever I want about you."

He shrugged again. "Be my guest."

I couldn't stop myself from showing a complacent expression. That was exactly what I'd hoped he would say. "Alright, then I bet you were a bedwetter as a kid, and you didn't stop until you were like, fourteen. Oh, and I bet you're really old, and you're wearing that mask to hide your wrinkles."

I grinned, pretty happy with my childish self.

He stopped and turned around to look at me, the expression on the part of his face that I could see anything but pleased. "That annoys me a whole lot more than it should."

I gave him my sweetest smile. "What does, sir?"

He sighed, frustrated but didn't respond and started walking again instead.

I could see Mom shaking her head at me, and I rolled my eyes and shrugged, as a way of apologizing for being so petty.

She ignored me and walked up to him. "So, Dayn… is it alright if I just call you that?"

He nodded politely. "Of course."

I clenched my fists. Why was his tone of voice, his whole attitude, so different towards her?

"Well then, Dayn, I really like your mask."

He stared at her for a moment, as if he were trying to figure out if she meant it or if she was making fun of him, but she showed him nothing but her honest, kind face, so eventually, he seemed to accept that as the truth.

"Thank you."

She put her hands behind the straps of her backpack, clearly already comfortable around him. "It reminds me of the masks the people in our village used to wear during carnival. Did you bring it from your home realm? Do your people all wear masks like that?"

He laughed a little and shook his head. "No, they don't. I don't think most of them would like it very much. I didn't bring it from home, I made it myself."

I looked up, that piqued my interest. I looked at Mom's back in front of me. Ask him more! I wanted to yell at her.

She pressed her hands together, honestly impressed. "That's amazing. Where did you learn how to do that?"

He opened his mouth to answer but then closed it again. After that, he shrugged. "I guess I just picked it up somewhere. It's not hard to do."

I sighed inaudibly. That was it. Within two sentences, he'd realized he was giving away information about himself and immediately stopped. That was the last thing we managed to get out of him for the rest of that day.

Everything about that first day felt awkward to me. The way old man Dayn would walk in front of us so full of confidence. The way Mom followed right behind him, overexerting herself to keep up with him. The way I walked behind her, instead of next to her, to close our little formation. The way he was still here, even after all these hours. The way that made me extremely aware of his presence, unable to keep my eyes off his back. As if I had to constantly make sure he was still there, that he wasn't going anywhere.

And it felt awkward when he suddenly stopped as the sun started to go down, turned around and told us we should make camp there for the night.

Mom and I nodded obediently as he divided the tasks that needed to be done before we could relax. All three of us had brought dried and prepared food, so there was no need to actually cook it. Still, we all agreed that it would taste better if we did, so Dayn disappeared between the trees to find firewood, and Mom started to unpack our small pot and several bowls while I set up the tent.

It seemed like a normal tent from the outside but was beyond beautiful on the inside. I sat down in the middle of it, with the tent flaps closed, and looked up at the canvas above me. The entire thing was painted in a deep, dark blue, like the night sky. Little white dots were spread all over it, like stars, but the rest was unlike any night sky I'd ever seen before. A whirl of beautiful, intense colors was painted above me, and all kinds of different, colorful globes were spread randomly over the canvas. Some of them seemed like they were on fire, some of them had colorful rings around them, some had even smaller globes next or even attached to them.

I lay down on my back and looked up at the incredible colors in front of me. I knew they weren't actually moving, but somehow those globes seemed to slowly move around, that whirl of colors seemed to slowly spin, the little stars seemed to really twinkle. It was mesmerizing.

Had Dayn infused it with his magic? Somehow, I found that unlikely.

"Pretty, isn't it?"

I bolted up, completely startled. Dayn snickered at my reaction and kneeled in the tent, right in front of the entrance, keeping an appropriate distance from me for a change.

"It's awe-inspiring. What is it?"

He snorted in his usual mocking tone as if I'd asked something stupid. "It's the night sky."

I threw him a scowl, and he grinned. "It's the part of the night sky that's so far away you can't see it with your naked eye."

I allowed myself to frown slightly, breaking my earlier promise to myself. That sounded like a lie.

He laughed after seeing my expression and opened up the right tent flap. "Let's go eat. Your mom is waiting for us."

I followed him outside. "How do you know it's there then?"

He walked over to the fire and sat down on the ground, leaving the piece of tree trunk that we'd set up camp next to, open for Mom and me. I sat down and watched him as he crossed his legs and leaned over to see what was inside the small cookpot.

"Hm…" He pretended to think about it while he accepted a bowl of stew from Mom.

I let him think about what he did and did not want to tell me and instead took a bite from the stew that Mom had handed me as well. I closed my eyes. As always, one bite was all it took to take me to another place. For a second, and only for that first insane bite, the world around me disappeared, and it was just me, that bowl of stew and my spoon, and I couldn't wish for anything more.

Dayn's chuckling pulled me back to reality, and I looked at him. "What?"

He shook his head. "No, nothing, I just realized I've never actually seen you eat before. It's good, huh?"

I felt myself turn red. "Yeah, it's really good."

I looked at the stew in my hands. Mom had prepared it, which meant that the ingredients she used had been infused with magic beforehand. Was that safe? Both Mom and I had left behind all our clothes and everything that had magic in it, but that seemed pointless now that we were carrying around magic-infused food.

I looked at Dayn. He was the one who'd brought the magical food, and, I looked at his tent over my shoulder, it probably wasn't him, but someone had definitely fused their magic in that thing with all their heart and soul as well. Did that mean that he wasn't worried about it at all? Or maybe he felt that there was no use hiding it anyway since he carried magic inside of him too?

I turned back to him. Dayn was better at hiding than any other person I'd ever met, and his magic definitely had something to do with that. Maybe this little amount of infused magic wasn't something we had to worry about.

"It's something I saw once. A long time ago."

I blinked a few times to refocus my attention. He was staring at the fire in front of him now, but he must've mistaken my earlier look at the tent as me subtly pushing him into continuing our conversation.

"That sounds conveniently vague." I tried to be as nonchalant about it as I could and casually took a bite to emphasize that. The one thing I'd noticed about Dayn in the few times we'd met was that the more desperately I wanted to know something, the less likely he was to tell me.

He looked up at me and grinned slightly, clearly seeing right through my obvious tactic. "You spent a lot of time in Raven's library, right?"

I nodded.

"Have you learned anything about the realms of the special continent there?"

I nodded again. "I know most realms are named after their leaders, which is why the one we're in now is called the Realm of Dreams, after Raven's magic. Although not all realms are named after their Keeper's magic, sometimes they're also named after their accomplishments or just something they find important."

I stirred my stew with my spoon while listing what I knew. "There are twenty-one other realms on this continent. There are two more continents besides this one. One is the human continent. The other one is called the continent of eternity. Although opinions about whether that one really

228

exists are apparently divided, and I've only been able to find one faded drawing of it.

As for this continent, the realm next to this one is the Realm of Healing. Next to that is the Realm of Ruins." I narrowed my eyes. "And you call human territory the Realm of Filth."

He laughed, completely ignoring both mine and Mom's insulted expressions. "Right, except that the Realm of Ruins is known only to a handful of people as the Realm of Magic."

My eyes widened. "Because that's where the Magic's Source is, somewhere in between the ruins?"

He tilted his head slightly. "You could say somewhere in between, yeah. Underneath is another word, or among, in betwixt. They all kind of describe it, and yet none of them really do. There aren't many people who can find it, even if they know where it is."

I put down my emptied bowl and folded my arms. "So, we'll cross the Realm of Healing and enter the Realm of Ruins, and somewhere over there, you will lead us to the Source, so I can try and ask it for magic?"

He picked up my empty bowl, stacking it on his own, so he could wash them when Mom was done as well. "That's pretty much the plan."

"What about those Boreans that have been following me?"

He didn't seem very worried, as if he knew something I didn't. "They haven't noticed we left yet, so all we have to do now is outrun them to the Source."

My mistrust of his plan got deeper. "And then what?"

He turned his head away from me as Mom handed him her empty bowl, and he got up. "Then… I guess I'll bring you home."

I stared at him, unable to find any words.

"Home?" I turned to Mom, her voice had sounded small, and her eyes showed slight signs of panic.

I looked back at Dayn. "You... know where I came from?"

"Yeah... Kind of." He walked away towards the small brook that wasn't far away from our camp.

I sat there silently, not ready to move or talk. The most I'd hoped to gain out of all of this were some answers. Who had my parents been? Why had they abandoned me? Who was sending these mercenaries after me, and why? I rubbed my forehead. Until that very moment, I hadn't realized that I'd always thought of my biological parents in the past tense. Why had I automatically assumed that they were dead?

Had I really thought that the only possible explanation for them to leave me behind was that they weren't alive anymore?

I lifted my head. Technically Dayn hadn't mentioned my parents or if they were alive or not. I folded my hands, frustrated.

I felt my hope quickly melt away. If I were going to meet my parents, why did I have to risk my life to get some magic first? Why did I need magic to face my biological parents? Was it because I needed it to protect us from the boreans and other mercenaries that were after us on our way there, or because something much worse was waiting for me at 'home'? A chill moved through my body, giving me goosebumps. Part of me desperately wanted to know the truth, but I was too scared to ask Dayn anything else about it.

"Thera-"

"You're my mother!" I'd turned to her and pretty much yelled the words in her face before I even realized it. I took a deep breath and calmed myself down, so I could give Mom a comforting look. "*You're* my mother, no matter what."

She shook her head and put her arms around me, hugging me tightly. "I know, sweetie, nothing can ever change what you mean to me, no matter what. It's okay to want to know where you came from and who gave birth to you, but…"

She squeezed my shoulder.

"But what?" I pressed, unsure if I wanted to know.

She softly stroked my arm. "But this world is a dangerous place full of dangerous people. I just think that you'd be smart to keep in mind that there has to be a reason you grew up with us, not them."

I buried my head in her shoulder, breathing in her scent that always calmed me down.

"I wish Fionn and Mori were here." I released myself from Mom's embrace and sat up straight. "Do you think we made a mistake leaving them behind?"

She sighed heavily. "Honestly? I'm not sure. I'm relieved that they're safe behind that barrier, instead of out here in the open, but whenever I think about them being so far away from us, under the care of someone we barely know, my heart starts racing so fast I can hardly breathe."

I watched the fire as it was slowly dying. "Yeah… me too."

"Thera."

I turned around to see Dayn stand behind us with the now clean bowls in his hands. "What?"

He opened my Mom's bag to put the bowls away and then turned back to me. "When we reach the Magic's Source, I think you should be aware that there's only an extremely small chance it'll actually grant you any magic."

I nodded. "And an even smaller chance I'll survive, right?"

Dayn sat down next to the fire again. "When you do survive, and you've received magic, it's probably best not to tell anybody, no matter how much you trust them. Until we're absolutely sure we're safe, we should keep that knowledge between just the three of us."

I narrowed my eyes. "Why?"

"For now, let's say just because."

"Okay." I couldn't help but feel just a little pleased. "You seem to be pretty sure that I'll have no problem with both surviving and getting the Source to grant me magic."

I'd expected him to make fun of me for misunderstanding or to turn my words into some kind of joke, but instead, he gave a strangely warm smile. "I am."

14

I woke up early, far too early for my liking. I rubbed my eyes and lifted myself up halfway, leaning on one elbow. Mom was still asleep next to me. This first night hadn't been easy for her. After she'd made it very clear that she would be the one sleeping in the middle for the entire journey, I'd felt her tossing and turning all night. I'd tried moving away from her, closer to the tent's canvas, but it hadn't helped much, so as a result, neither of us had slept well.

I crawled out of the tent, carefully not to wake Mom up, and stood up straight, looking around. It was a fresh, somewhat dewy morning, but it wasn't cold. It was one of those mornings that promised to turn into an extremely hot day after only one or two more hours. I lifted my arms in the air to stretch my body after sleeping an entire night on the ground and then looked at Dayn. He'd made a small fire and was now clumsily trying to cook something.

I walked towards him and leaned over to look inside the small cookpot that he'd hung far too low over the fire. I grimaced, I wasn't sure what he was trying to make, but I was pretty certain that it wasn't supposed to be this black and clumpy.

I turned to him with a smirk. "Do you not know how to cook?"

He lifted his chin. "Of course I do. I'm just not used to the pot you brought."

I laughed, such a flimsy excuse. "Then use your own."

He didn't look up to me but instead tried to stir the dark, clumpy mess in the pot. "It's too small for three people."

I shook my head laughing and took the ladle out of his hand. "Plus, I'm guessing it's infused with magic, so it won't burn and maintain a perfect temperature or something like that?"

He lifted his shoulders, his lips no more than a vertical line. I felt my smirk broaden; he couldn't get himself to admit I was right.

I took the pot off the fire and handed it to him. "How about this; we go to the brook, so you can throw this monstrosity out and wash that pot, and I'll catch some fish for breakfast?"

He took the pot from me with a defeated sigh, and we walked towards the brook together.

The day before, I'd walked about five steps behind him the entire day, so for some reason, it felt strange to walk beside him now.

"If we keep our pace up today, we'll be in the Realm of Healing before sunset."

I looked at him from the corner of my eye. It had caught me off guard when he suddenly started talking.

He held the dirty pot under his left arm while putting his right hand to his chin. "If possible, I'd prefer to be able to set up camp in the Realm of Healing instead of staying in this awful place for another night."

I looked in front of me again. I could already hear the brook's babbling from here. "You really don't like Raven, do you? What ever happened between you two?"

He dropped his hand next to his side and turned his head to me, his mouth slightly open, as if he were completely caught by surprise. "Me? Not liking Raven? Why ever would you think such a ghastly thing?"

I couldn't help but chuckle lightly. "That's probably overdoing it a bit."

"Yeah, well… the truth would probably just make you mad, so I figured."

I lifted an eyebrow. "Saying that makes me want to know it even more."

We stopped by the brook, and he kneeled on the bank, holding the burned pot underwater so it could soak. "I know, but I don't want to tell you. Besides, it's not just Raven I don't like. It's this whole realm. I don't like how it borders human territory."

I rolled up my pant legs, so I could stand in the brook. "What's so wrong with bordering human territory?"

He jerked his head towards me as if he couldn't believe what I was saying. "I guess you're not that aware of it since you grew up like that from the start. Plus, you've lived a relatively peaceful life up until now."

He poured out the pot and dunked it under again, this time scrubbing it with the brush he'd brought. "It's not that it's *bad* living next to humans, it's just that there's a certain tension in the air that you can never quite shake or ignore. I know Raven finds humans interesting and wants to learn about them, he wants to meet them, but he's interested in them in the same way you can be interested in a new animal species, not so much as people. He just wants to know how they work, how they differ from us, how they managed to survive for so long, even though they don't have any magic and their bodies are so frail."

I scowled. Even though I knew he was telling the truth, I still didn't like to hear it. Besides, Raven may think that about humans as a whole, but he always treated me as a person. He'd definitely taken the time to get to know me, Mom, Fionn, and Mori as people, not just as 'humans'.

Dayn's lip curled up, amused after seeing my rebellious reaction. "What I'm trying to say is that, despite Raven's charitable attitude towards humans, overall relations between humans and specials aren't even half as charitable. That goes for the specials that live in Raven's realm as much as for the rest of the realms. If they had the choice, they would prefer to get rid of the humans that, despite their many shortcomings, can pose a threat to them. And I suppose I don't have to explain anything to you about the way humans think about specials."

I lowered my head to think about it while I stepped in the brook and focused on the neatly camouflaged fish that swam by. He was right. Most humans were only aware of their existence as legends, but specials weren't exactly pleasant beings in those legends.

I'd read in Raven's library that many, many years ago, it had taken wars and a lot of diplomacies for us to live the way we did today. So, I understood what Dayn meant when he mentioned the tension that was always tangible. Who knew when the specials decided they wanted some of our lands back and attacked? Who knew if some teen specials would dare each other to enter human territory and ended up killing a human? Those stories Fionn and Mori's classmates used to tell them about specials that came to take you if you didn't

236

eat your vegetables or brush your teeth must've come from somewhere.

"So, it's different in the other realms? The ones that don't border ours?"

Dayn emptied the pot again and looked inside it with a pensive look on his face to determine if it was clean enough for his taste. "Yes and no. Some realms get along, a lot don't. But at least they're specials amongst each other. They understand each other, they know their place in the tapestry that is this continent, but humans don't really seem to fit in. They're considered lower beings, beneath lower specials even. Because of that, our kind doesn't like to mix with them, and they're not allowed into our territory, so we don't know much about each other." He hesitated. "I'm sure Raven knows a lot more about them by now, but most of that is about humans overseas. From before the treaties we have today, the role of humans in our history is vague at best. We, at least, were always taught it was better to stay away from them."

"Hm… Yet you still brought me to them."

He pressed his lips together, avoiding looking at me. "So, you figured out it was me?"

"No matter how much I think about it, that makes the most sense. So, why did you?"

He shrugged. "Because your kind looks like them. I thought you'd be able to fit in."

I scoffed. "You thought wrong."

He laughed wryly. "Well, we all make mistakes."

He put the pot on the ground in the sun, so it could dry and smiled at me as he put his hands on the grass behind him and leaned back, done with his task. "If you're curious about realms and whatnot, wait until we get to the Realm of Healing. It's a pretty magical place."

I lifted an eyebrow and bent over, my hands right above the water, ready to grab the next fish that would come close enough. "That sounds hard to imagine for me since everything here seems pretty magical as well."

He lay down on the grass and put his hands behind his head. "Trust me, you'll know what I mean when we get there."

"I can't wait."

Right at that moment, the biggest fish I'd seen so far swam by, and I slid my hands in the water, breaking the surface with barely any splashing. I grabbed it and, in the same movement, lifted it out of the water and threw it on the bank. Then I jumped out of the water, pulled my knife and with the same sting of pain in my heart I always felt, I stabbed it through its head, after which it stopped moving. I pulled the knife out and took the fish back with me to the brook to take out its guts and wash it.

We walked back to the camp, where Mom was already waiting for us, and I cooked the fish on a flat stone over the fire while Dayn broke down the tent. After we ate, cleaned, and gathered our stuff, we spent the rest of the day walking at a high pace.

For Mom, who didn't have the much stronger muscles and bones and the much higher stamina of a special body, it became increasingly harder to keep up, even after I started carrying her heavy backpack for her.

Mom was a proud and tough person; she wouldn't ask for a break for herself until she eventually collapsed. She was probably pushing herself at that moment, hoping we would reach our destination before that happened.

I looked past her at Dayn, who was walking in front again. I could ask him to slow down for Mom or to take a break, but she probably wouldn't appreciate that at all.

I sighed and stopped. "Dayn."

Both he and Mom stopped as well and turned around to look at me.

"I'm tired. I need a break." Mom wouldn't want us to stop for her, but she would probably wait as long as she had to for my sake.

Dayn walked over to us, clearly not happy. "We can't afford to take breaks if we want to reach the Realm of Healing today."

I sat down on a nearby rock, putting my own and Mom's backpack on the ground next to me. "Well, then I guess we won't reach it today."

Dayn folded his arms and looked me up and down. "You don't look tired."

I ignored his gaze and averted my face as I casually shrugged. "I'm tired on the inside."

Dayn pressed his lips together until they were barely more than a thin line, something I noticed he did when he was angry or irritated. Even at that moment, when I was sure that the look he gave me was an angry one, I was curious what it looked like beneath that pretty but annoying mask he insisted on wearing at all times. Would his eyes have the same light color as his skin? Were his eyebrows and eyelashes the same white color as his hair? Somehow, I imagined them darker.

"Doesn't it hurt to wear that mask all the time?"

That sudden change of topic seemed to startle him a little and he hesitated. He clearly had a reaction ready to my intrusive question, but if he answered, that would mean he accepted the change of topic, and thus the fact that we were going to take a break here.

Eventually, he let out a deep sigh as a sign of defeat and sat down on a rock on the other side of the path. "Not as much as your stubborn attitude."

I shook my head and took Mom's flask of water out of her bag, and handed it to her, which she accepted with a stern look.

"You didn't have to do that. I was fine." She whispered, although, from the way I saw Dayn lift his head, I was pretty sure he'd heard her.

"Do what? I just wanted to drink something." I gave her a small grin as I took my own flask out of my bag.

She lovingly pinched my arm. "You're looking far too happy with yourself, young lady."

I looked at Dayn. I understood why he wanted to keep this up, as it wouldn't be long before those boreans that had been hanging around Raven's land waiting for me would realize I'd left and would pick up on our trail. They were faster than us, even if they didn't hurry, and they would probably be able to keep going longer than us too, so the best thing for us to do was to create as much distance between them and us as possible.

Suddenly Dayn shot up straight. He lifted his head in the air and turned it a little as if he were trying to pinpoint something he'd picked up on. Before I had the chance to follow his example and listen for myself, he turned to Mom and me. "We have to go now."

I got up and pricked up my ears, but no matter how hard I listened, I couldn't hear any signs of anyone following us. Was Dayn's hearing better than mine, or was it part of his magic? Either way, it meant that even if we were being followed, they were still far enough away for us to outrun them. Probably.

Dayn turned to Mom and spoke to her much more directly than I'd done. "We're going to have to run. Will you be able to keep up?"

She looked dejected. "I will be for a while, but then what? Will they magically stop coming after us when we reach the next realm?"

She turned to me. "I'm sorry."

I put my hand on her shoulder. "Don't be. It's not your fault. We still have time; we just have to figure something out before they find us."

I looked at Dayn. "Why are they following us? What do they want from me? Are they getting paid for it? Is there something we can offer them to make them stop?"

He thought about it. "Yes, they are getting paid, but trust me, even everything we have combined won't be enough to outbid their client."

I nodded; I'd known the answer even before I'd asked it.

"How many are there?"

Dayn tilted his head, just as he'd done before, to focus on the sounds he was picking up on. "It's hard to say, around three to six, I think, definitely no more than ten. Their footsteps sound strange, mixed as if it's not only boreans."

That didn't give us much clarity. Three might've been possible. Judging from the way I'd been able to take down some of them before, I would even dare to take on five if I had Dayn with me, but more than that was too risky, especially if we had to fight while protecting Mom from the rest of them.

"Ahum." Dayn coughed awkwardly to regain my attention. "This is as good a time as any to let you know that I won't be of much use in a fight."

I glared at him. "Why not?"

He sighed impatiently as if I was stupid for even asking. "Because not all specials are built the same way. You, for example, are much stronger than those boreans, and those boreans are much stronger than me." He shrugged. "Most specials are, by the way, for future reference."

I looked down at myself, from one shoulder to the other and then looked back at him, kind of pissed. "Are you saying I look muscly?"

He sighed, and I saw Mom shake her head. She put her hand on my shoulder. "That's clearly not what he's saying, sweetie."

Dayn nodded. "What I'm saying is that when it comes down to a fight, I'll try to do what I can, but the second one of those boreans gets his hands on me, they'll snap me like a twig. It's just the way it works. Isn't it the same with humans?"

I didn't answer. He was right, but that really limited our options; I wasn't going to be able to fight off five of those monsters by myself.

Dayn seemed to have reached the same conclusion. He turned his look from me to the ground beneath us and back. "How fast can you dig a pit able to trap at least five guys?"

I wasn't exactly sure how to look after hearing something so insane. "Are you kidding? Because it's seriously not a good time for that right now."

He took a small, foldable iron shovel out of his backpack and handed it to me. "Dig as fast as you can. It doesn't have to be deep." He turned around as if he wanted to walk away but then changed his mind and turned back to me. "Stop digging the second you can hear them, no matter how far you got, and let us know as quietly as possible."

I unfolded the shovel and stuck it in the earth in front of me, which was a lot easier than I'd thought it would be, almost causing me to push it in far too deep. I lifted it up, again much easier than I'd expected, and saw that that small shovel held a lot more earth than I'd expected it to be able to. Dayn's plan to dig an entire trapping pit in the short amount of time we had, had seemed insane to me, but if I were working with what could only be a magic-infused shovel, we might actually be able to do it.

I quickly put my hair in a ponytail as Mom and Dayn disappeared between the trees to my right and started digging as fast as my body allowed me, carefully throwing the earth I dug up as far away between the trees to my left as I could. It wasn't perfect; all they had to do was look to their left, and they would see something strange was going on here. I tried to ignore that thought and kept digging my quickly widening hole in the ground. Considering how hiding seemed to be his biggest strength, Dayn might be able to deal with it when he got back from whatever it was he and Mom were doing.

I suddenly froze in the middle of a scoop and pricked up my ears. I heard them, not very clearly, they were still very far away, but I definitely picked up some movement. I dropped the earth that was still on my shovel and looked around me. I couldn't yell, but I also didn't have time to go run around looking for Dayn and Mom.

"Dayn?" It was somewhere between a whisper and a yell, and the second I did it, I felt my shoulders tense up. If I could hear those monsters from here, chances were that they could hear me from there as well.

"Ssht!" Dayn and Mom appeared from behind me, both their hands full of sharpened sticks.

Dayn jumped in the hole without saying anything else and started planting the pointy sticks in the earth. Mom stepped in the hole as well, handed me half of her gathered sticks, and followed his example. I kneeled in the sand, sticking the sticks she gave me in the ground one by one, working my way from the center to the edge of the hole. After I ran out, I got up and stepped out of it. It wasn't very deep, nor was it very big. It definitely wouldn't hold five people, and I highly doubted it would do more than inconvenience those monsters, but it would have to do.

"So, what now?" I was afraid to do more than whisper. "Should we put some branches or leaves over it to cover it up?"

Dayn, who was still sitting in the middle of our pit, shook his head. "No need, I'm taking care of it."

I narrowed my eyes as I observed him. He'd lowered his head, had placed his left hand on the stake that was closest to him, and buried the right hand slightly under the dirt. I would've thought he was calmly sitting there under any other circumstance, taking a rest, but at that moment after I focused all my attention on him, I noticed something flowing from him.

It wasn't something visible, I wasn't even sure if I was really feeling it, but I did smell it. The scent of oranges, the same scent his mask had, spread through the air. It circled him and seemed to be imbibed by the ground beneath him. It didn't last more than a few seconds, and as soon as he got up, the scent of oranges completely disappeared.

I didn't know how it worked or what he'd done specifically, but I was sure that he'd infused our pit with his

244

magic. I took a step back and looked at it while he stepped out. It had worked. Even to me, who was standing right next to it, the pit seemed blurry. It barely seemed to differ from the ground around me. It wasn't that I wasn't able to see it, but to me, it seemed almost normal that it was there, like it was part of a normal landscape, like it was supposed to be there. I didn't catch my attention any more than the trees around me did. If I hadn't known somewhere in the back of my head what it was, I would've definitely walked right into it.

I felt goosebumps appear on my arms. It was a disheartening thought. How many more specials were able to do that? How many traps were laid in this forest that I wouldn't be able to see?

I didn't ask Dayn, nor did he give me any time to. He grabbed my backpack from the ground and pulled one of my shirts out of it, which he threw in the hole. He smiled apologetically to me after seeing my aghast look. "It's probably better to leave something of yours on this exact spot, just to be sure."

I lifted an eyebrow. "I thought you said they didn't follow me by scent?"

He shrugged. "That's why I said, 'just to be sure'."

He didn't give us any more time to talk about it but handed me the bag and started walking away from the pit. "It'll slow them down, but it won't stop them, so we should still hurry and get as far away from here as possible."

Mom and I quickly followed him. We didn't run, but we weren't walking normally anymore either. It was something in between which, I was guessing, was his way of accommodating Mom.

As we hurried, the scenery slightly started to change around us, which probably meant we were close to the Realm of Healing. My breathing got heavier, and I could clearly hear my mother panting in front of me. I knew that reaching the Realm of Healing wouldn't change anything at all. Even if we crossed the border, we would still be in the exact same situation, but for some reason reaching that border was all I could think about.

"Oh no." Dayn stopped out of nowhere, nearly causing Mom and me to bump into him.

He turned around. "We have to go back right now."

He didn't explain, and he didn't give us a chance to ask. He just ran past us, back to the pit, at a tempo that neither Mom nor I could keep up with. Panic instantly spread through my body, and I looked at Mom, conflicted about what to do.

She nodded. "Go. I'll catch up from a distance."

I didn't like to leave her behind, but I ran after Dayn anyway. I had no idea what reason he could possibly have for suddenly going towards those monsters, but if what he'd said about how useless he was in a fight was true, then wasn't he running headfirst into some real, life-threatening danger?

Dayn was fast, a lot faster than I'd originally thought. I could still see him between the trees, but he slowly kept getting farther away from me until I could only see his light silhouette in the distance.

"Stop! Don't move!"

I narrowed my eyes. I didn't see Dayn very clearly, but his voice had easily reached me all the way there. I sped up even more and finally caught up to him. He stood still in the middle of the open spot we'd left not that long ago. I walked up to him to see the monsters he was talking to, and felt my

246

breath disappear from my lungs. Right in front of us, at the very edge of the pit trap, stood Fionn.

I stared at him with my eyes spread wide open, and a dozen emotions fought for priority inside of me. I was happy and so relieved to see him again, to see him safe. I wanted to run over and hug him tightly and never let go again. At the same time, I was extremely pissed that he had disobeyed Mom and me and followed us. But most of all, I was scared, scared he was here, where those monsters could appear at any moment. And they did.

15

Before I could even say anything to Fionn, the first one of what would turn out to be six boreans appeared from between the trees to his left and headed straight towards me, completely ignoring both Fionn and Dayn.

The monster reached me in a heartbeat and lifted his oversized fist to bash my head in. Dayn stepped out of its way, as graceful as ever, and in that same movement lifted up his leg and kicked the borean against the side of his knee, that bent into a strange angle as the borean fell down with an excruciating, inhuman scream of pain.

I jumped back, so the monster wouldn't touch me as he fell down and turned to the right to thank Dayn for his help, but he'd already disappeared. It didn't matter.

I slowly moved to my left to make sure I put the pit trap between me and the remaining five boreans heading towards us.

"Fionn," I whispered to him, without taking my eyes off the coming boreans, "move to the right and get behind me."

Fionn usually wasn't the type to listen the first time you told him to do something, but he instantly sprinted behind me. He grabbed the back of my shirt and held on for dear life. Part of me wanted him to hold on and stay there, close to me, but it was probably the most dangerous place to be at that moment.

"Sweetie, the second they attack, move back and keep going back until you can't even see us anymore, okay?" I tried talking as slowly and calmly as possible.

Fionn nodded, and I could hear him hold his breath. I felt my heart hurt. This must've been the most scared that he'd ever been, but I didn't have time to worry about it. The two boreans in front charged at me simultaneously, and I stared at them in disbelief as they ran straight into the pit.

One or two of the stakes actually did some damage, but the rest just broke or bent to the side the second the boreans fell on them. The only thing that pit did for us was surprise and confuse them, giving me a small opening to attack. I jumped inside the pit and kicked one of the boreans against his head as hard as I could, while I grabbed one of the stakes and stabbed it into the thigh of the other one, which I then also hit against his head as hard as I could. Rather than focusing on killing one of them, it was probably better to immobilize as many of them as them, increasing our chances of survival.

I picked up two more stakes and looked up in front of me. There were three of the six boreans left. All three of them were standing in place, looking at me with a hesitant look on their faces. In less than two minutes, we had taken out half of their forces.

I tried to show them the scariest look I had, to intimidate them even more, which wasn't very hard for me now that I was standing face to face with these monsters again.

"Thera!"

I turned around and started running towards Fionn before I even had a chance to see what was happening. He hadn't run away like I'd told him to. Instead, he still stood in the very same place, frozen to the ground, staring at the borean with the broken knee, who was limping towards him.

"Fionn run!"

Even though it only took three steps to get to Fionn, I was still too late. He flinched and lifted his arms in front of him to protect his face, as the borean lifted his left arm and slammed it against Fionn's side, literally causing him to fly over two yards through the air and slam into a tree. I heard cracking and air escaping his lungs as I reached the borean who had hit him.

"Fionn! No!" Mori appeared between the trees at the same spot Fionn had come from, but I didn't have time to give her any attention. Blind hatred was raging through my body, and I used all of it to kick the borean against his broken knee. He let out a deafening scream of pain and fell towards the ground, but before he even reached it, I jumped on top of him, lifted my stake and stabbed it in his neck. Blood started spurting out at quick intervals, telling me I'd hit an artery. I pulled out the stake, unable to avoid a spray of disgustingly green blood that drenched my shoulder and part of my neck.

All of me wanted to run to Fionn, but there were more boreans left, and I could feel them running towards me even from behind. I turned around to face them, two of them. As I'd expected, Dayn had jumped the last one from above and was now struggling to keep him pinned to the ground. I knew from experience that he would be able to keep that going for a while, although he didn't seem to be doing all that well.

I shook my head and focused on the two boreans walking towards me through the pit. I bent my knees and loosened

250

my grip on the two stakes I was still holding, one of them sticky and warm from the borean's blood. I forced myself to breathe calmly.

One of them suddenly shot to the side, trying to pass me, while the other one charged at me head-on. I turned to my right to stop the one that was clearly aiming for Fionn, even though I knew it left me open for the one that was attacking me.

I stabbed the one to my right in his left arm with my stake and hit him against the back of his head. He fell towards the ground at the same moment the borean in front of me slammed his fist against my own head.

For a moment, everything went black, and my ears started to ring, drowning out all other sounds around me. From somewhere far away, I realized I'd hit the ground with a scarily hard slam, and I heard several people yell in reaction to that. Two of them stood out above the rest.

One was Mom. She must've caught up with us.

The other one was Corean. He screamed something short, louder than I'd ever heard him do before. His scream got cut off and was instantly followed by a horrifying, cracking sound.

Suddenly, everyone around us stopped moving. I blinked a few times to get rid of the blurriness I saw and pushed myself into a seating position.

It was a complete, horrifying mess. Dayn had been thrown off by the borean he'd tried to hold down, and his right arm was hanging limply along his side. The borean that had hurt him had worked himself up and was standing quietly next to Dayn. Both of them were looking at us with an uncertain look on their faces.

I turned around. Fionn was sitting upright against the tree he'd been slammed into. His face was white as a sheet, but his eyes were open, and he seemed fully conscious. Mom sat on his left side, holding him carefully, while Mori sat on his right, her hands tightly clutched around his arm, a terrified look on her face. All three of them were looking at us too.

I turned back to see the borean that had hit me to the ground. He was quietly looking down at Corean, who lay eerily still in front of me, a small stream of blood dripping down from the corner of his mouth.

"No…" I got on my knees and crawled over to him, putting my index and middle finger against his neck. There was a heartbeat, but it was very faint and irregular. I suppressed a sob and desperately looked up at Dayn, even though I knew that he wasn't able to do any more than I was.

The borean in front of me kneeled next to us and moved his hands under Corean's neck and knees as if he wanted to pick him up from the ground, but I pushed him away with all my strength and grabbed one of the stakes that I'd dropped when he'd hit me nearly unconscious.

The four other boreans that had somehow survived jumped up, as much as their injuries allowed them to, and looked ready to start fighting again, but the borean in front of me stopped them with just one gesture of his hand. He turned back to me and said something in a language I didn't recognize. I stared at him silently, my body hovering over Corean's, my hands firmly planted on either side of him, protecting him from whatever the borean wanted to do to him.

"He says they can help him if you let them take him." Dayn moved forward slowly as all of the boreans instantly pointed their anxious gazes towards him.

252

"That's a lie." I shifted my look from Dayn to the borean. "I'd rather die than hand Corean over to these monsters."

Dayn sighed. "These monsters? He's one of them, Thera."

I gave him the most hateful look I'd ever given him. "He's nothing like them."

He kneeled on the other side of Corean's quickly weakening body. "Just because you like him doesn't make him any less borean, and I don't like admitting it any more than you do, but these guys actually have a pretty strict code of honor. They take care of each other." He gestured to the boreans around us with his hand. "Why do you think they all immediately stopped fighting the second this boy got hurt?"

I followed his hand and looked at the boreans staring back at me with a mix of anger and worry.

"They can't have him, Dayn." I turned back to him. "If they can really help him, then tell them to do it now, here, because I won't let them take him."

I couldn't see Dayn's eyes, but I knew he was giving me a frustrated look. "Why are you going this far for someone you barely even know? Just give him back to them. They're his people."

"No, they're not! He doesn't want to be like those bloodthirsty monsters!"

Dayn sighed again, and it filled me with red-hot anger. "Yeah, well, his existential crisis isn't our problem Thera, just give him back."

I stared at him in disbelief, barely able to contain the rage whirling inside. I lowered my voice, aiming it only at him, making sure he would know how serious I was. "You said you'd be there for all of us from now on, and Corean is part of that now, so decide, are you going to be here for us or not?"

Dayn pressed his lips together, he was pissed, really pissed, but he was also going to give in.

He straightened his shoulders, got up and took one step to the left, firmly planting himself between us and the boreans that were restlessly staring at us. He spoke to their apparent leader in their own language, making it impossible for me to understand them, but after a quick back and forth, he turned back to me.

"There's a place not that far from here, in the Realm of Healing, where there are small creatures that produce a liquid that heals nearly all wounds. They're willing to let us join them in going there, so you can see for yourself that they will help him, but they refuse to let you have him."

He kneeled in front of me again after seeing the doubt in my eyes. "This is our best chance Thera, if you really care about helping him, more than about being stubborn and hateful towards these guys, you should take it."

Every word out of his mouth made me want to hurt him, but part of me realized I didn't have another choice, or at least not a better one. I reluctantly moved back, allowing the borean in front of us to lift Corean off the ground. He pressed him against his chest in a surprisingly tender way and walked away from us, towards the Realm of Healing, in a high-paced tempo.

Two of the remaining four boreans followed him quietly, while the fifth kneeled down next to the one I'd killed. He picked him up in the same way their leader had picked up Corean and followed the other four as well.

I got up, trying really hard to pretend I hadn't seen that look of hurt and sorrow on the borean's face and ran to Mom and the kids. I kneeled in front of Fionn. "I'm going to carry you there too, Fionn, bear with me."

Mom held out her hand to Mori, which she accepted without a single word, and the four of us followed the boreans at a much slower pace, even though we were still going as fast as we could.

I could sense Dayn following us from a small distance and remembered that he'd gotten hurt during the fight too, but I didn't have the energy or the patience to even acknowledge him.

Dayn had said it wasn't fair, but we were walking for over an hour already before we finally entered the Realm of Healing, and with every second, my worries for Corean grew and cramped up my stomach.

Dayn had been right about the Realm of Healing though, it really was something else. Its name might've been a little cheesy, but it did fit. It was hard to explain exactly what it was that made this place suddenly feel so magical. Part of it was that everything around me seemed normal but more. All the trees and plants around us were beautifully green, for example, but they weren't just green. Most of them had a purple edge, or a bright yellow center, or little uneven dots of red. The same went for the rocks, they were grey, but nearly all of them had small and big veins of sparkling crystal that seemed to actually move through the rocks as if they were living beings that had liquid starlight instead of blood.

But there was also something else. The air was different here. I breathed in deeper; it had a very distinctive scent, one that I could only smell when I took a deep breath, but one that I recognized. Or I should say a combination of smells I recognized. I smelled freshly cut grass and herbs, combined with the very slight scent of alcohol disinfectant, that I remembered from the medical building in our village. It was a strangely calming scent, as if the air itself was telling me everything was going to be alright.

I looked at Dayn over my shoulder to see him smile at me ever so slightly confidently.

After about another half hour, we reached a big open field of grass. The boreans had already stopped there and were now standing in the middle of it, jumping around and slapping their hands like crazy people. It took me a few moments to realize they weren't clapping randomly; they were trying to catch something.

The meadow was a bright, almost fluorescent green in the middle, but was colored darker closer towards the edge and eventually bled from dark green into a dark, reddish purple that also colored the big trees surrounding it. Those trees weren't just big. There were also a lot of them, creating a dense wall of trees all around the meadow. Each of those trees grew inwards, and most of the tops met in the middle, above the open space, creating a sort of natural room, where only a few rays of the already setting sun reached inside.

The grass in the meadow, mostly the greenest grass, was covered in dew, and every other second, one of those dew drops grew into what looked like a soap bubble but with much more shine and much more saturated colors. Once the bubble was about as big as a fist, they started to move, coming loose from the blade of grass they were attached to, and floated up into the air. It was those bubbles that the boreans were trying to get their hands on.

They jumped in the air, slapped, or popped them and caught the tiny bit of spatter that came from it with their hands. They then kneeled down next to Corean, who they had lain down in the middle of the greenest part of the grass and poured the few drops from their hand into his mouth.

256

And it was barely noticeable, but very, very slowly, the light blue color started to return to Corean's face.

I felt a wave of relief flow through my body and carefully lay Fionn down on the grass in front of us. "Are you okay, sweetie?"

Fionn nodded but then averted his face from me. "I'm sorry."

I lifted an eyebrow. "Why? You didn't do anything wrong." I grinned. "Well, except for coming after us even after we told you not to."

He shook his head. "No. I just stood there and didn't do anything. If I'd run away like you said, you wouldn't have had to come to save me, and Corean wouldn't have had to save you, and he wouldn't be in danger right now."

I put my hand on his arm and squeezed it softly. "I told you, dummy, you didn't do anything wrong. You were in an incredibly scary situation. It's okay if you freeze up, I would've done the same when I was your age." I let go of his arm and lowered my head. "I'm the one who's sorry for not being fast or strong enough to protect both of you. I'm really sorry you got hurt, Fionn."

He tried to shrug but stopped halfway. "What part of me is hurt? I'm not even bleeding."

I shook my head. "Just lay still and let me catch some of these bubbles for you."

I reached out my hands to touch one of them, but Dayn stopped me by grabbing me firmly by my wrist.

I turned to him with a scowl. "What're you doing?"

He let go of me. "I know they don't seem like it, but these creatures are as much alive as we are. Don't kill them just because you want to use them."

I wasn't sure how to look. "These bubbles are the creatures you talked about?"

Dayn nodded slightly.

I turned around in shock and looked at the boreans, who were grabbing the bubbles out of the air by the dozens. "Then why are you letting them kill them like that? We have to stop them!"

Dayn looked at them over his shoulder and then turned back to me. "Thera, you don't seem to realize how lucky we were to get away from that fight alive. Nor do you seem to realize how much you pissed them off when you refused to hand that boy over. One misstep on our side, and they could instantly change their mind."

I clenched my fists. "So, you're letting them kill these creatures because you're scared about how they'll react if you try to stop them?"

"Yes." It was a resolute, unashamed response. "I promised I'd look after all of you, and no matter how much it pains me to let them do this, it's the best way to keep my promise right now."

I stared at him, desperately wanting to see the look in his eyes beneath that horrible, beautiful mask. "Then how can we collect some of that liquid for Fionn without killing these creatures?"

His face lit up. "Just let him lay there on the grass for a while and wait."

He put his hand against my shoulder to push me back a little, so I wouldn't be hanging over Fionn so much. I let him and stood there about a yard away from Fionn, together with Mom and Mori, and anxiously waited for what would happen.

We stood there waiting for what felt like hours, while my doubts and worries grew bigger the longer nothing seemed to happen until Fionn suddenly exhaled deeply, and his entire body seemed to relax.

I stared at him in surprise. Until that moment, his body had been tensed up a lot more tightly than I'd realized.

"Look closely. You'll see it if you focus." Dayn whispered the words right next to me, meaning they were only meant for me.

I breathed in quietly but deeply, and I instantly realized that the scent of freshly cut grass and herbs and disinfectant became stronger at intervals. I narrowed my eyes. Every time the scent became stronger for a moment, I heard a slight pop and saw a strangely colorful vapor floating down, landing on Fionn and the ground around him. Every time the vapor touched him, his face seemed to unclench a little more.

"They have a lifespan of about three minutes."

I looked at Dayn, who was staring up at the bubble creatures above us with a smile.

"You see, the funny thing about the Realm of Healing is that it doesn't have a Keeper like the other realms. It's a completely neutral zone, no one lives here, and any kind of fighting is absolutely forbidden, a rule that almost all specials actually obey."

He turned to me. "You noticed the veins of magic running through the rocks on our way here, right?"

I nodded, and he turned back to the creatures in front of us. "Well, these kinds of veins flow through almost everything that comes from the ground here, including the trees and the grass. On rare occasions, the magic coming from the ground permeates with something outside of it and gives birth to a new species, like these creatures."

I watched as a new drop of dew started to grow and eventually flew up into the air, to pop right before it reached the top of one of the trees that closed this space off.

"Only a handful of people know this, but these veins of magic branched off from the Magic's Source and for some reason only go as far as the Realm of Healing." He shrugged. "Although even I don't know how or why it has these incredible healing capabilities."

I looked at him, even from the side I couldn't see behind his mask to see the rest of his face, to see his eyes. "How do you know this stuff that almost no one else knows?"

He showed me a proud grin. "Because only two realms in our entire continent that I know of have such a privileged disposition, and the realm I come from is one of those two."

That piqued my interest exactly as much as he'd wanted it to. "Where is it?"

He thought about it for a second. "Very, very far away, but very easy to get to if you know where to go."

I narrowed my eyes. There was no use asking further if he started talking like that. "Does your realm have healing magic in the air too?"

He shook his head. "It also doesn't have the same ban on any kind of fighting that this one has, unfortunately."

After that, he walked away from us and sat down against one of the trees surrounding the meadow, slowly moving his injured arm up and down. I hadn't realized up until that moment, but it seemed that the bubble creatures had healed him too, even though he'd just been standing there talking to me.

I hadn't wanted to say it out loud, especially not after the look on Dayn's face, but to me, it made sense his realm didn't have the same ban on fighting. If it had an entire people living there, that meant it had a ruler and means to fight back and protect themselves when attacked, so why should they be treated differently from all the other realms?

"He woke up!" Mori had clenched Mom's arm, and both of them were looking in Corean's direction with an excited look on their face.

I followed their eyes and felt a second wave of relief roll over me when I saw him open his eyes and sit up slowly. I ran over to him, ready to hug him tighter than I'd ever hugged anyone, but one of the boreans around him jumped up and blocked my path. The others quickly followed his example, so I suddenly faced five boreans, who all looked anything but kind or welcoming at me. Not that I wanted them to. If I was completely honest, I still wanted all five of them to drop dead.

Dayn walked up to me and put his hand on my shoulder, breaking our silent standoff. "Remember what I told you before Thera? All it takes is one misstep."

I narrowed my eyes without taking them off the boreans. "I thought any kind of fighting was strictly forbidden."

He slightly pinched my shoulder as a warning. "Which is why they're waiting for you to make the first move. As long as you don't do anything, they won't either."

I frowned. "But they will the second we leave this realm. Ask them why they're trying to kill me, ask them who hired them."

"They won't tell you, even if you ask." Corean worked himself up to a standing position with a painful moan. The boreans standing between us looked at him over their shoulders but didn't move an inch away from me.

He walked past them and planted himself before me, bravely facing them head-on. "Thank you for saving me, but I'm not going with you. I'm going with Thera."

You're not going anywhere, except for back to the academy, I wanted to tell him, but there was no way I could interrupt what he was trying to do.

The leader took a step closer to us, and although it was barely noticeable, I saw Corean flinch. The borean yelled something at him in their own language, and I braced myself, ready for anything, but Corean stayed completely still, forcing himself to seem as calm as possible. He said something back to the leader in their own language. I looked towards Dayn over my shoulder, hoping he could translate where necessary, but he shook his head and gestured to wait and listen. So, I did.

They argued back and forth, in a surprisingly decent manner, until eventually the leader of the boreans growled something far too close to Corean's face for my liking and then turned around and walked away, just like that. The other four, one still with their dead comrade in his arms, followed him, and we watched them walk away until they'd completely disappeared between the trees.

Corean turned around to me and let out a huge sigh of relief, sinking on his knees in the process. "Thank the gods, I was sure they were going to kill us all."

I kneeled beside him and put my arms around him, pulling him close. "I'm so glad you're alive."

Corean chuckled. "What you should be happy about is that they will stop trying to kill you. Not that they were happy about it. It took some real convincing. Especially since they were not happy with my choice either. Or with the fact that they were going to miss out on the money they were supposed to make. And they also-" He stopped the moment he realized he'd started rambling again and moved back, so he could look at me. "I'm pretty glad I'm still alive too." He exhaled uncomfortably. "It was a pretty close call."

I shook my head. "I can't believe you did that for me. Please don't ever, ever, ever do that again. I don't want to survive knowing you died because of it."

His light blue cheeks turned green. "It wasn't exactly a conscious choice, my body just moved on its own, so I can't promise I won't do it again, but I'll try from now on."

I got up and held out my hand to him to help him to his feet, then I turned around to Mom. "What now?"

A nearly palpable silence fell between the two of us. We both knew what we should say, what was probably the right thing to say, but I was also pretty sure about what we both really wanted to say. Let's take the kids with us. Let's not send them back. It was selfish. It was a selfish thought that neither of us wanted to say out loud but that we were both hoping the other one would say.

"Hey, Mori."

We both turned around to Dayn, who was nonchalantly standing next to Mori with a big smirk on his face. "I'm impressed you managed to escape Raven's clutches." His little play couldn't possibly be more obvious or be more obviously aimed at Mom and me.

Mori, who wasn't exactly sure what he was trying to do, chuckled hesitantly. "Thank you, sir." Polite as ever towards everybody but her own family.

Dayn's smirk got even worse. "Say, how many more times would you say you'd be able to pull that off again?"

Mori, who now realized what he was doing, didn't hold back anymore, showing us a possibly even bigger smirk than

Dayn. "Oh, I'd say about… as many times as it takes until we won't be sent back again."

Mom accidentally laughed and quickly put her hand over her mouth.

I sighed, no longer able to bear it. "Fine, I'm ready to give in." I turned to Mom. "You?"

She nodded and walked over to hug Mori. "I'm a little scared of what's going to happen from here on out, but staying together is the right thing to do."

"Does that mean I can stay with you too?" Corean stood a little farther away from us, clearly separating himself.

Mom gave me a look, making it clear that this would be my decision. I walked over to him. "Are you sure that's what you want, Cor? We don't know how long we'll be gone or what's going to happen. You'd be giving up on school, and you were so happy there."

He shrugged. "I wanted to be different from those other boreans by going to school and learning all I could learn, but the truth is that I already know more than everyone in that school combined." He smiled at me. "Besides, you were the only person who treated me normally, even though you had more reason to hate me than any of them." His smile widened. "I can sit in a library and learn from books whenever I want, but right now, I want to learn more about life and who I want to be, and I feel I can do that a lot better if I go with you."

I put my hand on his shoulder and gently squeezed it. "Well, that's enough for me."

16

It took us two more days to cross the Realm of Healing. After that, we crossed the smallest part of a broad river and then finally set foot in the Realm of Ruins.

Its name fitted it only after a few hours when old, overgrown pieces of what must've once been enormous buildings were scattered all over the place.

With so many more people, my nerves were much more on edge, but so far, no one else seemed to be following us. And even if they did, I just had to trust that Dayn would pick up on it long before we were in any real danger.

On the other hand, now that the kids were with us, things felt less awkward. Especially since Fionn and Corean talked a lot, both to each other and to us. And even when Fionn was done talking, Corean seldom was.

With her sarcastic sense of humor, Mori had found an ally in Dayn, who had no problem at all matching that sarcasm. Leaving me to close our formation again, this time with Mom, who was usually looking around just as fidgety as I was.

"Mom." I put my hand against her arm, and she turned to me with a nervous look on her face. "It's okay. We're almost there."

She lifted an eyebrow. "How do you know? We've been following Dayn for three days already."

I thought about it. How did I know? I saw Dayn look at me over his shoulder and give me a quick smile. Then I took a deep breath. I smelled it; it was a strange mixture of many scents mixed together. I smelled freshly baked bread, the rose-scented soap we used back home, the scent of cut grass and herbs I'd smelled in the Realm of Healing, the scent of oranges that belonged to Dayn's magic, the sweet sugary scent of pastries, I even smelled the salty scent of the ocean. Suddenly I grimaced. There were a lot of good scents, but also a lot of bad ones. I covered my nose; I smelled bloodshed and festering wounds and even stables that had to be cleaned out.

That was the first time I started to have doubts about this whole thing. Dayn had said he believed I would be able to do this, but what if I wasn't? What was going to happen to me if I failed? Suddenly death, or worse, seemed very real.

I looked at him again, ready to go over there and quietly discuss it with him, but he suddenly stopped and turned around.

All of us stopped as well and looked at him as he lifted his hand towards a bunch of willow leaves that reached all the way to the ground. "Before we go any farther, I should warn you not to come too close to the Source. Magic is beautiful and has a strong attraction, but it's also dangerous, especially for humans. So, don't come too close and don't touch it. Understood?"

We all nodded obediently, and he turned to me. "Thera, that goes for you as well. Make sure you keep some distance between you and the Source when you ask it for magic. It might be enchanting, but you absolutely cannot touch it, understood?"

I nodded again, annoyed that he'd felt the need to give me a double warning like that.

He put his hand through the willow leaves and pushed them aside, showing us the most beautiful, most terrifying thing I'd ever seen.

It was about as big as one of the wells in our old village except that this well standing on a pedestal in between dilapidated, white ruins, was in a much worse state.

Whatever came out of it somewhat reminded me of the orange crystal of Aleaxia's seafaring guild, in the way that the upper half was a smooth globe, not solid, but flowing into itself.

This… thing… there was nothing in the entire world I could compare its beauty to. It was an enormous clear crystal, with a different pearly color from every direction you looked at it, but in alternately liquid and gaseous form. It was continuously swirling around in every direction but somehow contained in that half globe shape. It sparkled in the sunlight that shone down on it, but I felt like I was looking at liquid starlight, alternating with stardust, and it tried to pull me in like nothing, no other form of magic, had ever done before. It literally took me all of my strength, all of my willpower, not to walk towards it and throw myself into it, to drown myself in it.

I felt Dayn's cold fingers wrap around my wrist, but I wasn't able to tear my eyes away from the Source of all magic to look at him.

"Don't touch it," Dayn whispered the words close to my ear, but they seemed to come from miles away.

"Don't touch it!" He repeated the words, louder now, more demanding, aimed not only at me but at Mom and Fionn and Mori as well. Only Corean didn't seem to need to be reprimanded.

"Why not?" Fionn responded bravely, and from the corner of my eyes, I saw him move closer to the source of beauty and attraction, of everything I could ever want.

I nodded, at least I think I did, I wanted to. I couldn't agree more. Why on earth would we not touch it? Why wouldn't we want to feel it? Would it be cold to the touch, like the crystal from the Aleaxia Seafaring Guild? But I felt such a warm, inviting sensation coming from it, floating towards me through the air, surrounding me.

"You." Dayn aimed his words towards me, strengthening his grip around my wrist. I could feel the pressure coming from it, but somehow it didn't hurt. I wondered if I was even able to feel any kind of pain while I was faced with something so breathtaking.

"You shouldn't touch it because it could break you." He pulled on my arm, and I felt how I had no other choice but to take a step back, to my deepest regret.

"And you," Dayn turned towards the rest of the family, "shouldn't touch it because it could kill you."

I heard those words. Somehow, I registered them more clearly in my mind than everything else that had been said since we came here.

"Thera, we shouldn't stay here for too long. Move closer to it, without touching it, and ask it for the kind of magic you want to possess. Sit on your knees, close your eyes, and wait until it bestows it upon you. Afterward, get up as fast as you can and walk away from it. I'll take the family further away, back into the woods, where we'll wait for you." He moved his face closer to mine, so he could put some extra weight in the words he whispered. "Be careful."

Somewhere in the back of my mind, I think I registered it as a warning, not him being worried about me.

He let go of my hand and walked past me to offer Mori his hand instead, which normally would have annoyed me, but at that moment, I just hoped she would accept it, and they would all leave. She took his hand very ladylike, and they turned around and started walking away, followed by Corean and Mom, who took Fionn's hand. I smiled, only a few more moments and I would be alone with it.

"No!" That was somehow loud enough for me to turn my head and finally take my eyes off the miracle before me. Fionn had pulled his hand out of Mom's grip and had taken a step back, closer to the Source.

"I'm not going! Why does Thera get to be the only one who gets magic? Why is she the only one who gets to be useful? Why should she be the only one who can protect us?" Tears streamed down his face.

I took a step closer to him, slowly. "Fionn…" I wasn't sure what to say, it was hard to think with the magic pulling at me.

"No!" Fionn's voice broke, and I immediately stopped moving. "It's not fair! You were the only one who knew our village would be attacked. You were the only one who got to go back for Dad!" His voice became softer. "You were the only one who got to see him one last time."

He looked up at me. "That's not fair, Thera," he pointed behind him, to the Source, "if this 'magic' can make you stronger, strong enough to fight to protect us, then I want a part of it too. It owes me that." He looked me straight in the eye, unwavering.

"Fionn," Dayn took a step forward, "it doesn't work like that. Magic doesn't owe you or anyone anything, and it doesn't give magic to humans, if you touch it, you will die."

Fionn slowly moved his eyes from me to Dayn, and for a second, I saw a sliver of doubt, but it immediately disappeared, and he shrugged. He was even able to force himself to show us a small, confident smile. "We'll see."

With that, he instantly turned around and jumped into the Source. It wasn't like jumping into water. There was no sloshing or splashing. He just dissolved and changed into the same gaseous liquid as the Magic's Source itself, which he became part of and disappeared into. I stared at it. It'd happened so fast. In that incredibly short moment, I had lost my little brother.

"No!" Mori sprinted forward, trying to grab Fionn out of the source as if he hadn't completely disappeared. I started running. I knew Mori. I'd held her mere minutes after her birth. I'd spent my life loving and taking care of her. She could act cynical and even grumpy at times, but I knew her through and through. She was going to jump in after Fionn. In that one instance, that one second, I was going to lose them both.

I jumped and threw myself with my whole body against Mori, making both of us fall on the hard, cold floor. I quickly got up and tried to grab Mori's hands, but Dayn pulled me back.

"Don't touch her!"

I turned around to look at him, completely enraged that he tried to separate me from Mori.

"Look at her hand." He stared past me, to Mori's hand, and I followed his example. It was gone. No, that wasn't the right way to describe it. It had changed into the same kind of gaseous, liquid crystal as the Source itself, and it was spreading. More of her arm started to disassemble the same way Fionn had done.

I released myself from Dayn's grip and wrapped my hands around Mori's upper arm, squeezing it as tight as I could, as if it were possible to tourniquet it to stop the magic from spreading.

Dayn pulled on my arm as Mom fell onto her knees next to us, tears streaming down her face, calling out Mori's name as she lifted up her head and pulled her closer.

"Please stop, both of you!" Dayn sounded desperate as he tried to pull me back. "The magic will spread to you too!"

"Let it!" I swung my arm back, hitting him against his chest.

"Nayana, please, if it spreads to her, Thera will die as well!" He yelled at my mother, clearly hoping she would listen to him if it were for the sake of her only child that at least had a chance at surviving this. Corean followed his example and wrapped his hands around Mom's arm.

"It won't!" I squeezed harder on Mori's arm, to the point that she moaned in pain, despite the trance-like state that the magic seemed to have lulled her into.

"It really won't, look!" Mom put her hand on my shoulder. Her voice, which was suddenly calm and full of relief, forced me to look to the left, where Mori's disappeared hand slowly but definitely started to take form again. The gaseous parts of the crystal-like substance turned into liquid, and the liquid melted together and became solid in the exact shape of Mori's hand. It was like it had never changed, never disappeared. The magic moved over her body, shortly changing, disassembling it, taking it in as a part of itself, just to change it back as if nothing ever happened to it.

Mom moved back, carefully placing Mori's head back on the floor, making sure she wasn't touching her anymore, and gestured to me to do the same.

Both of us moved back and watched as the magic disassembled and then reassembled every inch of Mori's body, with no idea of what it would do to her.

I held my breath as the magic reached her heart and her head. Was it inspecting her, deciding there was no need to do anything to her? Was it changing her? Or… I swallowed, not allowing myself to even think about that one last option. It had to be the first thing. There was no other way. And why wouldn't it be that? Magic wasn't useful to humans, or humans to magic, that didn't have to mean it would kill them.

We watched in silence until the magic put back her fingertips, after having gone over her entire body, and then disappeared into thin air. On the opposite side of Mom, I kneeled next to her and carefully reached out my hand and placed it on hers, the hand she had stuck into the Magic's Source. It was cold to the touch, but that didn't have to mean anything. I moved my fingers down to her wrist and pressed them against her skin. An enormous weight got lifted from me instantly. There was a heartbeat. It was small and slow, but it was clearly there. Mori was alive.

Mom started crying the second she saw the relieved look on my face, but I didn't allow myself time to do the same. Instead, I turned around to look at the Source. If the magic didn't kill Mori…

"No." Dayn put his hand on my shoulder, pushing me down. I looked at him, surprised; I hadn't even realized I'd started to get up.

"Dayn, if Mori survived this then-"

"No," Dayn cut me off. "Those are two completely different things, Thera. Mori only scraped the magic with her fingertips and looked at what it did to her. She might be alive for now, but she is definitely not fine."

His eyes flashed to the Source for a second and then back to me. "Fionn threw his entire body in it, and the magic devoured him. It didn't reject him like it did with Mori. Everything he is, everything he was, is part of it now. There's nothing for you to get back."

I quietly stared at the Source, and I felt Mom's eyes burn in my back. I could almost hear the thoughts going through her head. She'd lost her son, she'd nearly lost her daughter, and she'd do anything not to lose me as well, but if there was even a millionth of a chance that I could get Fionn back… I knew she would never ask me, but she also couldn't get herself to tell me not to do it.

I pushed Dayn off me, hard enough for him to lose his balance and fall back. In that same movement, almost as nimble as Dayn usually was, I got up and let myself fall forwards into the magic, which pulled me in and completely absorbed me.

It was a strange feeling, being magic. I was everything and nothing at the same time. I whirled around inside that well, but at the same time, I also whirled around the whole earth, and the sky and the entire universe. I was that well. And I was the universe. I was everything, and I was nothing.

I'm not sure how long it took me to realize that I was me as well. But the moment I became aware of the me that was inside that whirl of magic, I became only me. And I remembered what I'd come for, what I was looking for. Instantly, the magic whirl I was before took solid form and became my body, inside which I resided once again.

The world around me had changed as well. I was in a big room, about the size of a warehouse, but the walls and ceiling and floor were made out of light. Out of the same soft, cold, crystal-like material that had become equivalent with magic to me.

I got up and looked at my body, moving my hands over my arms and face and stomach. I'd been disassembled and put back together the same way Mori had, but I didn't feel any different. If the magic had changed me in any way, I didn't notice it. Did the same thing go for Mori?

It hasn't changed you because we haven't decided how we want it to change you yet.

I turned around and felt my eyes widen. There was a creature standing in front of me, made out of the same crystal-like substance that radiated light as everything around me. I squinted my eyes as I tried to take a better look at it. It was a woman, who was a man at the same time, who was a child at the same time, who was a deer, and a tree, and a bird, and a fire. I closed my eyes. Looking at it made me dizzy. It was one person, but at the same time, it was also everything alive in our world. They weren't constantly switching between different forms; they were all these things contained in one form that was simply undefinable.

An untouched.

Their voice was the same as their form, and it was equally hard to explain. I was listening to a beautiful melody, as well as listening to the pouring rain, as well as listening to every single voice of every living creature in this world, talking, chirping, growling, singing, all at the same time. Still, somehow it was also just one voice talking directly to me.

I closed my eyes as I tried to wrap my head around what I was hearing. It was as if all things, everything in existence was all collected in this single creature in front of me. Suddenly I spread my eyes wide open, ignoring the pain that the light coming from the creature cost me. It didn't just seem like it was everything, it *was* everything, this was the earth's core.

It smiled. It was a burst of terrifying laughter, as well as an adorable giggle. *We prefer earth's essence.*

I nodded slowly. That felt right. That was what magic was, everything. The essence of everything, the energy of everything, the source of everything.

We think this is what you were looking for. It stepped aside, and behind it, I saw Fionn lying on the ground, crawled up into a little ball. I wanted to run to him, but the Source lifted up its arm, or paw, or branch, to stop me and smiled at me again, somehow scaring me as well as making me feel special as if this was an honor bestowed only upon me. I tore my eyes away from it and looked at Fionn. He didn't seem conscious, but he was clearly breathing.

He is quite a fearless boy to jump in like that. It turned its head from Fionn to me. *And you are quite brave to jump in after him.*

I wavered. The words it spoke were clearly praise, but it didn't feel like praise. Although it didn't feel like it was angry or lecturing me either.

"Will I be able to take him back up with me again?" It was the first time I'd spoken since I came there, and somehow it felt strange to hear my own voice, which was only that, my one voice.

It tilted its head. *Will you be able to take you up there again?*

I frowned. The way it had put so much emphasis on the word up made me realize that we weren't in a room somewhere beneath the well. We probably weren't even somewhere in the core of the earth. Were we even anywhere?

Thera, it spread its arms as a welcoming gesture. Hearing it say my name sent me into a near state of ecstasy.

What kind of magic is it that you seek?

I stared at it with a blank look on my face. What kind of magic? Dayn had said the same thing, but I hadn't had time to think about it yet with everything that had happened. Was I supposed to think of something on the spot?

The Source laughed. *You came here without knowing what kind of magic you want?*

I frowned, Dayn teased me daily, but somehow the Source's teasing made me feel dumb and humiliated.

"I want all of it." The words came out before I could stop them.

Its face barely changed, but somehow, a feeling of dread crept up on me. *You're an impudent one, aren't you?*

I swallowed, too scared to say anything back.

It walked towards me. Even if I'd been able to see its face clearly, I still wouldn't have been able to make out what it was thinking.

You want all of it? It repeated my words, honestly curious, angry, and mocking me at the same time. *All of the magic?*

I opened my mouth but closed it and nodded instead. Slowly, carefully.

Do you even know what that means? It stopped, close to me, far too close. It affected me in a way that was hard to explain. My breath halted. I felt my insides starting to whirl, the way they'd done before when I'd become magic itself. Was this something the Source was doing to me or was this just what too much magic did to a person?

I shook my head. "I don't." My voice was hoarse as if I hadn't used it in a long time, but the second I did, my insides stopped whirling. I forced myself to look it straight in the eyes, no matter how impossible that seemed.

"I don't know what that means, but it doesn't matter." I looked past it at Fionn, who was still laying motionless on the ground.

"All I want is to be strong enough to protect him, to protect all of them, against anything." I shook my head. "No. Against everything."

The Source stayed silent but looked at me as if it were deep in thought.

"I know it sounds selfish, stupid even, but the last few months have been hell. Fighting for our lives against one thing after the other. Constantly being worried and terrified, even when we're not fighting. I'm so tired of being scared, of not knowing what the next thing will be that will come for us and how many of us will survive it." I felt my breath falter.

"I don't want to take any of this away from you." I gestured my hand to the side, pointing out the room around us. "I just want to be strong enough to protect those I love." I let my arm fall down next to my side again and strained my shoulders. "And being able to hide or to be physically strong or even to breath fire or to be able to live forever isn't enough."

The Source laughed again, loudly. *We see, so even becoming immortal wouldn't be enough for you?*

I pulled up my shoulders slightly. It seemed to be honestly amused, but at the same time, I felt a clear threat in its words. Asking something like this from it, what was it going to do to me?

It stepped aside, looking at Fionn over its shoulder. *Prove it then.*

Suddenly, it started to both dissolve and extend. *Prove to us that you are worthy of that kind of power.*

It turned into a gaseous liquid the same way Mori had done, but unlike Mori, it didn't put itself back together. Instead, it started to grow and whirl around until it had nearly filled the entire room with sparkling, flowing, crystal-like starlight.

Part of me couldn't help but weigh my options. Stay here in this perfect storm of beautiful, transcendent magic that made me feel like I was floating, like I was truly part of this world and it of me; or grab Fionn and somehow find our way out of here and bring him to safety. I'd honestly been hesitating, but the moment that last thought crossed my mind, I realized there was no choice to make at all. If it had been just me down there, I might have stayed, but not Fionn, nothing was more important to me than him, and I would never make that choice for him.

I worked my way through the whirlwind of starlight, although I wasn't sure if I was running or walking or flying, and kneeled next to Fionn, picking his lifeless body up from the floor and tightly pressing it against me.

I pushed his face against my shoulder and covered his body with my arms as well as I could, trying to shield him from the magic that was flowing all around us. *Prove to me that you're worthy of that kind of power*. Those had been its words, but how on earth could I do that? Was simply being able to resist the magic all around us enough? Should I somehow prove to it that I was smart enough to find a way out of this doorless room?

The magic came close enough to touch me, and the moment I felt my shoulder starting to disassemble, I understood. There was only one way out of this room, and it was the same way as to how I got in.

Becoming the magic had nearly destroyed me the first time; I wasn't sure I'd be able to resist giving in to it a second time, but I was convinced there was no other way. I looked down at Fionn and pulled him as close to me as physically possible while I stopped resisting and let the magic devour us. Just keep him close, just protect him, just bring him back to safety. Those were the only thoughts I allowed myself to have as our bodies dissolved and I completely forgot myself and everything around me.

I thought the first time had been an exhilarating experience, but it had been nothing compared to the second time. Being able to give in to it again, to return to it, I had no words to explain the happiness it made me feel, the completeness. Finally, I'd become one. I'd become everything. And suddenly, I felt everything starting to slip through my fingers. I was the earth, I was the universe, I was holding the universe in my hands, but it became heavier and harder to hold. It wanted to be free from me, it wanted to become one with me, it wanted to be me, it wanted to be everything around me.

I don't know exactly how I did it, maybe it was because I worried about losing what I was holding, but somehow, I managed to remember my thoughts. I remembered the head they belonged to. And then I remembered how to slowly shake it, from one side to the other. No. The word resounded from within me and all around me. No. I couldn't let go. It wanted to be me, it wanted to be everything, but it couldn't. I wouldn't let it.

I forced myself to remember my neck, and then my shoulders, and my chest, my arms and fingers, my stomach, my legs, and toes, and when I'd remembered my entire body, I started to remember his as well.

I remembered it being small, smaller than mine, and different. It was harder to remember someone else's body, it took me much longer, but the more I remembered it, the more it gained consciousness, an understanding of itself, and before I realized it, it took over from me and started to remember itself.

I opened my mouth, I remembered it had a function, something it could do, but nothing happened. I opened it again. It wasn't just my lips, I realized. My entire mouth and even my throat and chest and stomach had to move.

"Fff…" It was barely anything, but something had come out, and after it did, it was as if I suddenly knew what I was trying to do and how I could do it.

"Fionn." I opened my eyes wide and looked at my little brother before me. It was as if calling his name had made him remember himself completely, not just his body, but all of him, all he was.

He looked at me with his blue eyes and reached his small hand out to me, only slightly touching my arm, but it was enough.

I opened my eyes, which should've been open already, and looked around. I was laying on the cold, hard ground, clutching Fionn far too tightly. We were both awake and conscious, but neither of us dared to move. We barely dared to breathe. The magic was whirling in the well next to us. The world around us was dark. There were no walls of pure light, only stone pillars, ruins, trees, and night.

Hm... Its voice reached me from deep within, and somehow it was different from how it had been inside that room. It took me a few seconds to realize what it was. In there, the Source had spoken with the voice of everyone and everything at the same time, except for mine. In there, the only one who used my voice was me, but now I heard it mixed in there with all the others.

Good job making it out, now let's see all the ways in which you will disappoint me.

The voice disappeared, and as soon as it did, I wasn't sure if I'd ever really heard it, to begin with, and honestly, it was too much for me to think about at that moment. It was hard enough just being me; it was hard enough knowing who I was and who Fionn was next to me.

I tried to move one of my fingers. It worked, it moved exactly as I'd intended it to. I tried another finger and then my thumb and eventually my entire arm. Everything worked like it should. I let out a long sigh of relief and felt my shoulders relax.

"Fionn." My voice sounded hoarse as if it had been through a lot, but it worked. "Try moving a part of your body."

Fionn didn't say anything back but slowly lifted his arm a little. "It works." It was soft and short, but he was able to use his voice as well.

I clumsily worked myself into a sitting position and relaxed my arms, which had still been holding Fionn tightly.

He used his newfound freedom to lift himself off my lap and sat on his knees next to me.

"Are you scared to get up?" He asked me quietly, his eyes glued to the ground.

I grinned uncomfortably. "So scared."

He gave me half a grin as well.

I carefully lifted my arm and put my hand on his head. His hair felt soft and nicely cool to the touch. "Do you want me to go first?"

Fionn nodded eagerly.

I took a deep breath and worked myself up to my feet. It felt strange using my body as much as this. It wasn't tiring. Honestly, it didn't cost any more energy than getting up had ever cost me, but it was awkward. After not having a body for so long, after being something so much bigger, so much more, so much freer, it felt strange to use this small, compact casing.

Fionn had worked himself into a standing position as well, and I could see on his face that he was experiencing the same kind of awkwardness.

He looked up at me, and I could see a sliver of fear in his eyes. "What are we now?" He asked the one question that had been repeating itself in the back of my head.

I looked him up and down. He hadn't changed a bit on the outside. Did that mean that the magic hadn't changed him? The Source had kept him unconscious. Was it so disinterested in humans that it hadn't done anything to him at all? Or was it really not possible for humans to possess magic?

I looked down at my own hands. I hadn't changed either. I didn't feel different outside or in. Had I failed its test? Had

I not proven myself worthy? Had everything that had happened to us been for nothing?

I looked back up at Fionn. "How do you feel?"

He tilted his head, as if he had to deeply think about it. "I feel like I've lived an entire life, more than that, as if I've lived an eternity, as if I was eternity, and now all of a sudden I'm back here again, as just me."

I nodded in agreement. That was about as well a way to describe it as any.

"Thera! Fionn! Oh, thank the gods!" Corean came running at us from behind the dense willow leaves and nearly jumped me, hugging me as tightly as he could. It felt strange feeling his skin against mine. Had I ever hugged him before? I couldn't remember. I leaned forward. I couldn't remember his touch, but I remembered his scent. The scent of old books and wooden tables, the scent of a library. It both relaxed me and frightened me all at once. Being able to smell someone's magic was something only I could do as an untouched. Was I still able to do it despite having gotten magic now? Or did this mean that the Source had failed me after all? I let go of Corean and looked at the Source over my shoulder. I didn't feel untouched though, I felt touched by its magic to my very core.

"Thera…"

Dayn appeared from behind the willow leaf curtain and looked at me and Fionn in complete astonishment.

"I can't believe it… I thought you were gone." His voice broke, and he stopped talking. He just stood there staring.

I ignored him for now and looked at Mori, who was lifelessly hanging in his arms. I could see her chest move up and down slightly, meaning she was still breathing, but all color had disappeared from her face, and she was grimacing as if she were in pain.

Mom, who had come out from behind the willow leaves last, stared at Fionn and me with the same silent astonishment as Dayn for a moment but then blinked and ran towards us, wrapping her arms around both of us and pulling us to her, as close as possible. She pressed her head against mine and then against Fionn and then back against mine again, tears freely streaming down her face, her shoulders shaking violently.

Fionn wrapped his arms around her middle and started crying as well. All of a sudden, he wasn't the person I'd been magic with, who I'd been the universe with. He was just my little brother who had been in way over his head. And honestly, I was jealous of him. It had never been as hard for me to stop myself from crying as it had been at that moment.

I closed my eyes as I hugged Mom back and then opened them again to look at Dayn over her shoulder. "What's wrong with her? Why isn't she awake yet?"

Mom let go of me and turned to the side, so she was included in our conversation, although she kept her arms around Fionn, holding him tightly as he buried his tearstained face in her stomach.

Dayn slowly shook his head as he looked down at Mori. "I have no idea. I have no idea how you and Fionn are even alive. I just…" He pulled up his shoulders. "I've never seen this happen before; I've never even heard of it happen."

He looked at me. I couldn't see his eyes, but I could hear the desperate tone of his voice. "I don't know how to help her…"

I walked over to him and took Mori out of his arms, pressing her tightly against me. I closed my eyes and tried to

284

search within myself for any kind of sign that I had obtained magic. If the Source had given me what I'd asked for, there should be something, something I could do to protect my little sister.

"Thera…"

I opened my eyes and looked at Dayn, far too hopeful. I was immediately disappointed by his hesitant posture. Whatever he'd thought of was probably nothing more than a gamble.

"I can't help her myself, but I can take her to someone who might be able to, someone who has stronger healing magic than any other person I've ever met." The tone of his voice lowered. "I think we should take her to my home."

I frowned. "Your home? I thought you said it was extremely far away."

He nodded. "But I also said it was extremely accessible if you know where to go. It will still take us at least a few days, but I can take us there as fast as possible." He looked at Mori, who was lifelessly hanging in my arms. "She seems physically fine, which means that it's the magic that's keeping her unconscious. We should be able to keep her alive until we get there."

I turned to Mom, not knowing what to do or say. She stared back at me, desperation clearly visible on her face. "If there's a chance it'll help her, we have to go."

I agreed and turned back to Dayn. "Okay, if there's someone there who can help Mori, we'll go."

9 789083 107332